Andrew Leatham is a former national newspaper and television journalist, turned public relations consultant. He lives in Lancashire.

PRAISE FOR ANDREW LEATHAM:

'A brilliant page-turner' – Tom Kasey, best-selling author of *Trade-Off*.

'Chilling and realistic. A five-star read' – Robert Foster, best-selling author of *The Lunar Code*.

Also by Andrew Leatham:

Killing Another (Inspector Ray Wilson Thriller Book 2)

Body Market (Inspector Ray Wilson Thriller Book 3)

DEAD HARVEST

ANDREW LEATHAM

ENDEAVOUR INK

AN ENDEAVOUR INK PAPERBACK

First published by Endeavour Press in 2013

This paperback edition published in 2017
by Endeavour Ink

Endeavour Ink is an imprint of Endeavour Press Ltd
Endeavour Press, 85-87 Borough High Street,
London, SE1 1NH

ISBN 978-1-911445-83-8

Typeset in Garamond 11.75/15.5 pt by
Palimpsest Book Production Ltd, Falkirk, Stirlingshire

Printed and bound in Great Britain by
Clays Ltd, St Ives plc

www.endeavourpress.com

For The Real Rhodogune.
Whoever You Were.

Table of Contents

Chapter One

Carefully, precisely and with a gentleness bordering on reverence, the old man bent to his task, oblivious to the guttering candles that provided his only light and to the drafts of chilled night air that whispered through the many cracks and crevices in his surroundings. Some would say he was painfully slow at his work although he preferred other adjectives: methodical, meticulous, precise. To him preparing the dead for the afterlife demanded a certain deference that was not within the understanding of ordinary mortals. The secrets were passed down from generation to generation and it was a huge privilege to be among the chosen ones, although his very soul ached with the realisation he was probably the last person in his bloodline that would carry out this ancient duty. His wife had made the great journey to the afterlife many years before, leaving him childless, alone and with no male heirs to whom he could pass the knowledge.

The skills he exercised that night had been honed to perfection through thousands of years, each generation finding new materials, new ways and new techniques to ensure the remains of the departed stayed inviolate and did not suffer the degradation of the earth and the creatures that crawled within it. The procedure, from the embalming of the corpse to the wrapping of the mummy was normally a solemn ritual with pre-ordained steps scrupulously followed. This body, however, had come with a specific set of instructions. The young woman's liver, kidneys, lungs and intestines had already been removed, as had the heart, which struck him as odd because, as the centre of intelligence and feeling, the heart would be needed in the afterlife and was therefore usually left in place. All he had had to do was remove the brain using the traditional method of a long hook to drag it out through the nose, dry the corpse for 40 days using natural salts, then anoint and wrap it.

It was the wrapping of the body that now occupied him. As he prepared the strips of fine linen with which he would begin the process, he began to wonder who this young woman had been and why her mummification was required to be done in such an unusual manner. Even in death, she possessed a degree of handsomeness with long, black hair, high cheek bones and an olive complexion which, thanks to a generous application of palm oils, still held a certain sheen in the meagre candle light. Had she been someone's princess? Or who was the important person to whom she had been an important person? How did she die and where?

But all thoughts of her antecedents were lost as he concentrated on the labour of love before him. He began by individually wrapping her fingers and toes in fine linen. Then, the arms and legs were wrapped separately and in between the layers he placed amulets to protect the body on its journey through the underworld – an Isis Knot and a Plummet amulet – while all the time incanting spells to ward off evil spirits. When all four limbs were satisfactorily wrapped, the old man tied the arms and legs together and began the process of bandaging the whole body in more linen strips, this time carefully painting each layer with liquid resin that would bond them together. After the bandages, the body was wrapped in a single sheet on top of which would normally be painted a picture of Osiris, the god of the dead. But his instructions for the preparation of this young woman were different. Instead of the picture of Osiris, he had been given a small gold tablet, no bigger than the dead girl's hand, on which were a series of tiny triangular indentations that could have been a pattern or a language. He had never seen their like before and they were meaningless to him. All he had to do was secure the tablet to the mummy's final wrapping with a dab of the liquid resin before fastening it for all eternity with more linen strips that would run from head to toe and around its middle.

Mummification complete, all that remained was for him

to lower the preserved body into its ornate wooden coffin. His instructions from that point on were unequivocal – he was to leave the coffin on the mortuary floor, nail a square of linen to the door, which was to be left unlocked, and not return until the linen square had been removed. He knew not and cared not for whom he was working, the promise of a sum of money far beyond even his most excessive dreams having bought his co-operation and his silence.

His task complete, the old man blew out the stubs of the candles, secured the linen square to the door and walked off into the desert night.

For four days and nights he dared not venture near the mortuary for fear of what he might find. But on the fifth day curiosity overcame fright and he set off with his two faithful dogs into the desert. From a full quarter mile away he could see that the square of linen had gone from the door. When he reached the ramshackle building he saw immediately that there were no tracks marking anyone's arrival or departure. Nor was there any sign of his linen marker. Heart racing with trepidation, he pushed against the wooden door, which swung open without resistance.

Inside, the coffin and its mummified contents had gone. The mortuary had been stripped of every trace of his work; every candle, every scrap of linen; even the tiny spills of resin had vanished, concealing the building's secret forever and leaving it, once more, just another apparently abandoned desert shelter.

Chapter Two

The powerful overhead strip lighting in the windowless ante-room masked the fact the clock was showing that in the outside world it was two in the morning as Jack Denham scrubbed his hands and forearms with anti-bacterial soap under running water so hot it would have made a half decent cup of instant coffee. Ablutions completed, he turned off the long-armed taps with his elbows, hands held aloft to prevent cross infection. A nurse, already scrubbed, masked and gowned, held open a pair of fine latex gloves, into which he thrust his newly disinfected hands.

Slightly more than an hour previously he had been roused from a deep, dreamless sleep by a persistent sound that his unconsciousness mind took a few seconds to identify as his bedside telephone. His half-wakened grunt of an answer was ignored by the female caller.

'Good morning Herr Denham, I'm sorry to waken you but a donor heart has been identified,' she said, her voice businesslike and matter-of-fact, as if she made similar calls every day. 'The organ will be here in less than one hour and your patient is already being prepared. Your team is being assembled and you are required in theatre without delay.'

'Of course. I'm on my way.' A mumbled response as the enormity of what the caller had just said coursed the blood through his veins, shaking off the shackles of sleep. Twenty minutes later, after a lightning fast shower and a quick caffeine hit from a cup of microwave-warmed coffee left over in the cafetiere from last night, he was in his car heading for Frankfurt's main hospital.

The American Army was to blame for his life in the heartland of Germany. As a young officer in the Medical Corps, they had sent him to the Ramstein Air Force base in 1991 to help treat the serious casualties expected from the first Gulf War. In the event there were few but he fell in love with this corner of Bavaria, fought off every move to return him to his native Idaho and eventually married a German doctor alongside whom he had worked at Ramstein. He had retired 10 years later with the rank of Colonel, an expertise in cardio-thoracic surgery and a burgeoning interest in transplant surgery. That, coupled with a fluency in German that betrayed his home roots, had been enough to secure him a job as a consultant surgeon at the Johann Wolfgang Goethe University

Hospital in Frankfurt, one of the most progressive hospitals in Europe.

As the nurse handed him his theatre apron which he would wear over his bright green scrubs, his assistant Gustav 'Gus' Harvald appeared at the ante-room door.

'Patient's nearly ready boss.' There was no time for formalities and anyway, the pair knew each other well enough for it not to matter.

'What do we know about the donor then?'

'Young Kurdish girl. Eighteen. Killed in a road accident in southern Turkey apparently,' answered Gus.

'Southern Turkey? How long ago?'

'About six hours."

"So how did they get the heart here so quickly?'

'In the cockpit of an American Air Force F-16 it would seem.'

Jack let out an involuntary whistle.

'That's impressive. They don't normally use those babies as supersonic taxis.'

'Guess it helps when your old man is the US Ambassador to Germany though,' ventured Gus.

'Was there no suitable donor closer?' asked Jack.

'I don't know the answer to that one,' said Gus. 'But it seems that from the moment they opened up the dead girl, our guy's name was on her heart. We don't even know who removed the heart or where. We were just told it was earmarked for us. The F-16 was diverted from a combat mission over Iraq to collect it at Incirlik Air Base and blast it up here, flat out all the way to Ramstein then from there to here by helicopter.'

For an instant a chill gripped Jack. He was well aware of the activities of unscrupulous 'dealers' who preyed on the families of patients in urgent need of all kinds of organ transplants, offering to buy them their dreams for the right price. Frequently that price involved pain and even death to poverty stricken peasants who had been persuaded to sell a kidney or half a liver. It was even possible to buy a heart, the 'donor' usually simply disappearing, leaving a family bewildered and bereft. But, abhorrent as he found the practise, the truth was that the chance to save the 15 year-old life of James Vanderburgh, only son of Ambassador Hugo Vanderburgh and his wife Alicia, was in his hands and he was not about to let it pass him by, irrespective of where the heart had come from or how repugnant he found it.

In the operating theatre, he found James already anaesthetised, the endotrachael tube that would maintain his airway in place and the Swan-Ganz catheter, through which blood oxygen levels could be monitored, inserted into his jugular vein and threaded through to his pulmonary artery. A quick check around the theatre confirmed his team, each one hand-picked by him, was in place.

‘''OK everybody, he said. 'Sorry about the ungodly hour. Let's do this. Scalpel.'

The theatre nurse confidently placed the instrument in

his right hand and without a second thought, Jack made an incision along young James's sternum from just below his throat almost to his belly button. Then, using a miniature high-powered circular saw, he cut through the sternum itself, divided the rib cage and exposed the pericardium, the double-walled sac that contained the heart, which he opened using a second scalpel.

Now, the wonder of life itself, the beating heart of another human being, lay exposed to his gaze – although in James's case his heart had become enlarged by dilated cardiomyopathy, the cause of which was as yet unknown to medical science, but which left him breathless and at risk of suffering a build up of fluid in his lungs because his heart was too weak to properly pump blood around his body.

The surgical team now connected James to a heart-lung machine, which would take over his vital functions while the transplant itself was carried out. Once the machine was in place and working efficiently, Jack took another scalpel and, with a slight feeling of trepidation, sliced through the collection of primary blood vessels known as the Great Vessels. One by one the vena cava, the pulmonary artery and the aorta were cut from the diseased heart. Another deft cut transected the left atrium, leaving behind a circular portion that contained the pulmonary veins. Gently Jack lifted the useless, lifeless organ from James's body and placed it in a surgical tray.

The donor heart was now taken from its sealed

transportation case and inserted into James's chest cavity. The left atrium was trimmed to fit the circular portion of James's own atrium that Jack had left behind and stitched into place. The vena cava, pulmonary artery and aorta were stitched into place in the new heart.

Jack looked around his team and could see the anxiety in each pair of eyes.

'OK people. The moment of truth. Restart the blood flow.'

As the heart-lung machine's function was reduced, Jack gently massaged the new heart. As the warm blood began to flow through it, he could feel its increasing power through his fingertips. Then, a beat. And a second. And a third.

Within a couple of minutes, the new heart was functioning fully, pushing oxygen-rich blood around James's body. Beneath his surgical mask, Jack could not help but grin. He had rehearsed this operation a thousand times. He had practised on cadavers. He had read virtually every medical paper written on the subject of transplants, including those of Professor Christian Barnard, who had performed the world's first successful heart transplant back in 1967 at the Groote Schuur Hospital in Cape Town on a 59 year-old called Louis Washkansky.

But until today it had all been theory. Today was the first time he had ever attempted a heart transplant on a living person. And it had been a success.

'Great work everybody. Looks like the boy's got a

fighting chance now,' he told his team. 'Gus, close him up and get him into the cardiology intensive care unit. I'm going home to catch up on my beauty sleep.'

'Yeah, well, you need it,' quipped Gus, but Jack was already back in the ante-room throwing his scrubs into the bin for laundering.

Outside, in the comfortable cocoon of his Mercedes, he noticed the dashboard clock was showing 7.00am. Five hours out of his life but, hopefully, many years on James's. It was a good feeling.

Chapter Three

Pat Hills hated rain with a passion. In his personal paradise, the sun blazed unrelentingly from a cloudless sky and nobody had need for raincoats or umbrellas. Rain simply did not exist.

That was why, as the rain slashed across the windscreen of his parked patrol car, reducing the outside world to a blur, Police Constable Hills was elsewhere. In his mind he was soaking up the sun. The Cambridgeshire Fens and the trunk roads he was employed to police simply did not exist on this most miserable of Saturday nights. He saw only brilliant sunlight and felt only its gentle warmth caressing his skin.

That was also why he did not see the foreign-registered truck that hurtled by so close it rocked the patrol car and thundered on into the night, not showing any rear lights, as the law required it to.

'Christ, he's moving a bit. I think we should have a look at him.'

The voice of his colleague Brian Thomas brought Pat back to the real, wringing wet world.

'What?'

'That truck. He had the hammer down good and proper. And he'd no rear lights,' said Brian.

'Sorry, I didn't see him. I was miles away. Let's see what he's got to say for himself.'

As Pat turned the ignition key, Brian hit two buttons on a keypad, one which turned on the flashing blue light array on the roof and the supplementary blue lights concealed behind the radiator grill, the other which activated the wailing siren that warned other road users of their presence.

The fact that it was close to midnight and the truck was the first vehicle they had seen for well over 30 minutes made no difference. They wanted the truck driver to be well aware that they were behind him.

It took just over a mile for the police car to catch up with the articulated truck. But even though the road was deserted and Pat kept back at a distance from which the truck driver could not mistake the flashing lights in his mirrors, the lorry ploughed on, showing no signs of slowing down and making no effort to move over to let the police car pass.

'Right pal. If that's the way you want to play it . . .' Pat said to no one in particular.

The A1 was a dual carriageway and Roman road straight as Pat pressed the accelerator and pulled out to overtake. As they passed, Brian pressed a couple more buttons on his keypad and a red dot-matrix sign lit up the patrol car's back window. It said: 'Stop.'

They guided the artic into a nearby lay-by and, pulling on high-visibility waterproof jackets, got out to speak to the driver, who was already climbing out of his cab. He showed the pair a driving licence which identified him as a Romanian national, even though he was driving a truck that belonged to a haulage company in Bulgaria. His command of English could by no means be described as good, but it was infinitely superior to the policemen's grasp of his mother tongue. It therefore took several minutes to establish that he was carrying a load of sportswear to a warehouse in Leeds; that he had been on the road for four days and that he had crossed the English Channel via Euro Tunnel.

Pat had just begun his lecture on the legal requirement to display red lights at the rear of a vehicle at night when his partner put a hand on his arm.

'Did you hear that?'

'Hear what?'

'A noise. From inside the truck . . . Listen. That's it.'

The Romanian driver watched, utterly bemused, as the two officers of the law now pressed their ears to the side of his trailer and screwed up their faces, as if the gesture would somehow improve their hearing.

This time Pat heard it.

It was muffled and indistinguishable but sounded very much like something – or someone – moving inside the trailer.

'Right pal. I think you'd better open this thing up.'

As the heavy double doors at the back of the trailer swung open, the policemen could see that it was stacked from floor to roof with large, unmarked cardboard boxes. But a close look revealed a gap between the bottom row of the boxes and the side of the vehicle.

Pat shone his torch into the gap. The powerful beam fleetingly illuminated a human face before its owner ducked back behind the stack of boxes.

'Bloody hell Brian. He's got illegals in there,' he shouted. 'Call for back-up and ask for the Borders and Immigration Agency to attend.'

Turning to the bewildered trucker he added: 'And you pal, are nicked.'

It was more than four hours later by the time the Borders and Immigration Agency had removed six Turkish men from the trailer and taken them off to a detention centre for processing. The driver was taken away for questioning on suspicion of people smuggling and an inventory of the truck's cargo was being carried out by two probationer policemen.

Curses and oaths floated freely from the trailer as the

pair struggled to manoeuvre the heavy boxes. The task was almost over when one of the probationers called out: 'I think you'd better come and have a look at this.'

'What is it?' asked Brian.

'It looks like a coffin.'

Pat, born in Scotland, given an Irish name that his parents insisted on pronouncing like a girl's and raised in England, had had a lifetime of wind-ups.

'Yeah, yeah. Don't they teach you anything original at training school these days?'

'No, seriously. It does,' the young officer replied. 'Come and have a look if you don't believe me.'

Pat clambered into the back of the trailer, now almost stripped of its load, and stared in disbelief at the object over which the two officers were standing.

It was an oblong box, about five feet long and securely bound in bubble-wrap. Taking a small knife from his pocket, he cut through the wrapping and shone his torch into the slit. The light illuminated exquisite carving. Whatever it was the object was obviously very old and quite possible highly valuable.

And it may, or may not, contain a body.

'Brian, we'd better get CID here quick. We're out of our depth on this one.'

Chapter Four

'Excuse me Karen, I've got a policeman on the 'phone. A Detective Inspector Wilson. He wants to talk to you.' Margaret Jones worked in the Fitzwilliam Museum's secretariat and firmly believed in the direct approach so, instead of using the internal telephone, she had poked her head around the door marked: Curator, Egyptology.

Karen Bowen sighed. The Fitzwilliam, in the centre of Cambridge, was justly proud of its place as one of the best – and best-known – institutions in Britain when it came to ancient history. But sometimes, just sometimes, its reputation could be a pain in the neck when all sorts of people from journalists to MP's researchers rang up asking pointless, even plain stupid, questions that could be just as easily answered in half an hour on the Internet.

'Oh God. Do I need this on a Monday morning? What does he want?'

'I didn't ask him specifically but I think he wants your help.'

'Help? That's all I need to kick-start my week, a plod that needs help. OK. Put him through.'

She sat back and waited for the phone to ring, answering with curt: 'Karen Bowen.'

'Good morning. DI Ray Wilson, Arts and Antiques Unit at Cambridgeshire Police. I've got a problem and I'm hoping you can help me solve it.'

The voice was a rich baritone that retained just a hint of a Fenland accent. Even from his brief words she guessed it belonged to a man who could be very persuasive and did not accept no for an answer.

'I'll try my best. Fire away.'

'Well, we've come across this old coffin. Actually, it looks very old. We reckon it could be Egyptian. And I was wondering if you could take a look at it for us?'

'A coffin? Where on earth did you find that and why do you think it's Egyptian?' she asked, barely able to conceal the incredulity in her voice.

'Er, actually, it's a bit more than that. From the weight of it there's something inside. We don't know what but I suppose it could be a mummy.'

'What? I do hope you're not taking the mickey Mr Wilson. How does an Egyptian mummy, complete with coffin, manage to turn up in Cambridgeshire?' She found herself glancing at the calendar, just to confirm it wasn't April Fool's Day.

'I assure you this is not a joke,' said Wilson. 'One of our traffic patrols stopped a foreign truck on the A1 near Peterborough on Saturday night. When they searched it, they found it contained half a dozen illegal immigrants – and this coffin with its mummy. Naturally, the illegals claimed no knowledge of the coffin and the driver is saying he knows nothing about either the immigrants or the coffin. But if the coffin and the mummy are genuine – and with our limited knowledge they appear to be – they must be worth a considerable amount of money. We need to find out all we can then maybe we will have a clue as to who owns it, what it's doing in the UK and where it was going.'

'OK. I can't promise I'll be able to contribute anything positive to your enquiry but I'll have a look at it for you,' said Karen. 'Where can I see it?'

'Well, that's the other thing we were hoping you could help us with. We've got it in a police garage at the moment, which is not ideal. We were wondering whether there was any chance you could keep it in your store room. You know, look after it kind of thing, until we know more about it. After all, you're the experts. You know how it should be treated and handled. '

She felt her face colour up as she struggled to suppress the flash of anger that coursed through her. The presumption of the man. She didn't know him from Adam yet here he was asking her to take charge of a potentially priceless antiquity, precisely because, it seemed to her, he didn't want the responsibility of keeping it himself.

'Just hang on a minute Inspector,' she said. 'The Fitzwilliam can't accept responsibility for this, this artefact or whatever it turns out to be. It could be anything. It could be one the greatest finds in the history of archaeology. Or it could be stuffed full of drugs for all you know. And what happens when the drug dealers find out where it is and come to take it back? You could be putting me, my staff and all the collections we have here at serious risk. No. I'm sorry. I can't do it. I'll look at it by all means but you can't keep it here.'

If her unexpected reaction dismayed or annoyed Wilson, he didn't show it. His voice remained calm as he turned on his powers of persuasion.

'Look, I'm sorry, I didn't mean that you should take full responsibility for it. Let me put it another way. How about if we bring it round to the museum, you keep it for as long as it takes and we put a 24-hour guard on it so you are not responsible for its security? As soon as you've done all you can with it, we'll take it away again. Is that a reasonable compromise?'

'So all we have to do is examine it, then you'll put it back in your garage or wherever?'

'Exactly.'

'Alright Inspector. I'm probably about to make a huge mistake but ok, you've got a deal.'

'Terrific. I'll get it loaded up and we'll be with you about two o'clock. Looking forward to meeting you. Goodbye for now.'

Before she got chance to respond, the line went dead.

Trepidation mixed with excitement as she buzzed Margaret Jones. 'Margaret, can you pop in for a second? I need your help.'

As a distant clock chimed two, both women stood in the enclosed yard that served as the Fitzwilliam's access point for deliveries of all kinds, watching as four bewildered porters struggled to unload a bubble-wrap encased oblong box from the back of an unmarked police Ford Transit under the watchful gaze of two firearms officers, each wearing a bullet proof vest and cradling a Heckler & Koch MP5 sub-machinegun.

Within five minutes, the box was atop a stainless steel table in the Egyptology department's very own store room deep within the basement of the museum. Despite the apparent security of the location, Wilson was as good as his word and the two firearms officers remained on guard outside the door.

Karen walked around the heavily wrapped box, running her fingers over the surface, desperately resisting the temptation to squeeze and pop the bubbles, an act so satisfyingly trivial she usually found it immensely therapeutic. But with Detective Inspector Ray Wilson standing silent in the corner she thought it appropriate to adopt a more professional air. She noticed that parts of the wrapping had been ripped open, probably by the policemen who found it.

'Mr Wilson, tell me again everything you know about the coffin,' she said, taking in his toned frame and the little white lines radiating from the corners of his eyes, betraying a man who clearly lived an outdoor life; a man who hated being indoors.

'Please, call me Ray.' Obviously practised at putting people at ease, he was also a clear and effective communicator. He went on: 'Like I told you on the 'phone, one of our traffic patrols stopped a truck on the A1 on Saturday night. Apparently it wasn't showing any rear lights.

'The truck was registered to a bone fide haulage company in Bulgaria, although the driver turned out to be Romanian and the six illegals were Turks. They're currently in a detention centre but we've still got the driver in custody and he's being questioned about a potential offence of people trafficking.

'Both the haulage company and the driver deny all knowledge of the coffin although it was found underneath a pile of cardboard boxes containing sportswear that was the truck's main cargo, which would indicate it was loaded at the same time. The sportswear was destined for a mail order company in Leeds and they also say they know nothing about any coffin, ancient or otherwise.

'Our unit was called in when the officer in charge of the initial enquiry realised that the coffin could have some historical significance. My degree is in the history of art so I'm well away from my area of expertise with this one. Which is why we've come to you. Whatever you can tell us will be a bonus.'

*

'We can start by removing all this bubble wrap. Sophisticated as they were, the ancient Egyptians hadn't discovered polymers.' As she spoke, she picked up a craft knife and began to carefully slice through the duct tape that held the wrapping in place.

'Can you preserve it? Put it in a bin liner for me? It might just yield something useful later. Sorry. Copper's mind and all that.'

Within five minutes the plastic had been cut away, the revelation leaving Karen, Margaret Jones and Wilson open-mouthed in astonishment. There, before them lay the work of a master craftsman. The five-foot long oblong box was intricately carved with rosettes, trees and random patterns with joints so tight they were barely visible, but cut into its lid was the exquisitely sculpted death mask of a beautiful young girl, the painted, sightless eyes staring the stare of millennia. For a flash, Margaret Jones wondered if she was the only one puzzled by the fact that the eyes hadn't blinked in the intense glare of the neon strip lighting. Below the mask was a small plate, maybe 120cm by 70cm, on which were carved a series of small, triangular marks.

It was Karen who broke the silence.

'Mr Wilson, I suspect we may have something very special here. I propose that I spend the rest of the day enlisting some assistance and that tomorrow we try to find out what secrets this young lady has to reveal.'

Chapter Five

By the time Wilson arrived at the storeroom the following morning, photographic flood lights had been set up, along with two video cameras to record proceedings from different angles. Karen was already there with an olive skinned man in his early 30s who she introduced as her deputy, Salim Badawi and a photographer who she introduced simply as Eric. A microphone was suspended from the ceiling, linked to a digital audio recorder in the corner which was being guarded and operated by the woman he recognised from the previous day as Margaret Jones.

Karen began the examination by describing in minute detail every pattern, every mark, every cut, every blemish on the surface of the ornate casket. When she came to the carved panel with its triangular marks she stopped.

'Salim, take a close look at this for me. Tell me if it's what I think it is.'

Salim produced a magnifying glass from his pocket and examined the panel. For the best part of five minutes there was silence; then he stood, sliding the glass back into his left hand trouser pocket.

'Yes. I think it is, although it's badly worn. I can make out a few characters like 'adama' – I am – and 'ducta' – daughter. But reading it all is going to be very difficult, if not impossible.'

'Read what? What is it?' asked Wilson.

'It's cuneiform script Inspector,' said Karen. 'Which creates a major, major puzzle for us.'

'Why? What's the problem?' He made it sound like an interrogation rather than a straight forward question.

Salim gave him the explanation.

'Cuneiform was the written language of the ancient Sumerians, the Persians; the country we know today as Iran. Another powerful civilisation from roughly the same period as ancient Egypt. The puzzle it gives us is this. The presence of cuneiform script would indicate that if this is a mummy, it is of Persian origin. But the Persians didn't mummify their dead. And the Egyptians didn't use cuneiform script. So how has it come to be used on what appears to be an Egyptian mummy?

'The only obvious explanation is that the Persians have copied Egyptian mummification techniques, or that they brought in Egyptian embalmers to preserve a member of their own nobility.'

'And if that's the case,' interjected Karen, 'what we have

here is unique. There are no Persian mummies in existence. More than that, there are no records of any member of any Persian dynasty being preserved in this way.

'That means this casket and its contents are probably priceless.'

The silence was tangible as the full implications of Karen's last statement sank in with the people present.

Whether Wilson was overwhelmed by the enormity of what he had just heard or simply stunned was impossible to gauge. His professionalism did not slip as he asked: 'Just how priceless is priceless?'

'I'm not an experienced valuer,' said Karen. 'But I'd say if it's genuine it would be beyond the reach of any Egyptology collection in this country and probably any collection in Europe. You're undoubtedly looking at tens of millions of pounds.'

'Bloody hell.' The words slid involuntarily from the policeman, a hairline crack in his composure. 'So where do we go from here?'

A brief smile played around Karen's mouth as she looked at Salim for some gesture of support for what she was about to suggest.

'Well. I'd say that the first thing we need to do is end the speculation and find out what's inside our mysterious coffin.'

Salim nodded almost imperceptibly as he murmured his agreement, leaving Wilson little choice but to also agree.

'Alright, if you think that's the best way forward. But let's be bloody careful.'

Salim produced a long, wide-bladed knife that looked vaguely surgical and began to insert it between the coffin and its lid. Satisfied he had located the pegs that locked the lid in place, he repeated the process, this time using a chisel. After a few minutes levering, twisting, pushing and persuading the lid was loose.

'OK Karen. Let's take an end each.'

The lid came clear cleanly and undamaged, itself a thing of great beauty but as nothing compared to what its removal disclosed.

Inside was a perfectly preserved mummy, an elaborate gold mask covering its face, its resin-impregnated wrappings dried to a hard, protective shell. And on its chest, a gold plate covered in the same kind of triangular markings as the carving on the coffin lid.

Salim was aware of the whirr from the Nikon's motordrive as Eric the photographer recorded his every move as he again produced his magnifying glass and began to study the plate. It seemed like the minutes were hours, his lips moving silently as he worked to decipher the ancient writing. Finally, he looked up, enigmatically rubbing his chin.

'Amazing. I've never seen anything like it.'

Karen asked: 'Can you read this one?'

'Oh yes,' replied Salim. 'It's perfectly preserved. It's as clear as if it had been written yesterday.'

'Well what does it say then?'

From the look on his face, it was obvious Salim was having difficulty believing his own translation.

'It says,' he started, 'it says: "I am Rhodugune daughter of the great King Xerxes. Mazereka protect me".'

The effect was as if the whole room had suddenly become a freeze-frame in the motion picture of life. Nobody moved. Nobody spoke. It seemed that nobody even breathed. Wilson was the first to break the hush, prompted by his police training.

'Right, we need to take stock of what we've got here. Is there somewhere we can get a coffee and talk?'

'My office is as good as anywhere. Margaret, can you organise it and we'll see you there in five? Eric, I'll give you a call when I need you again.'

Karen, Salim and Wilson waited while the photographer packed away his gear. As they left Princess Rhodugune in peace – for the time being – Wilson issued a terse order to the armed men still standing guard at the door.

'Nobody and I mean absolutely nobody goes in there unless I'm with them. Understand?'

'Seems a lot of fuss over an old stiff if you ask me,' one officer muttered to his colleague as they watched the backs of the three disappear around the corner, heading for the staircase that would take them to Karen's first floor office.

In the relative comfort of the curator's office, the three of them sipped freshly made coffee at the meeting table, sunlight dappling the oak floor through the stained, leaded lights that topped off the pseudo-Gothic windows. Wilson consulted his note book.

'So. If I'm interpreting what I've just witnessed correctly, the mummy is genuine and appears to be of Persian origin, making it one of the most valuable archaeological discoveries ever made. And it fell off the back of a lorry near Peterborough. Amazing. You couldn't make it up.'

Salim said: 'The evidence is pointing in that direction but we need to do a lot more work before we can be certain of what we've got. One thing I can tell you is that Xerxes ruled a vast empire around 2,500 years ago. It stretched from the Mediterranean in the west to India in the east and, interestingly, to Egypt in the south. Xerxes and his father Darius built an extravagant city called Persepolis, the remains of which can still be seen today. It's a World Heritage site about 400 miles south of the modern city of Tehran, which, in case you're wondering how I know so much about ancient Persian history, is my home city.

'Hundreds of stonemasons worked on the construction of Persepolis, mainly carving decorative images on the royal palaces and undoubtedly some of them were Egyptian. So it's not beyond the bounds of possibility that other craftsmen and artisans – such as embalmers – also worked there. To my mind, just because there's no record of mummification in Persia doesn't mean to say that individual members of the royal family were not treated in that way. After all, no remains of Persian royalty have ever been found. Until now.'

'I accept what you say. But I'm more interested in the body inside that coffin.' The policeman in Wilson once more took over from the art historian. 'The cuneiform script tells us she was Princess Rhodugune, Xerxes' daughter but we need to know more about her. How did she die? How old was she when she died? And where has this mummy been for the last 2,500 years?'

'Well, from where I'm sitting there's only one logical next step,' said Karen. 'She has to go to hospital.'

'What?'

'X-rays. We need to see what the body inside the wrappings looks like. We need to X-ray it.'

Chapter Six

Dr Phil Bennett was a busy man and right now he was not in a mood to be toyed with. Things had gone badly from the moment he stepped out of his front door. His car and his driveway were so familiar that reversing out into the tree-lined avenue was second nature – so much so that this morning his exit was accompanied by that pained, expensive sound of gate hinge on shiny metal. Then the board meeting he had to endure for the thick end of five hours had reached some decisions he didn't agree with and which would, he was sure, affect his ability to carry out his work as senior radiologist at the Nuffield Hospital, Cambridge. And now he had this woman on the 'phone, a woman he vaguely remembered meeting at a barbecue weeks before, asking for something that sounded so corny Indiana Jones himself could have been making the request. He knew that one day he would regret saying to people he didn't properly know: 'If ever I can help . . .'

Now it looked like that day had arrived, wearing a greasy Homburg and cracking a bull-hide whip.

'Let me see if I've got this right,' he said, the disbelief audible in his voice. 'You want me to X-ray a woman who's been dead for 2,500 years or more? Just so you can see what the body looks like?'

'That's something of an over-simplification but, basically, yes,' answered Karen.

'Why would I?'

'Because it could be the single most important archaeological discovery in history. It would make your name.'

'Karen, what I don't need is to make my name. What I need is to make money. Who's going to pay if – and it is only an if – I agree?'

'I was hoping that given the potential for a place in the great pantheon of world history, the Nuffield might look upon it as an act of charity.'

'Now you are taking the piss. The directors would hang me out to dry. Radiology isn't cheap you know. It's not like knocking off a few frames with a digital camera. To do this job properly would cost a fair amount of money.'

'I'm aware of that Phil. But think of the prestige. You would go down in history as the man who helped solve the riddle of Princess Rhodugune.

'At least let us introduce you to her. Then you can walk away if you want to and we'll find somewhere else to help us.'

Determined and immovable as he liked to think he was, Phil Bennett had always been a sucker for the soft sell, especially when it was delivered by a female, which was how he found himself in a storeroom beneath the Fitzwilliam Museum, guarded by two armed policemen, staring in awe at the ornate casket and mummy of the only daughter of one of the most famous kings of one of the greatest ancient civilisations in history.

No further pleading, persuading or petitioning was necessary. The sight of Rhodugune in her coffin, beneath her elaborate gold death mask did the trick. The Nuffield's radiology facilities were put at the disposal of the combined archaeological-police team.

Karen, Salim and DI Ray Wilson crowded around the wall-mounted light table as Phil Bennett explained what they were looking at. The entire coffin had been X-rayed from every conceivable angle but the rays had been unable to properly penetrate the mummy itself so it was impossible to tell whether the body had been prepared for the afterlife in the ritualistic Egyptian manner.

'The one thing I can tell you though is that this girl was under 21 when she died,' said Dr Bennett.

'How can you tell that?' asked Wilson.

'If you look at this plate . . . this is the pelvic bone and this, the thing that appears to be a white sliver is called the epiphysus. It's actually where the bone is still growing. When women reach the age of 21 that growth is complete and the gap – the epiphysus – closes. Although I can't give you an exact age for this girl at the moment, I'm confident in saying she was under 21.'

'Very interesting but it doesn't take us much further forward,' said Salim. 'I was hoping we could find out more about the body itself. Is there anything else we can do?'

'As a matter of fact there is,' said Bennett, warming to his new role as archaeological investigator. 'We can put the coffin and its contents through the CAT scanner and see what the wonders of computerised axial tomography can reveal.'

'Pardon my ignorance doctor, but what will a CAT scan show us that the X-ray can't?' Typical PC Plod question, thought Karen, although Wilson appeared to be genuinely curious rather than merely sarcastic.

'Oh lots,' replied Bennett. 'Think of the CAT scanner as a 3-D X-ray machine. Instead of producing images in just one plane, it rotates around the body producing 360 degree images. The end result is a series of images that appear like slices through the body. I'll get a couple of porters to take our princess through to the scanner now.'

Close up, the CAT scanner resembled something from a bad science-fiction film. It consisted of what looked like a giant, electronic doughnut, through which a body-length table could be passed. The entire assembly was surrounded by dials, switches and flashing lights. The four porters gingerly lifted the coffin onto the table and secured it gently with restraining straps. In the control room next door, Bennett nodded to the scanner operator who pushed a large, red, oblong button marked 'Expose' and sat back.

Wilson imagined he could hear a faint electronic hum as the coffin passed slowly through the scanner. Apart from the blinking lights, the movement was the only outward sign that the machine was doing anything at all. With four pairs of eyes glued to its progress, it seemed to take an eternity for the coffin to pass through the machine. Then it began its equally slow return journey.

'Save them as 'Mummy' and we'll be back in 20 minutes. I need a caffeine injection,' Bennett instructed the CAT operator.

Duly revived by large cappuccinos, Karen, Salim and Ray Wilson stood in silent astonishment as Phil Bennett matter-of-factly talked them through the individual CAT scan images, where necessary explaining in detail what the miracle machine had unveiled.

'The first thing to say is that the body appears to be remarkably well preserved,' he said. 'Look here at the abdominal cavity . . . You can see what looks like a large aperture running from the middle of the abdomen round to the side of the body, probably where the internal organs were removed. And this . . .' using his Mont Blanc fountain pen as a pointer . . . 'would seem to be a bandage that has fallen down into the cavity.'

Before anyone could make any kind of comment or question his interpretations, he had flicked on to the next slide.

'So, here we are in the thorax and the first thing we notice is that there are no internal organs. In a normal body you would see the heart and lungs here but in this one there is some kind of dense material lying on both sides of the vertebrae. I suspect it may be the packing that the embalmers used to retain the body shape.'

'There's no heart?' asked Karen.

'No. Were you expecting one?'

'Well, yes,' she replied. 'The ancient Egyptians were very particular about the ritual of mummification and the preservation of the internal organs. Things like the lungs, liver and intestines were normally preserved in individual stone jars but the heart was left in place because they believed it was the centre of intelligence and would therefore be needed in the afterlife.'

Wilson put in: 'But you've said you believe this mummy is Persian. Did they believe the heart would be needed in the afterlife too?'

'What I've said is that there indications this could be a Persian mummy. Even if it is, it's almost certain it was done by Egyptian embalmers so I would expect to see the heart still in place.

'I need to do a lot more research but I'm beginning to get a strange feeling about our little Princess.'

Chapter Seven

Through the haze and fug of an alcohol induced sleep, it took her several seconds to identify the distant, shrill sound as the ringing of a telephone, an old-fashioned landline handset that actually rang rather than trying to recreate an orchestral symphony with electronic beeps. She tripped back into consciousness but it took several more seconds before her right arm extended in the general direction of the bedside cabinet and her hand fumbled to find the phone. There was a crash and a clatter of plastic and aluminium, closely followed by the faint but unmistakable hum of a dial tone, as the handset and its cradle arced to the bedroom floor.

The racket shocked her into sitting bolt upright and at exactly that moment a red hot stiletto blade lanced its way from the back of her skull through to her forehead, causing stars in yet-unopened eyes. Shit, shit, shit. Port.

Fucking port. It always did her that way. Especially in the quantities she consumed. Every time was the last. Until the next, of course. Friday night poker and port sessions with the girls had become the norm since she had restarted her life in her own little cottage in the village of Sawston after going through the trauma of splitting a previously happy home down the middle as the result of a divorce 18 months ago. Now aged 36, Karen still enjoyed a good time, enjoyed a few drinks and would probably enjoy love again one day, but she had never been fond of night clubs and believed her age was a barrier to the raucous pubs in the city centre that were the domain of the university's international conglomeration of students. So, for now, Friday night sessions with the clutch of women she held dear – and the spin-off invitations that came with their friendship – was just about the extent of her social life.

And then there was that bloody noise again.

This time she managed to locate the phone and pick it up without mishap.

'Yes.' It was neither greeting, nor interrogation, nor agreement. It was, rather, an acknowledgement of consciousness and, to those who knew, a warning to tread warily.

'Karen, it's Salim.'

'Salim, it's nine o'clock on Saturday morning.'

'Yes, I know that. I've waited a couple of hours to call you in case you were having a lie-in. I hope I haven't woken you but I've discovered something about the mummy that you need to know.'

'Well, make it quick so I can go back into my stupor.'

'No, Karen . . . this is really important . . . I, I . . . er, I think it might be a fake.'

A fake. It might be a fake. The words echoed through her brain like a cannon shot in a canyon. Her adrenal gland went into meltdown mode pumping adrenalin into her bloodstream ensuring that she was instantly wide awake and that Salim had her total, undivided attention.

'Explain what you mean.'

'I've been doing some research,' he began. 'And I've discovered that Xerxes' daughter wasn't called Rhodugune. She was called Wardegauna. Rhodugune is a later, Greek translation of the name Wardegauna.'

'Salim, sorry, but I'm not sure I'm following you.'

'Don't you see? Whoever carved the name Rhodugune used a translation from a later era. There's no way the master engravers of the Persian Court would have made that mistake. It means that whoever carved the cuneiform script on both the chest plate and the coffin did so after the Greeks had conquered Persia and long after Wardegauna had died. It means the mummy in the coffin cannot possibly be her.'

There was silence from the other end of the line.

'Karen? You still there?'

'Yes. I'm dumbfounded. I don't know what to say. Meet me in my office in half an hour.'

Just over 30 minutes later, Karen was at her desk drinking black coffee fortified, unusually for her, by two heaped teaspoons of sugar. She badly needed the double hit. Salim contented himself with a bottle of mineral water.

'OK. So accepting what you say about the wrong name, do we have anything else that might help us to prove, or disprove, the provenance of the mummy and the coffin?'

'No. There are a couple of minor grammatical errors in the cuneiform script but I don't believe they're significant. It's the name that's the biggest clue.'

'In that case we need to do some digging. I suggest you and I go over our little princess and her coffin with a fine tooth comb and look for anything that doesn't look right or doesn't add up. Anything at all that may have been missed on first examination. Then we can make a decision on how we proceed.'

As Karen, still clutching her by-now lukewarm coffee, and Salim approached the subterranean store room, the armed policemen still on guard appeared startled.

'Sorry ma'am,' said one. 'DI Wilson's orders are that no one goes in there without him.'

'You bloody idiot,' barked Karen, 'I'm the bloody curator. It's my bloody store room. Get out of my bloody way.'

'But . . .' the hapless policeman began, suddenly deciding against an argument when he spotted a barely perceptible shake of his colleague's head. 'OK. On you go.'

Inside, Karen switched on every light she could find, revealing the coffin and mummy lying on its stainless steel slab, the exquisitely carved lid standing silent sentinel in the corner. She went burrowing in a deep filing cabinet drawer, emerging with two powerful torches and two magnifying glasses and handed one of each to Salim.

'Right then. You start on that side, I'll do this side. We're looking for anything that may have been overlooked; anything that looks out of place; anything that's wrong or odd. When we've finished with the coffin, we start on the mummy. And there's no rush. We need to take our time and get this right so we can be absolutely 110 per cent sure.'

For close on 90 minutes neither of them spoke. Karen had begun on the left hand side at the head of the coffin and Salim on the right hand side at the foot. The intricate carving along the coffin's flanks made detailed examination difficult but they persevered, twisting their torches this way and that to illuminate every tiny crevice and using water-soaked cotton buds to clean away accumulated dirt.

It was Karen's audible gasp that broke Salim's concentration. He looked up to see her staring fixedly through her magnifying glass.

'Found something?'

'Yes I think so. Have a look at this.'

Salim crouched down beside her and took the glass from her hand.

'Where am I looking exactly?'

'There. Just to the left of the bottom left hand side of that rosette.'

At first he could not make out anything that looked awry. Then he saw it. He moved his torch to illuminate it from another angle. And another. He moved the glass backwards and forwards, as if the very movement would change what he was seeing. But it didn't and what he was seeing was unmistakable.

It was a pencil mark.

Chapter Eight

Even to a casual listener catching just a snatch of Ray Wilson's attempted telephone conversation, it was obvious that whoever was on the other end of the line was not best pleased with him. Try as he might, he was unable to stem the flow of invective and vilification that was mauling his ear.

'But . . .' Followed a few seconds later by: 'Hang on . . .' Then: 'That's just not fair . . .' And finally: 'Karen, it was weekend you know.'

Desperate to divulge the discoveries of Saturday, Karen had called him immediately she and Salim were satisfied that the mark they had found really had been made by a lead pencil, an implement that did not exist until the 17th century. She tried all day Saturday and throughout Sunday but all she got was the recorded message urging her to leave hers.

Blissfully unaware, Ray had spent the weekend more than 100 miles away in Lowestoft, racing in a friend's yacht. He had initially intended to simply drive down to his small cabin cruiser moored at Wroxham on the River Bure and spend a relaxing weekend doing nothing except enjoying the local pubs. If he had done that, his mobile would have been switched on and in his pocket.

But the invitation to go to Lowestoft and race a 32–foot yacht in two races each day proved too much, which in turn meant that the mobile stayed unheard and unmissed in the bottom of his kit bag. Even after the racing, it did not occur to him to check for messages. With the boat squared away, the seven-man crew headed for the bar of the Royal Norfolk and Suffolk Yacht Club to conduct the ritual post-race inquest, all thought of contact with the outside world forsaken. It was only on Monday morning that he realised he had missed 12 calls from a number that he did not immediately recognise.

Now he knew to whom the number belonged.

'Ray, I need you to get over here now,' her voice at last beginning to show signs of a descending calm. 'We've already wasted at least 36 hours because of your gallivanting on your silly boat. I'm desperately worried about the implications of what we've found. You need to see it. And we need to talk about where we go from here – which is obviously not going to be the direction we first thought.'

At least she had called him Ray, not Mr Wilson or

Inspector. Maybe that was a good sign, he thought as he climbed into his car.

In the Fitzwilliam Museum's store room – still watched over by two armed officers – Karen and Salim explained the mistake in the cuneiform script and showed him their startling discovery on the coffin.

'It looks to us like this rosette was probably traced from a stone carving,' explained Karen. 'That would explain its size too. And this mark is where that tracing was copied on to the wood so it could be carved.

'However, taken alongside the fundamental error in the naming of the mummy, it almost certainly means that the coffin – and therefore probably the mummy – are fakes. Which in turn raises its own questions. Who is the dead girl? Who mummified her? When and why?'

'And with respect Ray, that's a job for the police rather than us Egyptologists,' said Salim. 'Although, of course, we will be happy to help you and advise you wherever we can.'

Before Ray Wilson had the chance to reply, Margaret Jones brushed her way past the door guards.

'Sorry to interrupt you Karen, but I've had Dr Bennett on the phone. He needs to see you urgently. He's found something on the CAT scans that he says you need to see.'

Once again, the three of them found themselves clustered around a computer screen in the city's Nuffield Hospital as Phil Bennett explained what they were looking at.

'The first thing to show you is this,' said Bennett, his fountain pen still doubling as a pointer. 'These are the bones of the ear and this is the ear itself, so sound would travel in this direction. In the middle ear is this hour-glass shaped structure and two small bones called ossicles. As you can see, the ossicles are held together by very delicate tendons and ligaments.

'The point is, in an ancient corpse it would be impossible for these tendons and ligaments to survive, even if the body had been mummified. Yet here they are intact. Which, I have to tell you, leads me to the conclusion that this body cannot be ancient.'

He had no idea why his carefully rehearsed bombshell did not have the impact he anticipated, although he was briefly aware of a glance, a spark of recognition, almost of agreement, that passed between the other three.

None of them spoke, so Bennett continued.

'And actually, there's more. If we move on to the spine . . .

'You can see here at the top of the spine, the vertebrae are in a nice straight line. But if we look at it from this angle . . .' the screen switched to a full length side elevation of the body . . . 'You can see that the vertebrae begin to move forwards, abnormally forwards and there is significant disruption of normal anatomy.

'I would say that this girl received a violent blow to her lower spine. So violent that her back was broken. It appears to be a blunt force injury, rather than one caused by a sharp edge. The vertebrae are also rotating, moving to the left, which would indicate that the force that caused this injury was coming from the right.'

He looked up from the screen at three now obviously stunned faces, each with a clutch of questions racing through its brain.

The policeman got his words out first.

'Is the broken back the cause of death?'

'It's possible, although the body is in such a state we might never know for sure what killed her,' the doctor replied.

'But we could be looking at murder here?'

'Again, the best answer I can give you Inspector is that it's possible,' answered Bennett.

By the end of the day, the mummy was in the possession of the Forensic Science Service at their regional headquarters in Huntingdon, suddenly transformed from priceless Persian antiquity to potential murder victim and therefore duly attended by the mountains of paperwork and rivers of administration that accompanies those thought to have died in suspicious circumstances.

All thoughts of rocketed reputations, international lecture tours, fame and fortune had been cast aside in favour of one, as-yet-unspoken seemingly simple, shared aim – to get justice for this poor, mummified, possibly murdered, young girl. As yet, all questions remained unanswered and it was feasible they would stay that way but

Ray Wilson was now putting the emphasis on the 'Detective' part of his rank. He may have been a BA in the history of art; he may have been a senior officer in the Arts and Antiques Unit, but first and foremost he was a copper and his copper's sense was telling him this was a potentially exciting and exacting case.

As the coffin was being loaded into a police van for its journey to Huntingdon, he made a silent vow to do whatever was necessary to remain as investigating officer on this one.

Devoid of armed policemen, casket, mummy and mystery, the Fitzwilliam Museum returned to normal. For now.

Chapter Nine

As senior officer on the case, Ray Wilson was entitled to attend the post mortem but he had had to pull a few strings to get Karen Bowen and Salim Badawi in a position to witness the autopsy at the Forensic Science Service's Hinchingbrooke Park premises. Now, he stood masked and gowned in the autopsy room, watching at first hand the expertise of the Home Office pathologist, Dr Graham Marr. Karen and Salim could only watch from a glass-encased balcony some 15 feet above the autopsy slab. But at least they were there.

After an interminable succession of photographs – mirroring the ones Karen had had taken five days earlier – Dr Marr indicated he was ready to remove the body from its casket. A hoist, exactly like the ones hospitals use to lift invalid patients, was rolled up to the table and broad, strong straps were passed beneath the mummy.

When Dr Marr was satisfied the corpse was secure, a silent electric motor winched it clear of the coffin, which was rapidly removed for examination by forensic scientists. The princess, or whoever she turned out to be, was lowered back onto the autopsy table.

With the help of a scalpel, Dr Marr then removed the gold death mask and breast plate, preserving each one carefully in evidence bags.

Then came the task of cutting through the thick layer of resin-impregnated bandages in such as way as to not damage the fragile body inside. The pathologist opened a plastic case and removed what appeared to be a DIY electric screwdriver but was, in fact, a surgical saw with interchangeable circular blades. A quick reference to the original X-ray plates showed him the approximate depth of the wrappings, allowing him to select a blade roughly six centimetres in diameter, giving him a cutting depth of just over two centimetres. Briefly glancing at his audience on the balcony he got to work, cutting horizontally around the mummy from feet to head and back to feet in the hope of preserving the full body length of the wrappings. It was a painstaking task.

After three hours of delicate manoeuvring and recutting the tough shell was in two pieces and ready to be removed. Dr Marr and his assistant gently prised the two halves apart and lifted the top portion from the bottom, just as Karen and Salim had done with the ornate coffin.

The revelation was equally staggering.

Poking through the bandages, just above the shoulder on the right hand side of the body was a tuft of hair that had been trapped in the wrapping process. And it was blond.

Individually, each of the three observers felt a surge of excitement yet none said a word. Dr Marr betrayed no obvious signs that he had uncovered something entirely unexpected beyond signalling the photographer to take more pictures, including close-ups of the blond tuft.

The removal of the shell also laid bare for all to see the details of how this young woman had been mummified. Each of her limbs, each of her fingers, had been bound separately, exactly in the manner employed by the ancient Egyptians.

Dr Marr now turned his attention to gingerly removing the bandage wrappings, preserving each length in an annotated evidence bag, just in case it should ever be needed at trial. One by one the crudely made linen strips fell away until, at last, the only ones remaining enclosed the corpse's head. As they too were removed, it became clear that in life the girl had possessed black hair.

For the first time since the autopsy had begun more than five hours previously, Dr Marr spoke to the trio of observers.

'I think I can guess what went through your minds when you saw the blond tuft poking out of the bandages but you can now see for yourselves what this poor creature's real hair colour was. I need to do tests, of course, but I'm fairly confident in saying that they will show that this blond colouring is the result of bleaching by whatever chemicals were used on the wrappings.

'However, I have to say that the body is in a remarkable state of preservation. The embalming seems to have done its job perfectly.'

The pathologist then proceeded to reopen the incisions made in the abdominal cavity, through which the internal organs had been removed. Inside was packed two different types of crystalline material, samples of which were bottled for analysis and the remainder saved in more evidence bags.

With the stuffing materials removed, the damage to the spine was plainly visible.

'A blunt force trauma that would have required considerable force,' said Dr Marr. 'It's caused considerable damage to the vertebrae.'

Wilson asked the question he had asked of Dr Bennett. 'Would it be sufficient to kill her, doctor?'

Dr Marr had lifted the delicate corpse slightly and was running his hand up its back, as if feeling the location of the individual vertebrae. Without answering the question he suddenly stopped, reached for a small high-intensity LED torch from the instrument tray and shone it on the throat.

'The spinal injury would have undoubtedly incapacitated her, Inspector,' he said. 'She would have been in excruciating pain. But I think this is probably the cause of death . . .'

Wilson looked carefully and saw the doctor's discovery – a very thin but unmistakable knife wound running from ear to ear that, in life, would have severed the young girl's jugular vein and carotid artery, bringing virtually instantaneous death.

Chapter Ten

By the time Ray Wilson's Saab 93 reached the Crown & Cushion on the outskirts of Huntingdon, it was dark.

'Don't know about you but I could murder a pint,' he said, half turning towards Karen as he switched off the engine.

'After this afternoon, a gin and tonic wouldn't go amiss.'

For reasons she couldn't explain she had instinctively said yes when Ray had offered her a lift home, even though she had travelled to Huntingdon with Salim who, without a word, had driven home alone.

Inside the pub, a clutch of locals were clustered at the bar enjoying an early evening drink. There was a marked break in their conversation as Ray's bulk pushed through the door, half a pace ahead of Karen's slender frame. In the background, indistinguishable pop music was barely audible. Satisfied that the visitors neither provided gossip nor posed a threat, the locals returned to their conversation.

'I'll have a pint of IPA,' Ray said to the balding, overweight character behind the bar, spotting the familiar green and white shield of his favourite Greene King brewery. 'And what will you have Karen? G&T?'

'Yes, that would be nice. Thank you.'

A couple of minutes later the pair were sitting at a table that Ray had identified the moment he walked in, comfortably out of sight of the locals but still with a view of the door. Old habits, he thought to himself, really do die hard.

Karen spoke first.

'So, what do you make of this afternoon's proceedings?'

'Well, it seems fairly certain that we are not dealing with an ancient mummy – there are too many things wrong like the error in the cuneiform script, the heart not being left in place, the hair left outside the wrapping, not to mention the pencil marks.

'But I think we need to wait for the forensics to come back and the results of the carbon dating tests on the bones and bandages before we make a decision on where we go from here. What do you think?'

'I have to agree that the mummy isn't what we first thought,' she answered. 'But that raises the question in my mind, if it's not genuine what's it for? Why would somebody go to the trouble – and expense – of making a fake mummy? The only answer I can come up with is that it's a deliberate attempt to defraud a museum somewhere.

'Like I said when I first saw it, if it was the real thing it would be worth an absolute fortune. But that raises other questions I'd prefer not to think about. Like who is the dead girl? Where did she die and when? And, given what Dr Marr has just found, who killed her?'

'Whoa, hang on. Let's not get too far ahead of ourselves. We need to wait for the test results before we go down that route. Just because the body appears to have a slit throat doesn't mean we can jump to conclusions.'

'I would have thought there was only conclusion to jump to, knowing what we do. She's hardly likely to have cut her own throat is she?'

'Of course not, but remember what Dr Marr said. We will probably never know the exact cause of death. And without a cause of death it's very, very difficult to prove anything.' He paused. 'Anyway, that's enough shop talk. Tell me about you. I don't know anything about you and I'd like to.'

Karen could feel the blush rising in her throat.

'Oh, I'm not very interesting. Why don't you tell me about you?'

'Because I asked first.'

Anyone listening would have recognised the early steps in a flirtation but it either did not register with Karen or she chose to ignore it.

'Well, I've been curator of Egyptology at the Fitzwilliam

for just over a year. Before that I was assistant keeper of Egyptology at the British Museum in London.'

'So how do you come to be in Cambridge?'

'Divorce. John and I were married for five years but it all fell apart when he left the RAF. He was a helicopter pilot. Very glamorous to an impressionable, donnish young girl like me. I was 27 when we first met, working at the British Museum. He was stationed in Oxfordshire officially but most of the time I never knew where he was. We'd get together maybe twice a month, always in London. And every time he would sweep me off my feet.

'We went on that way for nearly two years then, out of the blue, he proposed. Not long after we got married he left the Air Force and took a job flying with a commercial company so we could be together. But he couldn't adjust to civilian life. He hated his job – called it 'fucking bus driving' – and then he started drinking. The rows started soon after that and one night when he came home drunk he hit me. I packed my bags and left and the next conversation we had was through our lawyers.

'I spotted the Fitzwilliam job advertised in The Times. I was at uni in Cambridge so it was a place that held a lot of happy memories for me so I applied. I was astonished when I was offered the post but here I am, with my life just about back on an even keel.

'And that's about it really. So, go on . . . Your turn.'

Ray took a draft of IPA and tried to sound nonchalant.

'There's nothing much to tell. I'm very much a small

town boy – I went to university in Norwich, where I grew up. I did the history of art. I don't know why. When I'd got my degree all the jobs I was qualified for were a bit boring. Sorry, I didn't mean your job is, you know, boring but . . . So I joined Norfolk Constabulary – my Dad was a copper – as a graduate fast-track recruit, which meant I should be at least a Superintendent by now, if not an Assistant Chief Constable somewhere.'

'So why aren't you?'

'They discovered that I'm actually a very good detective. What they used to call "a natural thief taker"' – he made little quotation marks in the air with his fingers – 'so they kept me in CID and put me on undercover work. I had quite a bit of success and then they asked me to infiltrate a gang smuggling illegal immigrants. I don't know what went wrong but my cover was suddenly blown and I was lucky to get away with my life. The gang got what was coming to them but my undercover career was over.

'Then I read in Police Review that Cambridgeshire were recruiting people for an Arts and Antiques squad and, like you, I applied not expecting too much and was accepted. And that's how I come to be here in this pub with you and this pint of IPA.'

'So is there a Mrs Wilson?' asked Karen tentatively.

'No. Never has been and probably never will be. I'm 40 in a few weeks time, probably a bit late in life for settling into a routine that means sharing with somebody else. I'm quite happy with my life. I've got my little cabin cruiser and I've got my sailing so my social life is OK. I just don't have a permanent lady in the mix.'

Karen suddenly realised that both of them had probably revealed too much about themselves for what was, after all, just a casual drink after work and tried to steer the conversation back to the afternoon's autopsy.

'How long will the forensics and carbon dating results take?' she asked.

'Carbon dating is a fairly complicated procedure so I'm not expecting anything back inside a month. The forensics depends on what else the lab's got on. If they get a more urgent enquiry, a murder for instance, they will have to concentrate their resources on that. If they don't, probably two to three weeks should see a result. Will you have dinner with me on Saturday?' The question came out of the blue, unattached and without even so much as a pause for breath.

In a millisecond a thousand thoughts and a hundred excuses raced through her mind. But the one word that came out was 'Yes.'

Chapter Eleven

In the three weeks that followed their dinner date, Ray and Karen met up for drinks every two or three days and even managed a night at the cinema as their friendship grew. But, it seemed to Karen, it was going no farther than friendship. Ray had behaved at all times like a perfect gentleman. He offered her his arm and insisted on walking on the outside as they trod the streets of Cambridge. But he never made one attempt to kiss her or even to hold her hand. She found herself wishing that he would be a bit more forward, a bit more like her ex-husband's fellow officers, who had treated any female in their company as 'target for tonight,' irrespective of to whom they were attached. Then she felt immediately guilty for disrespecting his old fashioned sense of decency and integrity.

Now it was Monday morning and she was sitting at her desk in the Fitzwilliam, trying to concentrate on the work she had to do but unable to stop thinking about Detective Inspector Raymond Wilson. Had she done something that had put up a barrier between them? Had she said something? Maybe he didn't fancy her. Maybe he just wanted to be friends. Maybe he was gay.

She was dragged back to reality by Margaret Jones' tousled, greying head appearing around the door without a knock.

'Karen, there's a reporter from the Evening News on the 'phone. Says he wants to talk to you about the Egyptology collection.'

Her sigh could have meant anything from 'What have I done to deserve this?' to 'Why can't he just Google his question like normal people?' The resignation in her voice was palpable as she said: 'Put him through.'

Seconds later a voice that was far too bright and cheerful for a Monday morning was introducing himself.

'Miss Bowen. Good morning. My name's Barry Preston. I'm a reporter with the Evening News here in Cambridge and I understand you've got an interesting new addition to your collection. I'd like to ask you a few questions about it.'

In the coming weeks and months, Karen would be astonished, with the benefit of hindsight, that she did not instantly make the connection.

'I'm sorry I think there must be some misunderstanding. We haven't got any new additions.'

'I'm talking about the mummy. The one you thought

might be Persian but turned out not to be. I know it's been examined by Dr Graham Marr, the pathologist. I was wondering what you now think the origins of the mummy could be?'

The chill that ran through her could not have been more intense if someone had injected liquid nitrogen into her arm.

'How do you know about that? It's not public knowledge.'

'Sorry. Can't reveal my sources and all that. But you have got a mummy that's something of a mystery haven't you?'

'I'm, I'm sorry . . .' she stammered. 'That's got nothing to do with the Fitzwilliam. You will have to speak to the police. I can't tell you anything.'

'But you can confirm that the mummy isn't what you first thought it was,' pressed Preston.

'Yes. No. I'm not in a position to confirm anything. I've told you. You'll have to talk to the police.'

'But you must have an idea where the mummy's come from or how old it might be?' Tenacity to the point of rudeness.

She answered his question by simply dropping the handset back on its cradle. Immediately she picked it back up and dialled Ray Wilson's mobile. When he answered she by-passed the pleasantries.

'Ray, we've got a problem. I've just had a journalist on the 'phone asking about the mummy.'

That night's edition of the Cambridge Evening News carried nothing about the mummy. Nor did Tuesday's. But on Wednesday, the lunchtime edition carried the front page splash headline:

MYSTERY OF THE
'PERSIAN MUMMY'
Exclusive
By Barry Preston

Alongside the by-line was a small photograph of a young man in his early 20s sporting a fashionably foppish hairstyle and a worldly-wise expression that belied his youthfulness.

The story began:

'A mysterious mummified body in an ornately carved casket is puzzling Cambridgeshire Police.

'The body and its coffin were discovered in a lorry found to be carrying illegal immigrants after it was stopped for a routine check by a county traffic patrol on the A1.

'At first experts told police the mummy could be that of a Persian princess who died more than 2,500 years ago, making it a priceless relic.

'But after a detailed CAT scan, carried out in the Nuffield Hospital, Cambridge, and an autopsy by Home Office pathologist Dr Graham Marr, detectives now believe the mummy is a fake.'

The story went on to give details of what the CAT scan had revealed and what Dr Marr's autopsy had contributed, including the discovery of the blond hair swatch. It also reported that bandages from the body and bone samples had been sent for carbon dating while scientists at the Forensic Science Service laboratory in Huntingdon were conducting tests on the coffin. It quoted Karen as saying: 'Now we have examined the mummy, it does not appear to be what we first thought it was but we still don't know exactly what it is.'

And an unnamed source was quoted as saying that detectives trying to establish where and how the girl died had not ruled out the possibility that she was murdered.

Karen had just finished reading the story when her mobile buzzed into life. The single name 'Ray' was illuminated on the screen.

She answered simply: 'Hi.'

'I take it you've seen the Evening News?' he asked.

'Yes. It looks like Mr Preston has a very good source. And I want you to know right now that it's not in this organisation.'

'OK, OK, don't get het up. No one's pointing the finger at you or your people. As a matter of fact two of my guys have just gone to interview Mr Preston, for what it's worth. He won't tell us anything but we can make him sweat a bit. My concern is that the story will get picked up by the nationals and it then becomes something bigger than a local investigation.'

'I know it's annoying that the story's come out this way,' said Karen. 'But maybe a bit of publicity won't do us any harm. You never know what might turn up now it's in the papers.'

'I wish I could share your optimism Karen but in my experience, all this kind of thing does is bring every nutter and his brother out of the woodwork. We'll get swamped with people claiming they know who the girl is; they know who killed her and even that they killed her themselves. Every call has to be investigated, just in case of the highly unlikely event that one of them really does know something useful. It's time consuming and pointless and ties up officers who could be contributing something positive to the enquiry.'

'That aside, if the story does get picked up by the daily papers, we're going to get loads of calls that, frankly, I don't want to deal with. I'm an Egyptologist and I'm afraid I'm not very media friendly. What are we going to do?'

'Don't worry,' his voice soothing and reassuring. 'If you get any calls all you need to say is that it's a police matter and you are not in a position to comment and refer them to our Press Office. I've already given our Head of Press & PR a statement that confirms we have a mummified body of unknown origin and says we are not going to speculate at this stage about who the dead girl is or when or how she met her death. It also says the investigation is on-going and that we will issue a further statement when, and if, we have something more to say.'

They made an arrangement to meet for a drink after work and no sooner had Karen tried to return to her routine work when Margaret Jones appeared at her office door.

'Er . . . Sorry about this but I've got a freelance journalist on. Organisation called Fenland News. She says they work for all the national dailies and she wants to talk to you about the mummy.'

It had started. But at least, thanks to Ray, she knew what to do and reiterated his instructions to Margaret, adding: 'I don't want to talk to any journalists about this Margaret. Can you please field all the calls and tell them what I've just told you?'

Inside the next 30 minutes, Margaret had dealt firmly but politely with requests from the BBC, ITV and Sky News – the latter wanted to film Karen with the mummy – and half an hour after that, she had successfully fended off the Daily Mirror, the Sun and the Daily Mail.

By 5pm, she had dealt with the Daily Express, The Guardian, the Daily Telegraph, The Times and four local radio stations – one of which had been extremely rude to her – and the Today programme on BBC Radio 4, which wanted Karen to do a live interview at 6.30am the following day.

As the clock struck 5.30pm, she put on her coat and walked the half mile to her flat where, for the first time since she couldn't remember when, she took out her only crystal tumbler and dusted off a treasured bottle of

Bunnahabhain single Islay malt. She poured herself a very large one, slumped in an armchair and awaited the embrace of oblivion.

Karen also left the office at 5.30pm. But she went to meet a craggily handsome police officer of whom, she realised, she was growing increasingly fond.

Chapter Twelve

The large brown envelope that Ray Wilson tore open with the eager expectation of a child opening a birthday card was franked: 'FSS, Huntingdon.' Inside were five, single spaced sheets of A4 paper with a covering letter, bearing the logo of the Forensic Science Service and the address of the Hinchingbrooke Park laboratory, where he, Karen and Salim had witnessed the autopsy on the mummy three weeks previously.

He went straight to the report, speed reading it until he found the first bit he was looking for. The coffin was made from Lebanon Cedar – it even gave the wood its Latin name, Cedrus Libani – and was constructed using wooden dowels, a system that was first identified almost three thousand years ago but was still in use today in some parts of the world. Although now a very rare species in its native Lebanon, Cedrus Libani is found in abundance in Turkey and Syria and also grows in significant quantities in other areas of the Eastern Mediterranean. It had not been possible to pinpoint precisely where the tree from which the coffin wood came had grown.

Damn. Not much to go on there. He read on.

Using dendrochronology, the scientists at Hinchingbrooke Park had tried to establish the age of the timber used in the coffin. However, because the wood had been cut into planks, it had proved impossible to determine its exact age, the calculation for which requires the original bark to be intact. The best that could be achieved in the circumstances, therefore, was an estimate of age. In this particular instance, the scientists' assessment was that the wood was between 150 and 200 years old.

Again, nothing to take the enquiry forward, but at least there was apparent confirmation that the coffin was not an antiquity.

The report then turned its attention to the pencil mark that Karen had found. The mark was one of seven that the scientists had found, some of them only a millimetre long, mainly in the areas around the carvings on the outside of the coffin. Tests had determined that all the marks had been made by the same pencil, a 4B manufactured in Sao Paulo, Brazil, by the German company Faber-Castell, the world's biggest pencil producer. Again, accurate ageing was not possible but the composition of graphite and clay powder that made up the pencil lead indicated that it been manufactured sometime within the last 10 years.

Ray turned to the report's final page. As his eyes scanned the closely typed lines, he became increasingly animated. Whether by accident or design, the Hinchingbrooke scientists had saved the best until last. On the inside of the coffin, close to where the mummy's right shoulder would have rested, they had found a fingerprint. A check against OPUS, the computerised database of fingerprints and DNA samples used by police in the UK, proved fruitless, so a check had been made with Interpol at its headquarters in Lyon, France. The e-mailed image had been of sufficiently good quality to allow Interpol to come up with a match.

The print belonged to Kamil Behar, a Turk with dual British nationality, thanks to the fact his mother was born and brought up in Birmingham. He was 35 years old and, although a frequent visitor to Britain, his last known address was in Istanbul. He had known links to a people smuggling gang that used the so-called 'Balkan Route' to bring desperate Asians to Western Europe via Iran, Turkey and the Balkan states.

Reading the name of Kamil Behar started alarm bells ringing in Ray's head, so much so he could barely control his trembling hands as he picked up his mobile and pressed the one button that would connect him to Karen.

When she answered he blurted out his news. The forensic report had arrived. It was largely inconclusive except that the pencil marks proved the coffin couldn't be more than 10 years old. And they'd found a fingerprint.

'A fingerprint? In the coffin?'

'Yes,' he confirmed. 'And it gets better, or worse, depending on where you're sitting. They've put a name to the print.'

'What? That's astonishing.' Karen had the feeling of living inside a cheap, late-night TV thriller. 'How did they manage that?'

'It seems to have been a long shot. They checked the UK fingerprint database without success so they then checked with Interpol and they matched the print to a Turk called Kamil Behar. But Karen, the thing is . . .' a second's hesitation, as if he was rapidly assessing whether to continue with his revelation. 'The thing is . . . I know him. I know Kamil Behar. And he's a very nasty piece of work.'

'You know him? How? How do you know him?'

'Remember when we were in the Rose and Crown in Huntingdon and I told you I'd gone undercover to infiltrate a people smuggling gang? Well, Kamil Behar was the Middle Eastern end of that gang. He lived in Istanbul and he made all the arrangements for smuggling the illegals out through Iran and Turkey into Bulgaria, Bosnia and Croatia from where they would be taken to Western Europe.

'I met him a few times. When my cover was blown, he was one of the ones that got away. But he rang me on my mobile and told me that if ever we met again he would kill me.'

When she responded he could hear the fear in her voice.

'Ray, we're out of our depth here. You need to tell someone higher up. It's not safe for you to be involved in this. What are you going to do?'

'Well, before I do anything else, I'm going to speak to Interpol.'

Luckily for Ray, Inspector Gaston Terray spoke faultless English. From his office inside the Interpol headquarters in Quai Charles de Gaulle in Lyon, which looked out across the pleasant Parc de la Tete d'Or and its huge ornamental lake, Terray was responsible for collating information from all over the world on people trafficking, one of the six priority crime areas under constant investigation by Interpol and its 186 member countries. Terray's speciality was monitoring the gangs that controlled people smuggling into Western Europe.

Deciding not to go into detail, Ray simply told Terray that Kamil Behar's fingerprint had turned up on an antiquity and had been identified from Interpol's database, which had also pointed to his links with people smuggling. He asked what more Terray knew about Behar. Thanks to the clarity of the digital telephone connection, he heard the Frenchman tapping a keyboard.

'Ah yes Inspector,' Terray said at last, with just a hint of an accent that meant the last word came out as Inspectere. 'I have his file here. I suspect you will already be aware of the basic details, his age, dual nationality and so on.'

'Yes I am. I'm really trying to find out what you know about his current activities and whereabouts.'

'It is very interesting . . . it appears he has, as you English say, fallen off the radar in the area of people smuggling. He still maintains contact with some of his former gang but no longer takes an active part. However, there are reports that he has links to one of the gangs involved in the black market in human organs.'

'Human organs? You mean for transplants?'

'Yes Inspector. Sadly it is a burgeoning market. The gap between supply and demand is wide and there are many, many wealthy people willing to pay any price for the chance to cling to life. There are also many, many people living in poverty whose only chance of life is to sell a kidney or half a liver.'

'But surely selling human organs is illegal.'

'In some countries, yes. But in others, no. And even where it is illegal it is possible to find an unscrupulous surgeon willing to carry out the operation. Sometimes the surgeon isn't told the truth about the origin of the organ. I have heard the trade referred to as post-modern cannibalism.'

There was a pause as Ray absorbed the implications of what he had just heard.

'Are you talking here purely about organs that a person is able to donate and carry on a reasonably normal life, such as a kidney. Or are other organs, hearts for example, available in this black marketplace?'

'All things are possible in this world Mr Wilson. Even stolen hearts. Just think of the number of peasants in places like Iraq, Iran, Turkey and even closer to home in Romania and Chechnya who would not be missed if they were to mysteriously disappear.'

By now Ray's mind was racing, his imagination in overdrive.

'Monsieur Terray, you've been very helpful. Thank you. Just one last thing. Is it possible for you to find out how strong the evidence is that links Behar with the organ transplant black market? And his last known whereabouts?'

'For you I will try,' said Terray. 'It will take a few days but I will call you.'

Ray gave him his mobile number then used the same instrument to call Karen and invite himself round for dinner.

Chapter Thirteen

He struggled up the garden path, desperately trying not to drop the two brown paper carrier bags containing the takeaway Indian food they had compromised on, or the two bottles of Zinfandel he had bought to swill it down on the basis that it was probably the only wine strong enough to compete with Kashmiri butter chicken, lamb rogan josh and prawn bhuna. The thought occurred to him that he had probably bought too much.

He was puzzling how he was going to knock on the door with this arms loaded down, when she opened it, a glass of red wine already in her hand.

'Saw you get out of the car,' she said. 'I was amused by your juggling act.'

'You could have come and helped me,' he said, feigning hurt, at the same time taking in the tight denim jeans, expensive looking linen top and stiletto-heeled ankle boots.

'You looked like you were having enough fun on your own.'

To Karen's surprise, he put down take takeaway food and the wine, slipped his arm around her waist and kissed her firmly on the right cheek. Not a passionate kiss but not the false air-kiss of celebrity either. Just a kiss.

Before she could say anything Ray said: 'I've got some news about your Mr Preston. We've identified his source. It was his girlfriend – probably ex-girlfriend by now – she was a secretary at the Forensic Science lab.'

'Was?'

'Yes. She was fired this morning.'

'Serves her right. But if she was only a secretary, how did she manage to give him so much information?'

'She worked in Graham Marr's office. And if you remember, we had to tell the FSS everything we knew about the mummy. She simply photocopied all the documents, including Dr Marr's autopsy report, and handed them over to her boyfriend.'

Over curry, nan bread and Zinfandel, he told her everything that Inspector Terray had told him that afternoon, including the fact that Kamil Behar was suspected of being linked to the international black market in human organs. He recounted Terray's resume of the trade and his description of it as 'post-modern cannibalism' and he reminded her of his own dealings with the Turk. Throughout the meal she said little, seeming distracted, her mind elsewhere, her thoughts returning to his apparently changed demeanour towards her. To the kiss.

Afterwards, as they relaxed on her sofa over the second bottle of Zinfandel, she casually handed him two magazines from the coffee table, each with a page marked out by a little yellow Post-It note.

'I've come across these. You might find them interesting,' was all she said.

She sat silently as he read.

The first magazine was called 'Antiquity' and on the marked page he found a short story circled in red. It told how the Kunsthistorishies Museum in Vienna had been offered a mummy that appeared to be of Persian origin. Austrian academics were very excited because, if true, it would be the first recorded case of Persian mummification in history. At this stage, they had only been shown photographs of the mummy by an intermediary, but the potential contribution the mummy could make to the museum's collection was such that the museum had asked the Austrian government to consider making a grant towards the asking price of US$35 million.

The second title was 'Asian Art' and it reported how the Archaeology Museum in Karachi had been asked to examine what appeared to be a unique Persian mummy that had been seized by police in a raid on a house in the city, following a tip-off. The man who lived in the house had been arrested but was claiming he had found the mummy after an earthquake in the mountains close to the border with Afghanistan. Experts at the museum were quoted as saying that if the mummy proved to be genuine it would be priceless.

Ray took a long draft of wine and read both stories again. He refilled his glass and read them a third time, then he spoke.

'How long have you had these?'

'They'd been on my desk for about a week,' she replied. 'I just hadn't had chance to open them until this afternoon.'

'Why didn't you call me?

'I was going to; then you called me and invited yourself round for dinner. So I thought I'd save them. In case conversation dried up.'

'Do you understand the significance of these stories? What they mean to us and our mummy?'

'Yes. It means we are not alone. There are others out there.' This accompanied by a singsong Do-Do-Do-Do-Da.

'Karen, be serious. This is no laughing matter. The implications are very worrying. It means that for whatever reason, somebody out there is churning out fake mummies. It means somebody out there is running a mummy factory.'

Karen awoke to the realisation that for the first time since she walked out on her drunken husband nearly two years previously, she was not alone. She could hear him breathing. She could feel the heat of his body next to hers. She could feel the remaining dampness of their lovemaking. She also had a feeling that was not immediately identifiable: it could have been excitement, trepidation, guilt or fear in the wake of what had happened in the vastness of the king-sized bed. After his little outburst on reading the magazines, she thought she was in for a row but he had simply put his arms around her, hugged her and asked: 'Can I stay?'

Whatever the feeling was, it passed unresolved as she became aware of him stirring. Seconds later, he was propped on one elbow, scratching at his mop of dark hair, which gave him a vaguely comical look.

'Morning sweet pea.' The first time he had called her anything other than Karen. 'Fancy some tea?'

'That would be good. Give me a minute and I'll go and make it.'

'It's OK. I'll do it,' he said, throwing his legs from under the duvet and standing up, seemingly unconcerned by his nakedness. 'Milk and sugar?'

'Just milk thanks. Do you know where everything is?'

'Course not. But I'll find it.'

Ten minutes later he returned with two mugs of tea and two slices of hot, buttered, wholemeal toast on a tray, which he passed to her while he clambered back into bed, where they ate and drank in silence. She drained her mug and leaned out of bed to put the tray and its detritus on the floor, aware that she, too, was naked.

'So. Where do we go from here?' she asked.

'Is that we as in me and you or we as in me, you and the mummy?'

'From what those magazines said and what your French mate said, I think the mummy needs to take priority, don't you?'

'You're probably right, but it won't be half as much fun,' he replied. 'I think what we need to do is make contact with our counterparts in Austria and Pakistan and tell them about our mummy and what we've found out about it. Pooling information will be vital if, as we suspect, these cases are interlinked.'

'I agree. I'll make it a priority when I get to work.' She glanced at the bedside clock. 'Speaking of which, I need to get a move on.'

'So do I. But there's something I have to do first,' he said, running his hand softly up her inner thigh as he leaned to kiss her breast.

Chapter Fourteen

By 9.30am, thanks to the speed of the worldwide web, Karen had identified the people she need to communicate with and had sent e-mails to the curator of the Archaeology Museum in Karachi and the keeper of Egyptology at the Kunsthistorishies Museum in Vienna, telling them of the mummy that had turned up in Cambridgeshire, which at first she too took to be Persian but had subsequently proved to be a fake. She spelled out for them the errors in the Cuneiform script discovered by Salim; the pencil marks found on the casket; the absence of the heart revealed by the CAT scan; the blunt trauma injury to the mummy's spine; the slit throat and finally, the fingerprint. Her message suggested that their mummies could also be fakes, advising the Vienna museum not to proceed any further with their proposed purchase and indicating to the curator at the Karachi museum that he might want to carry out a rigorous examination of the mummy and casket in his charge.

At almost the same moment Karen had clicked the 'send' button, Ray Wilson was staring at the results of the carbon dating tests on the bone and bandage samples that the Forensic Science Service had ordered and which had now been forwarded to him. Even though the results were not entirely unexpected, they still made bleak and disturbing reading.

The bandages were made from a poor quality linen that was of middle-Eastern origin and, although difficult to date precisely, was no more than 20 years old. The bone sample was from a female, aged around 19. And she had been dead for no more than three years.

The phrase 'no more than three years' reverberated through his brain as he picked up the 'phone and dialled Gaston Terray's number. The Frenchman was obviously sitting at his desk, for he answered on the second ring and seemed genuinely pleased to hear again from the disquieted English detective.

'I know you said you'd ring me but there have been a couple of developments I thought you should know about,' said Ray.

He had decided to tell Terray everything he knew, from the discovery of the casket in a truck carrying illegal immigrants, through the autopsy report, the carbon dating test results and the discovery of two potentially similar mummies in Austria and Pakistan. Terray listened patiently, without interruption. When Ray had finished he asked: 'What you say is very interesting Inspector but from what I've just heard there is no proof that these three mummies are linked in any way. Couldn't their discovery be just a coincidence?'

'No. We don't think so.' Ray realised he had subconsciously included Karen in this statement. 'Ancient history does not record one single instance of mummification by the Persians as a method of preserving their dead. Not one artefact even vaguely connecting Persian aristocracy to mummification has been uncovered in the last 2,500 years. And now we have three mummies – by the sound of things very, very similar – mysteriously coming to light within the space of a few weeks. It cannot possibly be a coincidence. But, at the moment, we can't think what the link between them could be.'

Inspector Terray did not volunteer any suggestions, instead subtly moving the conversation onwards.

'Last time we spoke Inspector, you asked me if I could help find the last known whereabouts of Kamil Behar and to determine the strength of his links with the black market in human organs. I have made some good progress. I was going to call you later today. Through our affiliates in Turkey I have obtained an address for him Ankara. They also have intelligence that links him to address in the city of Leeds in your country, although it appears to be an address he visits regularly rather than a property he owns.'

'Leeds? That's where the truck that was carrying the mummy was heading.'

'That too may also be a coincidence Mr Wilson. However, our affiliates in Turkey tell us they are confident that in the last six months Behar has organised at least two kidneys for transplantation, one in Jordan and one in Egypt. They are 99.9 per cent certain that he brokered the deals to provide both organs. Within the same time scale, it is believed, although the evidence is weaker in this case, that he facilitated a liver transplant in Greece. The indications, as yet unsubstantiated, are that all three organs came from the same donor.'

Ray was stunned by what Terray was telling him.

'Are you saying that Behar somehow had access to a recently deceased person and was able to sell-on their organs?'

'Apparently the investigation is focusing on whether Behar was in some way responsible for the death of the donor.'

'What? You mean he may have murdered somebody for their body parts?'

'He may not have done it directly. He may have paid someone to do it for him. But that is still murder.'

'Christ, he's moved on a long way since I came across him people smuggling. How long has he been into this kind of thing?'

Terray's reply filled him with dread.

'On a commercial scale, comparatively recently. But

there is evidence that three years ago he did a deal with the CIA to supply a heart for transplantation into the son of the US Ambassador to Germany. It is said the heart came from a young Iraqi girl that Behar had killed. It is also said that the American military authorities in Baghdad have a statement from a witness who claims he saw a teenage girl run down from behind by a car. She was dragged into the vehicle screaming in pain. The witness assumed she was being taken to hospital. But there is no official record of such an injured girl ever arriving at hospital.'

It was as if the scales had suddenly fallen from his eyes in a kind of Pauline revelation.

'Oh my God,' stuttered Ray. 'Gaston' – he felt able, all at once, to use his counterpart's first name – 'I think we may have unwittingly fallen upon a crime of dreadful and terrible proportions.

'I don't know whether this is going to be possible but we need to ascertain how many organ transplants have taken place, as purely commercial transactions, throughout Europe and the Middle East in the last, say, three years. Then we need to compile a list of children and young people reported missing in those same areas in the same period. Do you think that can be done?'

In Lyon, Inspector Terray was unsure whether the man on the other end of the line had suddenly been struck mad or whether there was some validity in this strange request.

'I do not know, is the short answer. But I will ask my colleagues. What are you thinking?'

'I'm thinking, Gaston, that there may well be a link between the black market in human organs and the mummies.'

He needed to talk to Karen. He needed time to think. And he needed air. So, rather than call her, he decided to walk the half mile or so to the Fitzwilliam Museum from his office in Cambridge's Parkside police station. As he left, he simply called to the unit secretary: 'If anybody wants me, I'm on my mobile. I'll be back in an hour or so.'

Outside, September was still resisting autumn, the day dry, bright, clear and warm as he crossed Parkside and took the footpath that ran diagonally across Parkers Piece, one of the city's most famous park areas. At the far side of the park he turned right into St Andrews Street, his mind distracted by what Gaston Terray had told him to the point where he stepped, unseeing, into the path of a passing cyclist, who, although unhurt, called out a few choice names as he continued his journey. Ray ignored the insults, puzzling over the route that had taken Kamil Behar from people smuggler to potential killer and body part black marketeer as two more left turns brought him to Fitzwilliam Street and the museum on the corner of Trumpington Street.

Without difficulty he remembered the way to Karen's

office, walking straight past Margaret Jones, asking rhetorically 'Is she in?' and nodding at Karen's door before opening it to find out for himself. She was at her desk, engrossed in something on her computer screen, a delicate china cup and saucer, containing the dregs of green tea, by her right hand. She looked up startled as the door opened.

'Ray. What are you doing here?' she asked in surprise.

'I needed to see you. I've been talking to Gaston Terray at Interpol again and I'm deeply concerned by what he's told me. I need to talk to you about it.'

'Well, before you do, I've got something you need to know too. I've got a response from the Archaeological Museum in Karachi. They've opened their mummy and it has a gold plate on its chest, just like ours. And it has a cuneiform script inscription that appears to say exactly what ours does.'

'What, that she's Rhodugune, daughter of Xerxes the Great?'

'Exactly. Final proof, if any more were needed, that both mummies are definitely fakes.'

'What about the museum in Vienna?'

'Well, I haven't had a response from them yet but don't forget they only saw photographs. But I think it's a pretty safe bet it will be the same. So what has Monsieur Terray told you that's brought you over here unannounced?'

'Better get some more tea in. This is going to take some absorbing.'

Chapter Fifteen

Over the next 30 minutes, Ray wore his policeman's hat as he told her, in that deadpan monotone that senior officers usually reserve for juries, everything that Gaston Terray had imparted, including the rumoured deal with the CIA to supply a heart for the US Ambassador's son, Behar's address in Ankara and his frequent visits to Leeds. Finally, he told her of his suspicions of links between the fake mummies and the trade in black market body parts.

'Ray, I can't believe this,' she said when he finished. 'Are you seriously telling me that you believe the mummies are the by-product of some sick trade in human organs?'

'That's exactly what I'm saying, yes.'

'It doesn't make sense. The mummification process isn't quick or easy and timing is critical, especially in hot countries where decomposition of a dead body would begin within hours. If what you're saying is correct, it would take a fairly sizable team to get everything ready, long before they've even got their hands on a body. For a start, they'd need somewhere to carry out the process. Then they'd need close on half a ton of chemicals, the resins, bandages. All of which would have to be stored. And they'd need a goldsmith to make the death mask and the chest plate; a cabinet maker to build and carve the coffin, plus the guy who knew cuneiform script and could inscribe the chest plate and coffin lid. All this after the major organs had been surgically removed – and you can't do that in a shed at the end of the garden you know. Sorry Ray, it's just not possible.'

'Yes it is,' he replied. 'We've got the proof right here in Cambridge. You know it and you're deluding yourself if you think that the Rhodugune mummy is anything else. You're thinking like an academic. You need to think like a criminal.

'Put yourself in Behar's position. You've wormed your way into this fantastically profitable black market where people with limitless amounts of money are willing to pay you virtually any price you demand for a kidney, a liver or even a heart, that will give them, or someone they love, a chance of a new life. The downside is that there isn't an endless supply of organs and willing donors aren't exactly queuing round the block. So you set up your own supply chain.'

'What? By killing people?' The incredulity was apparent in her voice.

'Yes. You're already a ruthless, international thug with well-established routes for smuggling people and you're not above meting out a bit of violence when you feel like it. Having people killed to meet a specific demand is just one more step. The clever part is what you do with the remains after you've had the saleable bits harvested.

'Turning them into fake mummies that have a potential market value of $35 million each is pure genius.'

'You sound like you almost admire this Behar character,' said Karen brusquely.

'That's the last feeling I have for Behar,' replied Ray. 'He's a vicious, nasty piece of work and I would love nothing more than to see him get his just deserts. But you have to admit that if that's the kind of organisation he's stitched together, it's brilliant.'

Karen was speechless. For some time she had accepted the fact that the mummy was a fake but had spent many hours pondering who had made it and why. The best idea she had come up with was that it was an attempt to dupe some wealthy but unsuspecting museum. The notion that it was a leftover from a gruesome killing revolted her and the fact that that opinion had been advanced by a man to whom she was growing increasingly close, a man to whom she had willingly given herself, did nothing to quell her nauseousness. However, she silently agreed that the information from Interpol was capable of the interpretation Ray had put on it, irrespective of how distasteful it was to her. And if Behar was at large in the Middle East and Europe, butchering young women to feed this transplant monster he had created, how many more of the unfortunate, the unloved and the unmissed would die before he was brought to justice? In the circumstances, the only thing she could do was bury her revulsion and support Ray in whatever way she could.

After a silence that had seemed an age to her, but had, in fact, been less than 20 seconds, she spoke.

'It's not brilliant. It's a disgusting revolting crime. The question is what are you going to do about it? I'm guessing this is potentially far too large for a lowly detective inspector to deal with on his own.'

'You're right there,' said Ray. 'But I'm very keen not to let go of this one so I need to come up with a very good strategy that will keep me involved in the enquiry. Look, I've got to be getting back. Why don't you meet me in the Prince Regent after work and we can talk about it over a beer?'

'OK. See you about quarter to six.'

By the time Karen got to the Prince Regent, Ray was already a third of the way down a pint of Greene King IPA. He kissed her gently on the cheek and without reference to her, ordered a large gin and tonic. He topped up his own drink with another half of IPA and suggested they take advantage of the still, warm evening and take a seat outside at the rear of the pub.

They sat on opposite sides of a wooden table with

bench seating attached, making her thankful she had chosen her pale green linen trousers to wear that day. For a moment neither spoke as they looked out over Parkers Piece, watching young children playing and students sitting on the grass chatting. An archetypal end to an archetypal English summer day. Except it was September and supposed to be autumn, which caused a politically incorrect thought to briefly stray across her mind. The thought remained unspoken. Then Ray disturbed her reverie.

'Do you know,' he asked, 'what Parkers Piece is famous for?'

'I know it's named after a local bloke called Edward Parker who sold the land in the 17th century, but that's about all.'

'Well, the story is that students from the university used to play a game on here, kicking a ball about and eventually they devised a set of rudimentary rules that they called 'The Cambridge Rules,' which apparently are the basis of the Football Association rules that are still used today.'

'How interesting,' she replied, barely disguising her sarcasm.

'No, it's not a game I care for much either. Ball's the wrong shape.'

'So, you're a Rugby man eh? And a sailor. And you like cask beer. Anything else I need to know about you?'

'Oh, lots probably. But all in good time eh?'

The silence descended upon them once again, but not the silence of people who have nothing to say to each other; rather it was the silence of two people who feel comfortable in each other's company; to whom small talk is an irrelevance.

Eventually, Karen broke the hush.

'Have you given any more thought to what we discussed this afternoon?'

'Yes I have. I need to talk to the ACC Crime and tell him everything that's happened and everything that we've found out so far, including what Interpol have told me. He might well say I should have spoken to him earlier but I can claim the enquiries took a quantum leap after I'd spoken to Gaston Terray and that's why I'm talking to him now. He'll probably want to head up the investigation in the UK and do all the liaison with his counterpart at Interpol, but I'm going to make the point that it was you and I working together that uncovered the fact the mummy's a fake and that others have appeared in Austria and Pakistan. And I'm going to make the pitch that he needs both our expertise on this one. Plus, I've got a sneaky trick up my sleeve.'

'That sounds ominous. Is it going to get us, or rather you, in trouble?'

'Not if I do it right,' said Ray. 'One of the guys I sail with has a brother who's a reporter for the Daily Mirror. My thinking is to give him the whole story, fake mummies, body parts, transplant operations, Behar's suspected involvement, the CIA connection, everything.'

'What good will that do us?'

'Us? None. But what I hope it will do is escalate the enquiry and therefore help flush out Mr Behar. If I'm right, the story will get picked up around the world and much bigger fish than us will start asking questions. Someone out there knows where Behar is and what he's up to. We just need them to tell us. And there's nothing like a bit of international pressure to loosen tongues.'

He drained his glass at one pull. Karen tried, but was unable, to follow suit.

'Shall we have the one we came for?' he asked, rising from the bench.

Driving back to his own cottage in the village of Fulbourn, a touch over five miles from where he had bidden Karen goodnight outside the pub, he stabbed at one of the abbreviated dialling buttons on his mobile, which was securely plugged into its hands-free cradle on the Saab's dashboard. It rang twice before a disembodied voice boomed from the car's speakers.

'Hey, dude. How's it hangin' ?' Jonathan McVitie was an educated man but Ray never ceased to be amazed by his apparent fondness for American slang.

'Never been better Jonathan. How about you?'

'I'm finer'n frog hair and twice as fluffy, dude.' By which Ray assumed he was very well indeed. 'Whaddaya need?'

'Actually, I need to set up a meeting with your brother. The one that works for the Mirror.'

'Dominic? What do you want with him?' asked Jonathan, suddenly reverting to his native tongue.

'I've got something that might interest him. I think it might make a good story for him.'

'What's it about?'

'If you don't mind I'll tell him that. It's a bit sensitive and I don't want too many people knowing about it just now.'

'OK. Just asking. You're in luck because he's coming to stay for the weekend with his new girlfriend. Australian apparently. He and I are planning to go to the Rugby match on Saturday while the girlies do shopping. Cambridge are playing Waterloo. Why don't you join us? Then you can talk to him at your leisure.'

'Great idea. See you in the bar about half past two.'

Chapter Sixteen

By the time Saturday arrived, Ray was having second thoughts. Maybe handing the whole story on a plate to a journalist, even if he was a mate's brother, wasn't such a good idea after all. He would be in serious trouble if his superiors ever found out. He could even lose his job. But then again, as he'd argued to Karen, they needed someone to rattle a few cages, to lift a few stones and see what was beneath. They needed someone to guide them to Kamil Behar. The problem he faced was that right then and there, he wasn't convinced that spilling the beans to Dominic McVitie was the best idea he'd ever had. Wouldn't it be better to leave the whole thing to Interpol? After all, they had links to the police forces of 186 countries around the world, including the whole of Europe and most of the Middle East. They already had some knowledge of Behar's movements. It should be simplicity itself for them to locate and track him.

He made himself a lunch of pasta and salad, washed down by a pint of iced tap water and decided that he would keep his counsel; that it was the best thing all round; that having the story splashed all over a national newspaper was to no one's benefit.

Much later, when everything was done and dusted, he would come to realise that what he should have done at that moment was to pick up his mobile, call Jonathan McVitie and excuse himself from the afternoon's jollities. What he actually did was to pick up his mobile, call a taxi firm and order a cab to take him to Cambridge Rugby Club's Grantchester Road ground.

The rugby club bar was crowded with people enjoying a pre-match pint and it took Ray several minutes to spot Jonathan and the man he assumed was Dominic standing by a window overlooking the pitch, each with beer glasses on the point of needing to be refilled. Rather than crush through the crowd, he managed to catch Jonathan's eye and made a drinking motion with his right arm, which was answered by an enthusiastic thumbs up. Five minutes later he was picking his way carefully towards the window, clenching three pints of bitter in the triangle of his hands. After an endless stream of 'excuse me, excuse me,' he reached his companions, who happily relieved him of his burden.

'Dominic,' began Jonathan, 'this is Ray Wilson. Ray, this is my brother Dominic.'

Both men muttered versions of 'Hi, pleased to meet you' and shook hands.

'Cheers,' said Dominic, raising his glass in Ray's direction. 'Jonathan tells me you're a pretty good mainsail trimmer.'

'Good of him to say so but it's not the most demanding task in the world. Do you sail?'

'I've tried it a couple of times but I'm afraid I'm not good on water. I have problems finding my sea legs, if you know what I mean.'

Rightly or wrongly, Ray immediately mentally branded Dominic as a city dweller, uncomfortable in open spaces and he could not help but be struck by the difference between the two brothers. There was probably only three of four years difference in age but Jonathan was about 5'10', powerfully built, with rapidly receding hair that he disguised by shaving his head, giving him the appearance of a Rugby forward or a nightclub bouncer. No one would be surprised to learn that he ran a building company. Dominic, on the other hand, was roughly the same height but, if he had been forced to give an official description, Ray would have said he was slightly built with a mop of unkempt, dark hair. His bookish demeanour was underlined by a pair of oblong, horn-rimmed glasses which, to anyone meeting him as a journalist, would have marked him out as a writer of gentile features for one of the more serious newspapers rather than a red-top tabloid hack.

The conversation drifted to that afternoon's match and Cambridge's chances of victory. While Jonathan gave his two companions the benefit of his expertise on the subject of Cambridge RUFC, Dominic took the opportunity to get in another round of drinks. With only minutes to go kick-off, Jonathan reciprocated, meaning each of them went out on to the terraces clutching at least a pint and half each. Another two pints followed in the first half and they managed to consume another one each during the break. The second half saw another two pints disappear so that when the final whistle blew at the end of 80 minutes and Cambridge left the field the victors 15-3, Ray was feeling decidedly unsteady on his feet. But the home side had won and he didn't take much convincing that there was only one proper thing to do – they went for more beer.

Jonathan had launched into his post-match analysis, not really caring whether either of his companions was listening, when Dominic said to Ray: 'He tells me you might have something that would be of interest to me. In my professional capacity, that is.'

Ray's heart sank. He had hoped the matter would pass unspoken; that he would somehow get away without speaking about the whole reason he set up the meeting in the first place. But now Dominic had backed him into a corner and he had to come up with something fast.

'Well, having thought about it, I'm not sure it would interest you. It might be a bit stuffy for Daily Mirror readers.'

'You'd be surprised,' said Dominic. 'It's not all celebrities and football you know. Give me a clue.'

'It's about an ancient mummy,' replied Ray, desperately trying to make it sound as dull as a wet Monday in January.

'Egyptian?'

'Persian. Well, at least we thought it was.' The beer was making him careless.

'Persian? I didn't know such things existed.'

'They don't. This one's a fake.' Another beer induced slip.

'A fake Persian mummy. In Cambridge. Sounds interesting to me. Tell me more.'

'No, sorry Dominic. I really can't. I've already said too much.'

'Ray, you can't do that to me. You've dangled the worm. I've taken the bait. You've got to tell me more.'

'I should never have started this. I realised it was a bad idea as soon as I suggested it. Us coppers are always taught never to trust a journalist you know.'

Dominic's frustration was mounting. 'Look Ray, let me tell you how I work. It's not the way some national newspaper journalists work, but it's the way I operate. If somebody tells me something in confidence, it stays that way. I don't tell a soul. I've never understood the point in shitting on a contact just for the sake of a story. And you're more than a contact, you're Jonathan's mate. I know we're all half-pissed but I give you my word that whatever you tell me will remain between the two of us. I won't even tell him if you don't want me to.'

Ray could feel his resolve beginning to weaken. Deep down inside he still believed that the quickest resolution to this case would be to flush Behar out into the open so he could be arrested. They already had evidence linking him with the coffin, which would be enough to hold him while more detailed enquiries were carried out.

'All right,' he heard himself saying. 'But you mustn't breath a word of what I'm about to tell you to anybody. Understood? If you let me down I'll stitch you up tighter than a fish's arse. Clear?'

'Perfectly. Shall we step outside?'

Unseen by Jonathan, who was voicing his opinions to a small group of Waterloo supporters, telling them where their side had gone wrong, the two of them stepped out of the clamour of celebrations on to the now deserted terracing.

He told Dominic the whole story in chronological order, starting with the truck that was stopped on the A1 for having a defective light, through the forensic examination of the mummy, the conversation with Interpol and the revelation of Kamil Behar's involvement in black market body parts, right up to the carbon dating test results. Throughout, Dominic listened with ever-widening eyes but uttered not one sound. As Ray finished speaking,

Dominic's face was flushed with a mixture of beer and the almost child-like excitement that overcomes a journalist who realises he has just chanced upon the greatest story of his life.

'Fuck me, Ray,' he stumbled. 'It's like a movie plot. Ray, you've got to let me use it. It's a bloody fantastic story.'

'No, you can't. Not yet anyway. There are certain things I need to do first, people I need to speak to.'

'Like what? How long will they take? Do any other journos know about this?'

'Steady tiger. You are the only journalist that knows the full story and I promise you I'll keep it that way as long as you stick to your end of the bargain. I'll ring you when I think it's safe to use but I've no idea how long that will be.'

Dominic gave him his card which contained his direct line number at the Mirror's headquarters in Canary Wharf – the former London docklands development that is home to at least four national newspapers – and his mobile number.

'Call me on either of those numbers,' he said, then turned way and stepped back into the clubhouse, immediately coming face to face with Jonathan.

'Where have you pair of bastards been?' he slurred. 'I thought you'd buggered off and left me. Come on Dom, it's your round.'

Chapter Seventeen

On his way into the office on Monday morning, Ray stopped off at the village newsagents and bought a copy of the Daily Mirror, half expecting to see the story of the mystery mummy all over the front page. He found it was actually devoted to a story about some pop singer he had never heard of and who barely looked old enough to be out alone, being admitted to a clinic to undergo treatment for drug and alcohol abuse. A quick skim through the rest of the paper reassured him that, on that day at least, Dominic had kept his word.

His doubts about speaking to Dominic had been reanimated after he told Karen what he had done. Still fuzzy from the previous day's excess of beer, he had arranged to take her for Sunday lunch and took the opportunity to let her into his secret in the uncertain hope that she would not fly off the handle in a busy restaurant. In the event, she had not rounded on him. In fact, she had been rather supportive. But she kept on asking: 'How do you know you can trust him?' In the end he was forced to admit that, other than the fact that Dominic was Jonathan's brother, he didn't know.

When he reached Parkside police station, he dumped his car in its allocated spot then used his force identity card to swipe through two security doors that gave him access to a staircase that led to his first floor office. Once there, he dropped his briefcase and the copy of the Daily Mirror on his desk, slung his jacket over the back of his chair and headed off for the department's small kitchen to make himself a much-needed cup of tea. Back at his desk he skim-read the newspaper and let the hot tea revive him.

Suitably refreshed, he pulled a small wire bound directory from his top right hand drawer, flicked through it until he found the page he needed, then picked up the telephone and dialled an internal number. Almost immediately, his call was answered by a crisply efficient female voice that contained no hint of warmth or welcome. 'ACC Rattery's office.'

Bill Rattery, a forthright Ulsterman who had worked his way through the ranks since joining Cambridgeshire Police more than 20 years previously, was the force's Assistant Chief Constable (Crime) and, as such, was ultimately responsible for every criminal investigation, for counter terrorism and for serious and organised crime, as well as keeping the force's political masters happy, a task that occasionally proved more difficult than catching criminals.

'Good Morning. DI Wilson, Arts and Antiques unit,' he began. 'I need to see Mr Rattery urgently.'

'Can you tell me what about?' Again, the impression was of cold competence rather than a desire to help.

'It's about an investigation that I'm involved in that has potentially got international repercussions.'

'I need to know more than that.'

Ray had never been able to easily handle the rudeness of others and in the face of this secretary's almost open hostility he had to stop himself making a totally inappropriate response.

'It's far too complicated to go into,' he snapped. 'But, in a nutshell, it involves fraud, extortion, a black market in human organs and potentially murder. Is that enough?'

The woman made no reply but he could hear her turning the pages of what he assumed was a desk diary and wondered how many days would pass before she would deign to let him in to the presence of ACC Bill Rattery. Her eventual answer surprised him.

'In the circumstances, I can switch a couple of appointments around. Can you be here at nine thirty tomorrow morning?'

'No problem.'

'Fine. Just ask for me, Veronica Barnes, at reception.'

'OK. I'll see you in the morning.'

He put down the 'phone slightly bemused by the speed with which he had got to see the ACC. He had assumed an appointment a couple of days hence would have been reasonable but the following day was fine. It just meant he had a lot of work to do.

For the rest of the day Ray worked solidly on producing a weighty briefing document that not only included a run down on everything that had happened so far – without mentioning Dominic McVitie or the Daily Mirror – but also the names and contact details for everyone who had been involved, from Karen right through to her counterparts in Vienna and Karachi. When the document was completed he hit 'spell check' on his keyboard, made the couple of amendments it highlighted and re-read the document all over again. When at last he was satisfied, he e-mailed it to the unit secretary and asked her to print and bind four copies, with the instruction that one copy was to remain in the office safe.

With the other three copies safely stashed in his briefcase, he turned out his office light, drove home to collect an overnight bag then headed South towards Sawston and Karen's cottage on the basis that, even though it was further away from police headquarters at Hinchingbrooke Park, he felt in need of some tender loving care before facing Bill Rattery.

The digital clock in the dashboard was showing just before 9.15am when Ray turned into the huge complex near

Huntingdon that the police force headquarters shared with the Forensic Science Service. He parked in the first available space he spotted, checked the contents of his briefcase and walked off, following the signposts to reception.

By the time Veronica Barnes arrived, he had completed the signing-in formalities and was wearing his force ID badge in a neat leather holder that clipped to the breast pocket of his jacket. He had imagined what Ms Barnes would look like and he wasn't disappointed. From the dark hair tinged with grey piled in a bun on the back of her head, to the gold-rimmed reading glasses on a chain around her neck, the plain white blouse, the skirt that ended just below the knee and the sensible shoes that had just the merest hint of a heel, she was the picture of controlled efficiency that he and Karen had generated, helped along by a bottle of red wine and a couple of large ports. She exuded the air that her sole mission in life was the personal protection of ACC Bill Rattery from all outside interference, especially from lowly DIs in the Arts and Antiques unit.

'Follow me Mr Wilson,' she said, spurning introductions and small talk. Even in the confines of the lift, she silently stared straight ahead.

From the lift, she preceded him into a small office, which he assumed was hers, from which a large oak door with highly polished brass handles gave entry to a much larger, grander office.

'Wait here,' she ordered and tapped on the open oak

door before stepping inside. Ray heard her announce: 'DI Wilson is here to see you, sir,' at which point she stepped back and ushered him into the ACC's presence with a wave of her right hand.

The Assistant Chief Constable (Crime) was in civilian dress, sitting behind an enormous oak desk that matched his office door. He rose and extended a hand to Ray.

'Good morning Inspector. Can I offer you some tea?' The Ulster accent still strong, despite 20 years in the Fens.

'That would be good, sir. Thank you.'

Rattery pressed an Intercom button on his desk. 'Veronica, can you organise some tea for us please? And we'll have mugs, not those daft little cups of yours,' giving Ray a conspiratorial wink.

Even through the wall, Ray could feel her eyes burning into the back of his head.

'Now then Inspector, what was it you wanted to see me about? From what Veronica told me it sounds very serious.'

He was only going to get one chance at this. 'I think it's extremely serious sir. But it's such a strange story I feel like I should start it with 'It was a dark and stormy night . . .' 'His feeble attempt at a joke failed to raise even a flicker of a smile from the ACC (Crime) and he made a subconscious note to stick to the facts.

He went on to detail the Bulgarian truck, why and where it was stopped, the identity of the Romanian driver, the six Turkish illegal immigrants and the discovery of the coffin, encased in bubble wrap, under the vehicle's cargo. Before he got any further, there was a tap on the office door and Veronica strode in carrying two mugs of tea, one of which she gently placed on the blotter in front of the ACC, in noticeable contrast to the one she virtually slammed down on a coaster in front of Ray.

Over the next hour, ACC Rattery listened intently, occasionally interrupting to ask a question, as Ray went into great detail about how the story had unravelled to the point where what was originally thought to be a priceless Persian artefact was now potentially a murder victim. He ended by handing over the spiral bound briefing document.

'It's a fascinating and intriguing story Inspector, I'll grant you that,' said Rattery at length. 'But I don't see what it has to do with us as police officers in Cambridgeshire. I don't see that there's anything to be gained by spending any more time and resources on this one.'

'Sir, with respect . . . we've got the body of a young woman that shows very strong indications that her death was anything but accidental. There are also indications that she was murdered for her vital organs. And her body turned up here in Cambridge, three years after she died, made to look like an ancient mummy which, we believe, was about to be offered for sale at a fantastic, fraudulent price. I'd say that's at least three very good reasons for continuing the investigation.'

Rattery put down the plastic ballpoint pen he had been impatiently drumming on the desktop. 'I can understand your passion for this case and your very laudable desire to find out who this poor young girl was and what happened to her, Inspector. But look at it from my point of view. By your own admission, the victim is probably Middle Eastern or East European in origin. She was almost certainly killed, for whatever reason, and mummified in the Middle East. There is a rumour – and that's all it is – that her heart was transplanted into the son of the US Ambassador to Germany, in a Frankfurt hospital, within hours of her dying.

'But there is absolutely nothing that ties the girl, her death or the perpetrators of her death to our patch. We have no proof of any wrong doing. As I see it, there's no evidence whatsoever that would give me grounds to authorise an investigation. The Chair of the Police Authority would be wearing my balls for ear rings if I pursued this one.

'We've done all we can by notifying Interpol but you might want to speak to the coroner's office, just in case the old buffer wants to hold an inquest. I think it's very unlikely but we should give him the choice.'

Ray's heart was in his shoes. He couldn't remember the last time he had felt so disappointed. He decided to give it one last shot.

'But sir. We have the body. We have evidence that indicates she didn't die a natural death. We owe it to her, whoever she was, to at least try to find out who killed her and why.'

'Inspector, I appreciate the fact that you've come to see me to discuss this matter and that you've obviously already devoted a considerable amount of time and energy in the pursuit of the truth. But I've made my decision. You are to let this matter drop. I don't want you spending any more time or resources on this inquiry. And that's the end of it.'

Ray stood. 'If that's your final decision sir . . .' he extended his hand. 'Thank you for your time.'

As he left through the small outer office he couldn't help but notice a wry, told-you-so smile playing across the face of Ms Veronica Barnes.

Back in the car, he called Karen and told her what Rattery had said.

'I don't think I've ever felt as down as this,' he said. 'I really need cheering up. Can I stay with you tonight?'

'Course you can,' she replied jauntily, trying to lift his gloom. 'Bring a bottle of port and I'll put the smile back on your face.'

By the time he was driving into work the following morning, whatever smiles Karen had succeeded in bringing to him had gone, replaced by that thick-headed, foggy feeling that is peculiar to an excess of port. But she had cheered him up and had promised to support his resolve to seek justice for Rhodugune in whatever way she could.

It was as they approached the bottom of the litre bottle of Taylor's Late Bottle Vintage port that he made his mind up to do something he had never, ever done before. He was going to disobey a direct order.

In the cold light of his port-induced hangover his determination had not faltered. And so it was that after attending to the three or four administrative tasks that awaited him, aided by an attempt to kick-start his brain with several cups of strong black coffee, he checked his wallet to make sure the card was still there, put on his coat and walked out of the police station. Turning left into East Road he carried on walking until he came to a public telephone box. He pumped in a handful of coins and dialled the number on the card. It rang and rang and he was just on the point of hanging up when a voice answered: 'Dominic McVitie.'

'Dom, it's Ray Wilson.'

'Christ, 'replied Dominic. 'That's a surprise. I'd convinced myself I'd never hear from you again.'

'Oh ye of little faith. I told you I'd ring when I was ready and I'm ready now.'

'Brilliant Ray. But listen. We were both a bit pissed that afternoon and I want to be sure I've got everything right. Any chance we could meet up so you can go through it all for me again?'

'We could but you'd need to come to Cambridge.'

'Tomorrow's my day off as it happens. I can make it then. About two o'clock?'

'Fine. I'll meet you in the Queen's Head in Sawston. It's in High Street. Any problems call my mobile. And whatever you do, don't tell anybody where you're going.'

'OK. See you tomorrow.'

As the 'phone box door closed behind him, the feelings of trepidation returned. But it was too late now. The train was in motion.

Chapter Eighteen

Tucked away in a quiet corner of the Queen's Head, Ray and Dominic attracted nobody's attention. Although he made notes in a small notebook, Dominic took the precaution, with Ray's consent, of recording everything using a discreet Olympus digital voice recorder. By the time Dominic had asked his last question, Ray had told the story at least three times without variation. The journalist was satisfied he wasn't being set up and offered his informant another beer.

When he returned from the bar he asked Ray if there were any pictures of the mummy that he could have.

'Karen took a lot when we first took the mummy to her,' he said. 'I'm sure if I ask her nicely she'll let you have a couple. I'll get her to e-mail them to you.'

'That would be great Ray. I really do appreciate this you know. They always say that in national newspapers you're only as good as your last splash but this one should bank a few Brownie points.'

'My pleasure sunshine. I've never done this before, disobeyed a superior officer. It feels odd. But I feel very strongly that I owe it that young girl to do whatever I can to bring her killer to justice and I don't care where she was killed or when. When do you think you'll use it?'

'Well, I'll tell the newsdesk about it tomorrow first thing. If they go for it – and I can't see why they wouldn't – it will probably be in the paper in a couple of days time.'

As Dominic predicted, the Daily Mirror went into melt-down when he told them the story he had picked up on his day off. Charlie White, the News Editor, dragged Dominic into the office of the paper's Editor Jim Garside, long before the scheduled morning conference, at which the newspaper's individual department heads would discuss the day's news prospects.

'Jim, young Dom here's got a cracking exclusive,' he blurted. 'It's about a murder victim that was turned into a fake mummy. Dom, tell him what you just told me.'

Over the next 30 minutes Dominic recounted the salient points of the story, emphasising that it was believed the victim had been murdered so that her internal organs could be harvested and that there was a possibility that her heart ended up in the son of a former US Ambassador to Germany.

'Great story, Dom,' said Garside at last. 'Where's it come from?'

'A contact inside the team in Cambridge that first examined the mummy.'

'Who is he or she?'

'Sorry Jim, I can't tell you that. I gave my word.'

'Bollocks to your word Dom.' Garside was well known for his fiery temperament. 'The potential repercussions of this story are huge. If we're going to run it I want to know who the source is. And it had better be good. I'm not going with this one on the say so of some bloody secretary.'

'I really can't give you his name. All I can say is that he is a senior detective and he works in the Arts and Antiques Unit at Cambridgeshire Police, so he knows what he's talking about.'

'So why is he talking to us?'

'Because he's a personal friend. And he thinks publicity would be a good way of flushing out the guy he believes is behind it all. He knows what he's doing.'

Garside said nothing. He swung his big, black leather executive armchair around and stared out of his office window, across the River Thames, over the O2 Dome to Greenwich. After almost a minute of unbroken silence, he swung back to face Dominic and Charlie White.

'OK. I'll take the risk. We'll run with it. But if it goes tits-up on us, don't bother coming back to the office. Either of you.'

Dom and Charlie exchanged glances but before they could utter any kind of response, Garside came at them again, but this time on a more friendly tack.

'How strong is the CIA link? That they did a deal to get this heart for the Ambassador's son?'

'I have to say not very,' answered Dominic, not wanting to exaggerate an already incredible story. 'Apparently it's something that Interpol think happened but we don't have any proof.'

'Right. Here's what we do,' said Garside, making another of the snap decisions – not always the right ones – that had driven him throughout his career. 'We'll splash a 10-paragraph taster on page one tomorrow with a double page spread on page two and page three. But we won't mention the heart transplant. We'll save that for a follow-up on Friday. Have we any pictures?'

'We should have pictures of the mummy by this afternoon,' Dominic replied.

'Great. Charlie, get on to the New York bureau. I want pictures of this Ambassador Vanderburgh and his son and warn them to get ready to front up Vanderburgh with the CIA allegation when we give them the nod. Right, let's get to work.'

Without another word, Dominic went straight back to his desk, booted up his computer terminal and set about the task of distilling everything Ray had told him into the 2,000 or so words that would make up the Mirror's double page spread. While he waited for the computer to kick itself into life, he discreetly sent a text message to Ray that read: 'We're running it 2moz.'

By 6.30am the following day, Ray was up and dressed and on his way to the village shop. Inside, the Daily Mirror splash headline screamed at him:

MUMMY GIRL BUTCHERED
FOR BODY PARTS
Exclusive
By Dominic McVitie

Back home, he carefully read every word, looking for any hint, any clue that could tie him to the leak. But Dominic had been as good as his word. The story quoted only 'a source close to the inquiry' and faithfully recounted everything that had happened, apart from the claim that Gaston Terray had made about the CIA doing a deal for the girl's heart.

Showered, shaved and secure in the Saab, he set off for work with an inner glow of self-satisfaction. He had been on the road only a matter of minutes when his mobile rang and was answered automatically by his hands-free set.

'Wilson,' he said out loud.

'DI Wilson. ACC Rattery's office here.' He had recognised Veronica Barnes' voice the second she spoke his name. 'Mr Rattery wants you at headquarters immediately.

We've got a major problem with the media. He'll fill you in when you get here.'

'OK. I'm on my way. Should be with you in about 40 minutes or so.'

But by then Veronica Barnes had already hung up.

By the time he reached Hinchingbrooke Park, three TV satellite up-link trucks had beaten him to it and were parked line astern in the entrance drive. Outside one, an earnest young woman was talking animatedly to a TV camera. Just beyond the trucks, more cars were parked and a clamour of reporters and photographers thronged the grass verge.

Once inside the main building, Ray flashed his force ID card, anticipating the signing in procedure and the wait for Veronica Barnes. Instead, the receptionist simply told him that ACC Rattery was expecting him and to go straight up.

He entered the ACC's outer office, where Veronica Barnes shot him a look so frosty it would have chilled a snowman. Without saying a word to him, she tapped on the big oak door, opened it unbidden and said to someone unseen: 'He's here.'

On entering the massive office, Ray discovered that ACC Rattery was not alone.

'Ah, Wilson,' said the burly Ulsterman. 'Don't know whether you two know each other. This is Detective Chief Superintendent Norman Shields, head of CID. I've asked him to join us for reasons you are probably well aware of.

'Let me start off by saying that I want you to know that I know what you've done. I know what you've done but I can't prove it, because if I could your arse wouldn't touch the deck. But don't think you've got away with it laddie. You haven't. It's just that right now you're more use to me in here on my side than out there against me. Is that clear?'

'Yes sir. Perfectly,' was the only reply Ray could make.

'Good. Now you've seen the vultures gathering outside and whether we like it not we're going to be forced to talk to them about our mystery mummy, as the Daily Mirror helpfully describes it this morning. But I don't want to talk to them and Mr Shields here doesn't know enough to talk to them. That's where you come in. We're going to hold a Press conference at ten o'clock, which all three of us will attend. However, I plan to let you' – and here he stabbed a stubby index finger in Ray's direction – 'do all the talking and answer all the questions. We'll both be behind you and if the questions start to get too political, I'll step in to help. Otherwise, you're on your own. I take it you've done the media training course?'

'Yes sir. But it was a few years ago and I haven't really had any experience of talking to the media.'

'I'll pretend you didn't say that, Inspector. Well, it's quite straightforward. Keep it simple, keep it factual, don't get drawn into speculation or conjecture. And don't use any bloody jargon. We don't want you sounding like a crap actor in a crap television series.

'Right. That's all for now. Reconvene here in this office at zero nine forty five.'

'Right sir,' was what Ray said, although he was thinking: 'And he doesn't want me sounding like a crap TV series . . .'

The media briefing room consisted of a dais about 60cm high on which was a long table and four chairs, each with a microphone in front of it. There was theatre-style seating for 50 journalists with room at the back to accommodate up to six television cameras. Ray, ACC Rattery and DCS Shields were greeted in a small assembly room behind the dais by a woman who introduced herself to Ray as Jane Tillotson, the force's senior Press Officer.

'OK gentlemen,' she began. 'I don't need to tell you how much attention the story in today's Daily Mirror has attracted. All the nationals have sent staff men. We've got BBC, ITV and Sky TV news crews, plus a crew from APTN – that's Associated Press Television News. They supply news and pictures to television stations around the world. And, of course, we've got all the local media, including the two local television stations and three local radio stations. It's going to be a busy Press conference.

'You need to be aware that the TV crews will probably want to do one-on-one interviews after the conference has ended. Which one of you will do that?'

'He will,' said Rattery, pointing at Ray. 'And he's going to be doing all the talking in the Press conference.'

She looked a little taken aback that the ACC (Crime) would pass up on such an opportunity to get his face on TV but said nothing.

'Fair enough. I'll lead the way in and take the seat on the far side of the stage. Mr Shields, if you follow and sit next to me, then Mr Rattery and Inspector Wilson at the near end. I'll introduce Mr Rattery and he can then pass proceedings over to Mr Wilson. If it gets out of hand, I'll call a halt. You also should probably be aware, Inspector, that the microphones in front of you also feed a hard-disc recorder so we have a record of everything that's said from the stage. Unfortunately, the microphones are unidirectional, which means they will pick up virtually nothing from the floor so we won't have the benefit of hearing any questions. But I'll do my best to keep a note of who asks what and I will choose the questioner. I will also ask each questioner to state their name and where they're from.

'Any questions? Good. Let's go.'

And with that she turned smartly on her heels and led the way into the briefing room.

Bringing up the rear, Ray's thoughts were of Christians marching to meet the lions.

By lunchtime, he felt like he had been in a tumble dryer. His brain was mashed, his thought train off the rails, his concentration level zero. In addition to doing all the talking at the Press conference, he had done recorded interviews for BBC and ITV national news, a live interview for Sky News and a recorded interview for APTN that seemed to go on forever. He had also done interviews for the two local TV stations, the three local radio stations and BBC radio's World At One programme.

Jane Tillotson found him in the empty briefing room, sitting with his head in his hands staring at the floor.

'Bit of an ordeal, isn't it?' she ventured.

'A bit? That's a bloody understatement if ever I heard one. I've never, ever done anything as tough as that in all my life.'

'You did very well but I have to say that I was a bit surprised old Rattery didn't want to steal the glory for himself.'

'I think it's called internal politics,' said Ray. 'When I brought this case to his attention earlier this week he didn't want to touch it with a barge pole. But then the Mirror story this morning forced him to confront it and I was the fall guy.'

'Cracking exclusive for the Mirror, I have to say. They were obviously well briefed by somebody who knew the case inside out. Any idea where the leak came from? Who the source was?'

'Not a clue,' he said.

But the look in her eyes told him that she knew.

She chose not to pursue the subject. 'You look like you need a drink,' she said, 'and the sun's well over the yard arm.'

'I'm not going in that bloody officer's mess. I've had enough of my fellow policemen for one day.'

'Don't fret. There's a good little pub not far away. And I'll drive.'

Chapter Nineteen

The story of the mummy headlined every national television and radio news broadcast for the rest of the day, although the words and pictures package put together by the APTN crew only arrived in time for the breakfast news bulletins in TV stations throughout the Middle East, India and Pakistan. And by that time, the British media had another sensational development to follow.

That morning's Daily Mirror had splashed on the claim that the mummy's heart had been transplanted into the dying son of the US Ambassador to Germany three years previously. It quoted an un-named Interpol source saying it was believed the deal had been brokered by the CIA and, for the first time, put the name of Kamil Behar into the public arena.

It was an apoplectic Bill Rattery that rang Ray's mobile, seconds before his 7.00am alarm went off and in his semi-waken state he had to concentrate hard to understand what the Assistant Chief Constable was bellowing, his anger intensifying his Ulster accent to the point where he was almost incomprehensible. The gist of what his boss was saying was, however, not difficult to follow. What did he think he was fucking playing at? He'd really fucked up this time. His fucking career was at a fucking end. The Daily fucking Mirror had put the fucking top hat on everything. He'd started a fucking international incident and he'd better get his fucking arse into headquarters immediately, or else. Before Ray got the chance to explain he didn't have a clue what the ACC was talking about because he had not yet seen the day's newspapers, Rattery had hung up.

He decided against rushing. If this was to be his last day as a Cambridgeshire detective he wanted to at least set his own timetable for the hours ahead. So he made himself breakfast of two poached eggs on toast and a pot of tea before running a shower as hot as his skin could stand. Freshly showered, shampooed and shaved, he chose a plain, dark blue wool suit from his wardrobe and matched it with a deep cream shirt and a subtly patterned burgundy coloured silk tie. From the coat stand behind his front door, he collected his heavy, German-made woollen overcoat, which he casually threw on to the back seat of the Saab and set off for Hinchingbrooke Park, stopping on the way to buy the Daily Mirror. The story contained what scant information he had given

Dominic on the alleged CIA deal but it quoted only Interpol sources and a denial from Hugo Vanderburgh, the former US Ambassador to Germany, that he had any knowledge of where his teenage son's transplanted heart came from. Again, there was nothing to directly tie the story to him or the Cambridgeshire force. He made his mind up to brazen things out, no matter what Bill Rattery threw at him.

The disapproving look on Veronica Barnes' face marked him out as something less than she had accidentally stood in on the street as she ushered him, with words unspoken, in to Bill Rattery's office. He found the ACC seated behind his massive desk with Norman Shields, the head of CID, sitting at the end of the desk to the right and looking nervous. There were no pleasantries, no invitations to tea. Rattery launched straight in to the attack.

'Right, Inspector. What the fuck is this all about?' stabbing his index finger at a copy of the Daily Mirror on his desk. 'Have you gone completely mad?'

'Sir, I have to say that nothing that has appeared in the Daily Mirror has anything to do with me. It looks to me like something the Mirror has done on its own. I have no idea where they got it from.' He resisted the temptation to add *It's what they do you know, report the news.*

'From where I'm sitting Wilson, it's got your grubby fingerprints all over it. And it's causing mayhem. I've already had the Home Secretary's private secretary on the phone demanding an update and I wouldn't be surprised if the Prime Minister and American President are not having a cosy little chat at this very minute.'

Ray was determined in his own defence. 'Sir, I have to say again that I have no knowledge of where, or how, the Daily Mirror got hold of this story. They appear to have spoken to someone at Interpol so it would seem fairly obvious that's where the information has come from. I know from my own enquiries that Interpol suspect there was a link between Kamil Behar and the acquisition of a heart for Ambassador Vanderburgh's son. And if they gave me that information they could just as easily give it to someone else – even a journalist – if they thought it would suit their own ends.'

The pent up fury within ACC Rattery was visible in the puce colour of his face and the throbbing veins in his temples.

'Wilson, I know you're bloody well lying to me but right now I can't prove it. I am, though, determined to get to the bottom of this whole sorry mess and find out who the fuck squealed to the Press. I'm therefore going to invite the Chief Constable of a neighbouring force to come in and conduct a root and branch investigation. And woe betide whoever that investigation points the finger at. Now, get out of my sight. And I don't want to hear another bloody word about this bloody mummy. Right?'

'Yes sir. Thank you, sir. Goodbye.' And with that Ray

smartly turned on his heels and left as rapidly as he could without making his departure look like flight.

Back in the cocoon of his car, he called Karen to tell her of the latest development. As he did so, America was waking up to the news. CNN, NBC News and ABC News were all preparing to lead their breakfast news bulletins with the allegation that the CIA had brokered a deal with an international criminal to obtain a heart for the son of the former Ambassador to Germany.

CNN was going one step further. As well as having a video-taped interview with Hugo Vanderburgh, the news channel was also going to report that a USAF F-16 fighter had been diverted from a combat mission over Iraq to collect the heart from the Incirlik air base in Turkey and fly it to the air force's Ramstein base in Germany.

Within 18 hours of the Daily Mirror identifying him, the name of Kamil Behar was known around the globe, making it highly unlikely that the man who lived such a high risk lifestyle was unaware of what was being said about him. His only crumb of comfort would be that no one accept his close associates knew what he looked like.

But all that was about to change.

The Sunday Mirror – the Daily's sister title – had been beavering away quietly ever since the story had first broken on the Thursday and the diligence and tenacity of its staff had paid off. The newspaper's front page carried a large picture of Kamil Behar under the headline: 'The Body Snatcher.'

On a double page spread inside, Sunday Mirror readers were enlightened as to what had been discovered about Behar. That he was an only child, born and raised in Birmingham by an English mother and a Turkish father, both now dead. That he was known to Interpol and to several UK police forces as a people smuggler although he had never been arrested. Interpol also believed he had previously organised two kidneys for transplantation, one in Jordan, one in Egypt and was also suspected of having supplied a liver that was used in a transplant operation in Greece at the same time. Although he had addresses in Istanbul and Ankara, he was a frequent visitor to England, spending several nights each month at an address in Leeds.

The newspaper carried a photograph of a small terraced house which it said was in Thomas Place, Leeds, a non-descript row of solidly built Victorian homes in a warren of similar streets just off Kirkstall Road and not far from the city's university. It also reported that a young, dark haired woman who answered the door claimed not to know Kamil Behar and even when confronted with his photograph maintained she could not identify him. She refused to give her name, although neighbours named her as Ann Massey, who worked 'somewhere in the Town Hall.'

The clamour for the picture from the world's media was deafening. The Sunday Mirror never acknowledged the source of the image but by the end of the day, the syndication department had sold it around the world, raking in a massive amount of money.

There were, however, no repercussions from the newspaper's revelations. Indeed, although no one at the Sunday Mirror was ever told, their work had unwittingly proved to be of immense value to the forces of law and order. The previous day, the Home Secretary had ordered the Serious Organised Crime Agency to investigate Behar and uncover his links in Britain. The newspaper story had saved the Agency a considerable amount of time and effort. By Sunday evening, the little terraced house at 7 Thomas Place, Leeds, was under surveillance by SOCA officers who had confirmed the owner and sole occupant as Ann Massey, a 27 year-old who worked in the accounts department of Leeds City Council. They also knew that her mortgage and utility bills were paid every month from a numbered bank account in Zurich.

By the time the watery late winter sun was setting, SOCA had tapped Ms Massey's telephone, obtained permission to listen to her mobile telephone conversations and intercept her post and e-mails. When she returned home from work on the Monday, she was also unaware that listening devices had been hidden in her bedroom, living room and kitchen. If Behar made any attempt to contact Ann Massey, SOCA would know.

While the agency's staff was busy bugging the house in Leeds, almost 1,800 miles away in Ankara, Kamil Behar, by now the world's most wanted man, was glued to his television screen with a morbid fascination. Spurred by the furore that erupted in America over the claims that a Turk had been behind a deal to obtain a heart for a senior diplomat's son, Turkish state television had resurrected the story and pictures sent to them three days previously by APTN.

And there, on screen, talking about the discovery of what was initially thought to be a priceless Persian mummy but could now be a murder victim, was a man he recognised.

A man he once trusted; a man who was once part of his organisation; a man who turned out not to be what he claimed to be; a man he now perceived to be responsible for his potential downfall. Ray Wilson.

Even before the TV news had moved on seamlessly to the next story, Behar had picked up the telephone and was dialling a number in England. It was answered after just three rings. Behar did not even bother to say who he was.

'I need you to do something for me. And urgently,' were the first words out of his mouth.

'There is a man, a policeman, called Raymond Wilson. I think he works in Cambridgeshire. I need you to find out everything you can about him. I need to know where he works, where he lives, where he sleeps and who with. I need to know his habits, his preferences, his likes and dislikes, what he buys and where he buys it. I need to know as much about Raymond Wilson as he knows about himself.

'But most importantly of all, I need to know who he loves and everything there is to know about her – or him; I was never sure – because a very special destiny awaits whoever it is.'

The voice in England said only: 'Such information will take time to gather.'

'It doesn't matter. The fee is one thousand English pounds a day. But I want results. No results, no pay. Is that understood?'

'Perfectly,' replied the voice in England. 'Leave it with me. I'll be in touch.'

Chapter Twenty

Kamil Behar was a wealthy man and he had the trappings to show it. A penthouse apartment in Ankara; a harbour-side apartment in Istanbul; a mountain retreat in Italy, where he kept a beautiful, long-limbed, olive-skinned 25 year-old Italian woman whose only task in life was to satisfy his every whim, and, of course, a small house in Leeds, where Anne Massey fulfilled a similar role in his life. He drove a ridiculously fast, ostentatious, lime green Lamborghini supercar and had a 60-foot motor cruiser, moored wherever took his fancy.

But life had not always been good to Kamil Behar.

He had been born in a terraced house in one of the poorer parts of Birmingham. His father, a Turkish immigrant to Britain, stacked shelves in the local supermarket and worked as a waiter in a Turkish restaurant at night to make ends meet.

His mother, Birmingham born and raised, had failed every academic test set for her. She left school without a qualification to her name so when Kassim Behar tumbled into her life one rainy Saturday night – they were both drunk in a seedy nightclub – she thought she had found her passport to easy street.

How wrong she was. But she'd made a vow, for better or worse, and she was going to keep it in the forlorn hope that one day, one day, things might just get a little better.

At school, the young Behar's jet black hair, dark, deep-set eyes and exotic complexion led the other kids to taunt him. 'Paki' and 'Towel head' were two of the most common and not a single soul in the playground took enough interest in him as a human being to actually find out anything about his background.

The boy kept his head down and did what he needed to do but it was clear to his teachers that was never going to be an outstanding pupil. He left school with the minimum qualifications in maths and English but with a deep-seated desire to prove himself, to prove to his peers that he was worthy of their respect.

The opportunity came only days after he walked out of the school gates for good.

Another boy, probably the closest thing Behar had to a friend, told him that an older boy was looking for somebody to look after something for him – and he was willing to pay.

Behar volunteered and one dark evening in the local

park he was handed a package, sealed in plastic and secured with duct tape.

In the relative safety of his bedroom, anxious fingers and a small penknife opened the package to reveal a snub-nosed Colt revolver.

It was the beginning of Behar's new life in crime, of his escape from drudgery.

From minding firearms, he moved to minding drugs, graduating to supplying and eventually dealing, first of all locally, then nationally and finally, internationally.

By now money was no object and the jeers of his playground tormentors long forgotten memories. And it was about now that Behar discovered something he could smuggle that was far more lucrative and far less dangerous than drugs. People.

He was watching television news in his Ankara penthouse one evening when it dawned on him that the stories of human misery, of poverty, of starvation, of genocide that he was seeing actually provided him with an opportunity to make money.

There were thousands and thousands of people from countries in Africa, the Middle East and even Eastern Europe willing to part with every meagre thing they owned for the chance of a new life in Europe and especially a new life in Britain.

He had the contacts and the means to make those dreams come true.

So it was that almost overnight, heroin and cocaine

gave way to the down-trodden, the weary and the desperate. And Kamil Behar was on his way to having more money than he could ever have imagined.

The scale of his operation became so vast that, at one stage, police in Britain believed Behar was behind more than 80 per cent of traffic in illegal immigrants. In fact, the operation was so large that it proved easy for them to infiltrate an ambitious young detective called Ray Wilson into the organisation.

Behar had just poured himself a very large glass of his favourite single malt whisky and was tuning his satellite dish to pick up his favourite American sports channel when his flashing mobile silently indicated an in-coming call.

'Yes?'

The voice on the other end of the call dispensed with introductions and small talk.

'Your friend the policeman.'

'Yes?'

'I have the information you wanted.'

'OK. Go ahead.'

'It seems your Inspector Wilson has a new love in his life. A beautiful and very intelligent lady. An expert in Egyptology . . .'

Over the next 30 minutes the caller gave Behar Ray Wilson's life story and every detail in it. By the end of the conversation, Behar had addresses, telephone numbers, even bank account details and regular haunts not only for Ray Wilson and Karen Bowen but for their closest friends – shared and individual – and people that Ray would only have described as acquaintances.

At the end of the call Behar hung up without a word and began planning a trip to England and, more particularly, to Cambridge.

Chapter Twenty-One

As with all media feeding frenzies, the story of the Persian mummy and ambassador's son's new heart gradually worked its way from page one to obscurity and after a week wasn't even worthy of a mention. The media machine had moved on to subject someone else to its unremitting spotlight.

SOCA continued to monitor Ann Massey's movements closely, so closely that they knew intimate details of her life without any of them even coming within touching distance. The Zurich bank account continued to fund her mortgage, gas, electricity and council tax bills. Now that the calendar had clicked over into December, her post consisted principally of Christmas cards; her e-mails of messages about nights out with the girls, parties and shopping trips; her telephone calls mainly confirmation of the million minor details of life, such as changes to meeting times or locations. Of Kamil Behar there was no sign.

Through its member nations, Interpol had issued an All Ports Alert for Behar that included his photograph, description and the numbers of his British and Turkish passports. The alert was endorsed 'Notify but do not detain' which, in theory, meant that if Behar tried to leave whichever country he was now in, Gaston Terray at Interpol in Lyon would be told and his movements could be tracked. But Behar did not trigger any alarm bells at any airport or harbour that had received the alert. It looked like he was staying in hiding.

In Cambridge, life had returned fairly much to normal for Ray and Karen. Each of them filled their days with the routine of their respective careers. Away from work they spent an increasing amount of time in each other's company and had started to leave little parts of their lives – such as clean clothes, razors, toothbrushes – in each other's homes, which both of them saw as an indication of the strengthening of their relationship and commitment, although neither of them was prepared to suggest that they live their two lives as one.

They had, however, decided to spend the Christmas holiday together at Karen's cottage, where close friends had been invited to join them at any point they wished during the festive period, a loose, open arrangement that suited both them and their friends.

But now, the Christmas shopping had to be done. The

city centre streets were thronged with weekend shoppers and visitors, so much so that Ray had suggested taking a cab from Sawston rather than face the frustration of finding a parking space which, even at the quietest of times, were not easy to find. To a casual on-looker, Ray and Karen were love personified. They held hands, laughed and joked with each other and appeared to be deeply interested in what the other was saying or doing. After three hours, they were both laden down with bags from chain stores, from small individual shops and from supermarkets. They had reached the Lion Yard shopping centre, just a few hundred yards from the Fitzwilliam Museum, where the plan was to finish off the day buying some indulgent chocolate from Thorntons and enjoying a much needed coffee before searching for a cab home.

The shopping centre seemed packed to capacity. Surely, Ray thought to himself, they can't get any more people in here, volunteering to hold all the shopping while Karen went into the Thorntons store. He stood with his back to the shop window with its mouth-watering display of chocolates in every shape and size imaginable, casually glancing around, taking in his fellow shoppers, content with his life for the first time since he couldn't remember when, comfortable in the happiness that Karen had brought to him.

At first, it was nothing more than a feeling, a perception that made the back of his neck tingle. He turned sharply to his left and then to his right to see what could be causing it, to no avail. He had almost convinced himself it was his imagination when the feeling came upon him again. He was being watched. No, he was being observed. But observed by whom or by what? Unconsciously he slid backwards so that his heels were against the shop frontage. The primeval protection instinct. Don't give anything or anybody the chance to get behind you. Again, he swept the crowds around him but saw nothing and then Karen was at his side, clutching a Thorntons carrier bag.

'What's the matter? You look like you've seen a ghost,' she asked.

'Nothing. I'm fine,' he replied, gazing over her left shoulder.

Straight in to the eyes of Kamil Behar.

Within a split second the Turk vanished.

'Here, hold these,' he said sharply, thrusting the shopping at Karen. 'And don't move.'

There was no sign of Behar. He elbowed his way through the mass of moving humanity without so much as another glimpse. He finished up outside the shopping centre on the curiously named Petty Cury where, again, the pavements were packed with shoppers. And still no sign of the man he had hoped he would never see again.

He squeezed his way back to the chocolate shop where Karen was still standing looking puzzled and not a little angry.

'What was all that about?' she demanded.

He couldn't hide it. She had to know.

'I've just seen Kamil Behar. Right here. Standing about five yards over in that direction.'

'What? It can't have been. You must be mistaken.'

'Believe me Karen, it was him. I swear it.'

'But what's he doing here?'

'I don't know but whatever it is, it won't be pleasant. Come on, let's get out of here.'

He pushed his way through the crowds, out of Lion Yard along Petty Cury to a taxi rank where an empty cab had just pulled to a halt. Without a thought for anyone who may have been waiting, Ray ripped open the back door and, dragging Karen with him, ordered the driver to take them to Sawston. He spent the entire 15 minute journey in silence, looking over his shoulder making sure the cab wasn't being followed. Satisfied that it wasn't he gave the driver Karen's address in Sawston.

Once inside the house, he poured himself a large scotch and slumped in the armchair in the corner, facing the front door.

'Ray, this is stupid,' said Karen. 'If it was Behar you need to report it. You've already told me enough about him for me to know that he's not come here on an innocent visit. You owe it to yourself. And to me.'

'Let me think about it. I don't want people to think I'm panicking.'

'I don't care what people think, it's you and me I'm worried about.'

'Me too. But I just don't know what to do.'

'Tell you what. We'll stay in tonight, have a couple of drinks and sleep on it. If you still feel the same way in the morning, we'll report it.'

The following morning, Ray was coming round to the idea that he had been mistaken; that the man he saw in Lion Yard was not Kamil Behar and neither his life nor, by association, Karen's, were under threat. As the day wore on he convinced himself that what he thought he'd seen was just the result of paranoia. And by the time he left for work on Monday morning, he was cursing himself for his stupidity. Interpol had an all ports alert out for Behar. He couldn't have got in to the country without someone knowing – and he would have been told, maybe even offered protection, if Behar had been spotted.

In the security of his office, he hung the soft goose-down filled jacket he had been wearing all weekend on the coat stand and dropped his briefcase on the desk. No sooner had he sat down than the unit secretary appeared with a cup of freshly made tea and his post. Leafing through the envelopes he came across what was obviously a Christmas card that had been hand delivered, addressed, in almost feminine handwriting, simply to Detective Inspector Wilson and in an unsealed envelope.

He opened it to find a card about 12cms square with the traditional nativity scene on the front. But the words inside the card turned his legs to jelly and for the first time in his life he felt real fear grip his throat. In the same, looping, girlish hand as the envelope were written the words:

'Merry Christmas. From Rhodugune.'

For the best part of a minute, Ray was transfixed by the words on the card, unable to do anything but stand and stare, as if paralysed by the latent threat contained within what should have been a joyous message. Finally, the realisation of what needed to be done struck him and without moving from behind his desk he shouted: 'Jimmy, Jimmy, bring me a couple of evidence bags. Now.'

It was only a matter of seconds before Detective Constable Jimmy Ross was in his office, proffering a handful of robust, sealable plastic bags, each with a plain white panel on which the bag's contents could be noted. Even though he was only in his late 20s, Ross had a face that belonged to someone much older, the result of a 30-a-day cigarette habit and a penchant for regular, excessive drinking. 'Here you are boss,' he said. 'Have you got something good?'

'I'm not sure Jimmy. It depends on whether your definition of good includes getting a Christmas card from a girl who's been dead for 2,500 years.'

'What?'

'Don't worry about it,' Ray assured. 'It may be connected to a case I've been working on or it may just be someone's idea of a jolly Christmas joke. But I need to get this card and envelope over to forensics ASAP and get them checked for fingerprints and DNA.'

He dropped the envelope into one bag and the card into another and marked them both with an indelible marker, 'Exhibit PM001 – envelope' and 'Exhibit PM002 – card.' He then placed both plastic bags into a large manila envelope which he gave to Jimmy with an instruction to get them processed as a priority.

As Jimmy left his office he was already dialling Bill Rafferty's number.

To say that the Assistant Chief Constable's response to the predicament in which DI Ray Wilson now found himself was devoid of emotion would be a very large slice of understatement cake. Ray described his encounter in a Cambridge shopping centre with a man he initially believed was Kamil Behar and how he later dismissed it as a misapprehension until that morning when he had received the Christmas card, which had now been sent to forensics. He admitted that if he really had seen Behar in the Lion Yard shopping centre, he feared for Karen's safety as well as for his own.

There was not the slightest trace of sympathy or empathy in the ACC's reply.

'Well Inspector,' he began. 'I'm very tempted to say you've brought all this on yourself. If you'd obeyed orders in the first place you wouldn't be in this sorry position now, would you? Now perhaps you understand what they mean by those who sow the wind reaping the whirlwind.

If it was up to me I'd happily let you sink in this quagmire you've created for yourself but I can't do that because of the risk to Ms' – he pronounced it Mizz – 'Bowen.

'She is after all a civilian, albeit a misguided one, who has let herself be drawn into this web by your feeble attempt at self-aggrandisement, or whatever pathetic notion it is that's driving you. For that reason and for no other she is entitled to our protection.

'If it was Behar you saw in the city centre then I agree her life could be at significant risk so I'll inform SOCA of this development and I will organise for at least one armed officer to be on close protection duty for her at all times until we all agree that the risk has been eliminated. Are you still an authorised firearms officer?'

'Er, yes sir. I haven't carried a weapon since I joined the Arts and Antiques unit but I have kept up my qualification.'

'Good. Come to the armoury at headquarters. I will personally authorise the issue of a handgun and ammunition for you to carry at all times, even when not officially on duty.'

Although Ray was shocked and somewhat disturbed by this unexpected authorisation for him to carry a gun, he didn't show it. 'Thank you, sir. I really appreciate this . . .'

Before he got any further, Rafferty cut him off. 'A little bird tells me that you and this Ms Bowen are more than good friends. Is that true?'

'We, er, actually sir, yes it is.'

'Good. It'll save me a packet in overtime when you're with her. Now get off the line. I've got things to do, just in case Behar is in town.'

The force armoury sat alongside the target range and firearms training area in a deep basement below the main headquarters building. It was accessed through a series of heavy steel doors, each protected by electronic locks that could only be opened by swiping a current firearms authorisation card. Down here there was no natural light and no natural light-hearted banter. Down here the business was, literally, deadly serious.

Beyond the final door, Ray found himself in a stark, white, featureless, furnitureless room about six metres square with a small counter facing the door. Behind the counter was a sergeant, obviously approaching retirement, whose lined and craggy features betrayed a lifetime of experiences, most of them bad from his expression. No smile, no word of greeting, he watched in silence as Ray made the five or six steps that brought them face to face.

'Detective Inspector Ray Wilson. I've come to collect a weapon and ammunition.'

A brief glimmer that could have been recognition but could equally have been disdain flickered across the old sergeant's Dickensian gloom.

'Ah yes Inspector. I've had a call from ACC Rafferty's office. Can I see your firearms authorisation card and warrant card please?'

Ray put down the card he had used to gain access to this underground bunker and unclipped his warrant card in its leather pouch from the breast pocket of his jacket. The sergeant eyed them both before entering details from each into a computer terminal which sat on the end of the counter. He then produced an old, heavily bound ledger from under the counter and painstakingly duplicated the information by hand. When he'd finished, he looked up.

'Right sir. What can I get you?'

It's as if I'm ordering a bloody drink, thought Ray. 'I need a handgun.'

'OK. What sort of handgun?'

This is going to be like pulling teeth, was the unspoken thought. 'A semi-automatic pistol I think. What would you recommend?'

It was as if the question had unlocked a door in the sergeant's mind and turned on all the lights. His mouth expanded into the resemblance of a smile and his eyes began to shine with a fervour that was almost devout.

'This may seem like a stupid question given the nature of our transaction, but can I ask what the weapon is to be used for sir?'

'Yes. It's principally for personal protection. I have reason to believe that my life, and the life of someone close to me, is under threat.'

The fervour became even more acute.

'In that case sir, you will be needing a weapon that is

powerful but lightweight, virtually foolproof but extremely accurate and so well made as to be almost indestructible. You need a Glock G17.'

'A Glock? I thought that was the drug dealers' favourite weapon.'

'So it is sir but it is also the weapon of choice of police forces and military units around the world. And with good reason. It's made in Austria and has a polymer frame which makes it 86 per cent lighter than steel but even tougher. It's a 9mm so it has plenty of stopping power and it comes with a 17-shot magazine as standard. It also has something called a Safe Action trigger which removes the need for a safety catch. Simply squeezing the trigger releases a built-in triple safety mechanism which is automatically reapplied when you release the trigger. So, should you ever have to use it, you don't need to worry about releasing the safety. You just concentrate on your target. Oh, and another thing. It's not prone to jamming when it gets hot like the old Browning Hi-Power was.'

He might be a miserable looking old bastard but he knows his stuff, Ray thought to himself. 'OK. Sold. I'll take one please. And can I have a spare magazine and a box of ammunition?'

'Certainly sir. Give me a minute.' And with that he disappeared – in Ray's later exaggerated retelling it would become a shuffle – behind a screen at the back of the counter to reappear five minutes later carrying a small black plastic case, a 10cm square cardboard box that was heavily sealed and a shoulder holster.

'What's that thing for?' asked Ray, prodding in the direction of the holster.

'Well, even though the Glock is lightweight, it's still a substantial weapon and needs to be carried carefully and safely. You can't walk round with it stuffed in your trouser band like they do on the telly you know Inspector.'

Too late Ray realised that this was the sergeant's attempt at a wise crack and, the moment having passed, made no reply.

'Just one other thing Inspector,' said the sergeant, reverting to his staid self. 'You are required to load the weapon here. I need to check it before you leave.'

Ray suppressed a sigh of impatience, tore opening the packaging on the ammunition box and loaded one of the two magazines he found inside the black plastic case. With a satisfying click, the magazine locked in place in the grip of the Glock and he passed the gun to the sergeant, who examined it with the enthusiasm of a child chasing chips and beans around a plate.

'Thank you Inspector. That's fine,' he said at last. 'I should just show you this.' He pointed to what looked like a small pin at the rear of the cartridge ejection chamber. 'When there's a round in the chamber that pin is visible. Just an extra safety thing but worth knowing.'

'Well, thank you very much sergeant. You've been very helpful but now I need to be off.'

'Thank you sir. Best of luck. And I sincerely hope I get it back unused. Nasty things, guns. I hate 'em.'

Chapter Twenty-Two

The dark blue Northern Gas Networks van parked alongside a small pink and white candy striped tent pitched over part of the pavement attracted little attention from the residents of Thomas Place, Leeds. Only the most observant – or nosy – among them would have noticed that although it moved occasionally, it was never out of sight of the front of number seven. Equally, when vehicles from Yorkshire Electricity or British Telecomm were parked in the street they were also ignored as were the anonymous saloon cars that came and went, even when they parked up over night.

The Serious Organised Crime Agency had had Ann Massey under surveillance for the thick end of six weeks and, apart from the odd night out with the girls, which usually consisted of a pizza, drinks in one of the dozens of trendy bars that populated Leeds city centre followed by a nightclub and a taxi home, her routine was unwavering. She rose each morning at 7.30am, showered, had a light breakfast, dressed and then took the bus for the short journey into the city centre and her work in Leeds Town Hall. The red and white Mini Cooper, identified as belonging to her, remained parked outside her home. At lunchtime she bought sandwiches from a specialist shop close to her office and ate them at her desk. At 5.30pm she left work and caught the bus back home.

But this day, this Friday, things changed. She finished work at 4.00pm, jumped into a waiting taxi and was home by 4.30pm. The SOCA listeners, this time concealed in a Yorkshire Electricity van, heard her take a long shower, much longer than usual, which was followed by the sounds of cupboards and drawers being opened and closed. It was fully five minutes before the two agents inside the van worked out what was happening. She was choosing things, probably clothes, with great care. She was packing a case. But where was she going? None of her telephone calls, her e-mails or her letters had mentioned a weekend away, if that's what she was planning.

Inside the van, agent Dennis Wetherby picked up the microphone of an ultra high frequency radio that operated on a frequency well outside the capabilities of the thousands of radio scanners out there in the hands of criminals, journalists and the myriad of others who had an interest in knowing what the forces of law and order were up to, and pressed the 'send' button.

'Whisky Yankee control, Whiskey Yankee control. This is Mike One, Mike One. Over.'

Instantly his call was answered by a female voice that possessed such clarity of diction it would not have been out of place reading the BBC radio news.

'Mike One, this is Whiskey Yankee control. Go ahead. Over.'

'The target is on the move. I say again, the target is on the move. We need urgent back up to carry out travelling surveillance. Rendezvous will be our current location. Over.'

'Understood Mike One. Surveillance Unit Two is on standby to join you. Confirming rendezvous is your current location. Over.'

'That's correct. I will contact you again when the target is on the road. Mike One out.'

Half an hour later, Ann Massey emerged from her neat terraced home and even by the unflattering orange light of the sodium street lights, the two SOCA men could see she was dressed to kill.

'Looks like some lucky bastard's in for some fun this weekend,' Wetherby remarked to his colleague. 'Unlike us.'

She casually threw a small case onto the back seat of the Mini Cooper, climbed behind the wheel and drove off, taking the first turning that would take her down to Kirkstall road, where she turned left towards the city centre.

'Whiskey Yankee control, Whiskey Yankee control. This is Mike One, Mike One. Over.'

'Mike One, Whiskey Yankee control. Go ahead. Over.' Again, an instant response.

'The target has left home and is driving a red Mini Cooper with a white roof. Index number Lima Sierra Five Six Bravo Echo Hotel. We are following along Kirkstall Road, towards the city centre. Over.'

'Thank you Mike One. I will notify Surveillance Unit Two. Standby on this channel. Out.'

Whoever, or whatever, comprised Surveillance Unit Two there had been no sign of them when Ann Massey pulled out of Thomas Place. But, then again, Wetherby hadn't expected to see them. After all, following people without being seen was what they did.

Despite the heavy early evening traffic, the Ford Transit van managed to stay three vehicles back from the Mini Cooper. Even when she took the slip road that lead down to the inner ring road, they still had her in sight. After a mile or so, the ring road became the A64, a dual carriageway leading away from the heart of the city that would eventually take its users all the way to the coast. On the crest of a rise ahead, Wetherby could see a set of traffic lights and was struck by a feeling of impending doom.

Sure enough, as the mini approached, the light flicked to amber. Ann Massey accelerated across the junction but the Transit, five car lengths back and at least four times the weight, had no choice but to stop. Wetherby had barely uttered the first syllable of a long chain of expletives when an old Vauxhall Vectra in front of them, carrying what looked like two youths, each wearing baseball caps back to front, pulled out of the line of traffic and rocketed across the junction against the red light, a brief flash of flame flaring from its drainpipe sized exhaust.

'Fucking hooligans,' muttered Wetherby. No sooner had he done so than the UHF radio crackled into life.

'Mike One, Mike One. This is Sierra Uniform Two One. We have the target in sight.'

Wetherby felt his face flush as he realised his mistake. Far from being hooligans, the two men in the Vauxhall were his back up, part of SOCA's specialist surveillance section, highly trained and highly motivated, driving discreet but very powerful cars.

'Thank you Sierra Uniform Two One. Keep us informed of target's route and progress. We'll stay behind you. Mike One out.'

For the next half dozen miles, the Transit managed to keep the Vauxhall in sight, even in the heavy swell of traffic on the city's outer ring road. As the A64 passed from the Leeds suburbs into more open countryside, an unsuspecting Ann Massey put her foot down. The SOCA surveillance car went with her, leaving the Transit behind as the speedometer climbed through 60mph and then 70mph on the twisting and narrowing road.

By now the Vauxhall was nothing more than two pinpricks of red light in the distance but Wetherby and his colleague were kept informed of its every move by its crew. As the convoy approached the stretch of dual carriageway that would become the Tadcaster by-pass, a motorcyclist thundered out of the darkness and overtook the van, the rider giving a casual wave with his left hand as he passed. Seconds later, he too had vanished into the night.

Then, the Vauxhall voice was on the radio. 'Mike One this is Sierra Uniform Two One. Surveillance is being taken over by Sierra Uniform Two Five who has just overtaken you. He'll keep you informed of the target's route and speed. We'll drop back behind you as back up should we be required. Sierra Uniform Two One out.'

The convoy continued into the night, Wetherby and his colleague speculating on their final destination. 'It's either York or Scarborough,' mused Don Barker behind the wheel of the Transit.

'I reckon it's got to be York – she's too dressed up for Scarborough,' responded Wetherby.

'Oh, I don't know. I hear Scarborough's pretty trendy these days.'

'I'll bet you five quid she goes to York.'

'OK. You're on.'

Minutes later, the UHF radio was alive. 'Mike One, Mike One. This is Sierra Uniform Two Five. Target has turned left, left, left off the A64 onto the A1036 towards York. I have visual.'

'There you are bud. That's a fiver you owe me,' said Wetherby, barely able to suppress his feeling of superiority. Small things, he thought, small things.

The motorcycle was now no more than 20 yards behind Ann Massey with no other vehicle between them, but the rider was unconcerned. Car drivers never see motorcyclists, not even when they're filling the back window. Inside the cosy cocoon of metal, radio playing, heater on, motorcyclists just don't exist. And the dark only makes them more invisible. He felt confident he could ride alongside the Mini if he wanted and she probably still wouldn't see him.

'Mike One, Mike One. Target is approaching the city centre. She's turning left, left, left into Queen Street. Maintaining distance.'

And two minutes later: 'Mike One, Mike One. Target is turning left, left, left into Bootham, the A19 signposted Thirsk . . . Target is slowing . . . Target has turned left, left, left into the car park of the Cavendish Hotel. I say again. She has stopped at the Cavendish Hotel.'

It took another five minutes for the Transit to reach The Cavendish, an elegant looking, small hotel in a tree-lined road not far from the historic centre of York. Barker parked up in a spot where both agents could see the hotel entrance and the entrance to its car park. No sooner had the engine been switched off than there was a tap on the passenger window and there stood the motorcyclist, crash helmet in hand.

'George Brookes,' he said by way of introduction. 'She's inside. The car's round the back. I've had a nosy and there's no way out. The back door of the hotel opens on to the car park but this is the only exit. If she comes out you shouldn't miss her. Assuming you're still awake of course.'

'Not a problem George,' answered Wetherby. 'We're relieved at midnight and we're not back on until Sunday lunchtime so she'll be someone else's problem. Thanks for your help by the way. She would have lost us coming out of Leeds if it hadn't been for you boys.'

'No worries. It's what we do. Well, I'll be off. I've got a long distance job to do tomorrow. Good luck guys.'

And with that he had gone, leaving Wetherby and Barker to focus on the comings and goings at the Cavendish Hotel.

For the rest of the weekend, SOCA teams kept the hotel under constant surveillance so that when Wetherby and Barker returned on Sunday lunchtime, this time driving a five year old Ford Mondeo, they were told: 'She's not been out all weekend.'

'Have you been in to see what she's up to?' asked Barker.

The young SOCA officer was momentarily shocked, as if he hadn't expected his colleagues to question how the surveillance was conducted. 'We tried but the bar's for residents only. I got a quick glimpse into the dining room but there was no sign of her. We don't know what she's been doing in there but we do know she's not been out.'

Wetherby cut in. 'OK fellas. Thanks. Off you go. We'll take it from here.'

The pair climbed back into their Mondeo and settled

into the routine of a dull December day in York. It was a main road so there was a constant flow of traffic, mainly private cars, and people out walking, some striding purposefully, others dawdling in no particular hurry and others exercising their dogs.

Wetherby and Barker had been carefully observing the scenario for about two hours when a private hire taxi, driven by a young Asian man, pulled up at the front door of the Cavendish where it stayed, engine running, for several minutes until a woman dressed in a white Muslim hijab came out of the hotel carrying a small, leather overnight bag and got into the back. The taxi did a U-turn and headed back towards the centre of York. Without thinking of a good reason, Wetherby noted down the taxi's registration number and the name of the company that operated it.

Fifteen minutes later, the Mini Cooper with Ann Massey behind the wheel, pulled off the hotel car park.

Wetherby picked up the UHF microphone as Barker pulled out into the traffic behind the Mini. 'Whisky Yankee control, Whiskey Yankee control this is Mike One, Mike One. Target is on the move from the Cavendish Hotel. Request surveillance assistance please.'

The carefully modulated voice of the Whisky Yankee controller responded instantly. 'Mike One, be advised that Sierra Uniform Two One is already in position on the A1036. Call them direct on Channel Zero to liaise. Whiskey Yankee control out.'

Wetherby radioed his counterpart in the Vauxhall Vectra

and gave him a yard by yard account of their route and speed until at last the Vectra observer said: 'We have visual. We're pulling in behind you now.'

'I need you to take the lead and follow the target to her final destination,' said Wetherby. 'We have further enquiries to make here.'

Barker shot his colleague a quizzical look.

'Let's get back to that hotel Don. I'm not totally happy that we've got the full picture from there.'

The two men parked the Mondeo on the hotel car park and went in through the rear entrance. Behind the small reception desk they found a woman in her mid 50s who still retained an air of the attractiveness that had undoubtedly turned heads and broken hearts when she was younger, her make-up flawless, her hair expensively coiffeured. She carefully placed a pair of designer glasses on the desk in front of her.

'Yes gentlemen,' she enquired.

'We'd like to speak to the manager please,' said Wetherby.

'I'm Jackie Richardson. I own the Cavendish. Can I help?'

'Of course,' said Wetherby. 'We're from the Serious Organised Crime Agency' – both men flashed their identity cards – 'and we'd like to ask you a few questions about one of your guests. Is there somewhere more private?'

'Please. Step this way,' she answered, holding open the door to a tiny office that was almost filled by a desk, two chairs and a filing cabinet. 'Now. How can I assist you?'

This time it was Barker who spoke. 'You've had a young lady staying here since Friday, name of Ann Massey from Leeds. We'd like to know what you can tell us about her please. What she did while she was here, who she spoke to, that kind of thing.'

'I'm sorry gentlemen there must be some mistake. We haven't had a guest called Massey this weekend.'

'I assure you there's no mistake,' said Wetherby. 'We followed her here on Friday and we've had the hotel under surveillance every since. We watched her drive away about half an hour ago. In a red Mini Cooper.'

'Ah. Now I know who you mean. But her name's not Massey. That's Miss Benson. Deborah Benson. She's one of our regulars. Well, I say regulars. She comes to stay with us every three months. She always books her next stay before she leaves.'

'And what does Miss Benson or Massey of whatever she calls herself do while she's here,' asked Barker.

'Well. She usually has a long meeting with her business partner – he's based in Holland and comes over specially to meet her. Then they have a few drinks and dinner in the hotel. After that I don't know. It's their business. Although the chamber maid told me his bed hasn't been slept in.'

From a manila folder he was carrying, Wetherby produced a photograph of Ann Massey taken by the SOCA surveillance team using a long lens.

'Is this the woman you know as Deborah Benson?' he asked.

'Yes, that's her. Ever such a nice person. Always very polite.'

A gut instinct made him produce another photograph, this one supplied by Interpol, a tight head shot of Kamil Behar.

'And have you seen this man before?'

'Yes,' replied Mrs Richardson without hesitation. 'That's Amir, Deborah's business partner.'

'Amir what?' demanded Wetherby. 'What's his last name?'

'It's Amir Nazari. Just a moment, I've got his registration card here somewhere.'

A few seconds later she handed Wetherby the registration card filled in by the man who called himself Amir Nazari and giving an address in The Hague, Holland.

'Thank you Mrs Richardson. Do you mind if we keep this? It could be vital to our enquiries.'

'Not at all. I do hope they aren't in any serious trouble.

'Afraid we can't say anything about that,' said Wetherby. 'Just one more thing. Where is Mr Nazari now?

'Why he left just before Miss Benson. He was wearing his traditional Arab robes – I think he's from Dubai – I don't know how he does it in this weather. He must be freezing, poor thing.'

'How Mrs Richardson? How did he leave?' The excitement was becoming audible in Wetherby's voice.

'In a cab. He called a cab to take him to Leeds-Bradford Airport.'

The realisation hit Wetherby and Barker simultaneously. The bloody Asian woman! It was Behar all along.

'Thank you Mrs Richardson. Thank you. You've been very helpful,' called Wetherby over his shoulder as both men rushed for their car.

Neither man spoke to the other but Wetherby used his mobile to call the cab firm whose name he had noted while Barker radioed Whisky Yankee control and ordered them to arrest Ann Massey and ground every flight from Leeds-Bradford to any destination in Holland for the rest of the day. He then asked the controller to contact Interpol to get them to check out the address in The Hague that Behar had given on his registration card, even though he knew the chances of it actually existing were very low indeed.

The news from the taxi firm wasn't good. The driver had been expecting a hefty tip for driving all the way to the airport. Instead the man – and it had been obvious from his voice that he was a man – had asked to be dropped at the end of one of the many side turnings on the main road out of York back towards Leeds. The driver, who had been handed double the fare, hadn't dared to ask why his passenger was wearing an hijab and had simply left him standing on the pavement.

Kamil Behar had succeeded in evading the law once more.

Chapter Twenty-Three

'Well, thanks anyway. I knew it was a long shot but it was worth a try.' Ray Wilson put down the phone and absorbed what the manager of the Forensic Science Service had just told him. The Christmas card and its envelope were clean. No fingerprints. Not a trace of DNA. And the greeting had been written using the kind of cheap roller-ball pen that can be bought in any trinket shop anywhere in the world, making it impossible to identify.

His mobile rang and even though the caller ID read only 'Private number' he answered.

'Ah Wilson. ACC Rafferty.' The prickly Ulsterman's tones were unmistakable. 'Listen. I've got some bad news. It looks like you were right about Behar. He is in the country. Or at least he was over the weekend. SOCA positively identified him at an hotel in York but he got away.'

'York? And he got away? How?'

'Well, you may not be aware but SOCA has had this girl in Leeds under surveillance for weeks. Then last Friday she suddenly takes off and heads for a hotel in York. SOCA maintained surveillance and when she left on Sunday afternoon, the hotel's owner admitted she goes there every three months to meet her business partner. They showed her a picture of Behar and she identified him as the business partner, saying she knew him as Amir Nazari. Apparently he got away in a taxi dressed as a woman in a Muslim hijab.'

'Didn't SOCA see him going in?'

'No. According to the hotel he checked in Friday lunchtime so he was already there when his girlfriend turned up. Gave an address in The Hague in Holland which, as you would expect, turns out to be false. The wee girly's been nicked and is currently being questioned in Leeds but there's no sign of Behar. I've already alerted Ms Bowen's close protection officer to be extra vigilant and I'm giving you the same warning. Stay on your toes Wilson. I don't want this one going tits up.'

'Yes sir. Thank you sir. Will you let me know what comes out of Leeds?'

'I will if they tell me. Bye for now Wilson.' And with that the ACC had gone, leaving Ray to absorb the implications what he'd just been told.

Behar was in the country. Somehow he had evaded the All-Ports Alert. How had he got in? And when? And where? But these were questions that could be answered later. First, he had to talk to Karen. She had to be reassured. She had to know he was there for her; that the chances of Behar coming after her were low.

They met in the bar of the Prince Regent, Karen's bodyguard keeping a discreet distance but nonetheless attentive to his charge. Neither of them felt like eating and settled instead for drinks, the usual Greene King IPA for him and a large gin and tonic for her. The bodyguard ordered himself an orange juice and a ham and cheese sandwich.

'Ray, what's happening to me?' asked Karen immediately they sat down, her voice tremulous with anxiety. 'I don't know what's going on. I'm out of my depth and I'm scared. Just having him around' – she swivelled her eyes in the direction of the bodyguard – 'frightens the living daylights out of me. He's a nice bloke and all that but just knowing who he is and why he's there freaks me out.'

'Listen Karen, I know you're scared and you have every right to be but believe me, we – I mean I – I'm not going to let anything happen to you. You're too precious to me. You're all I care about. I know it's not nice being under an armed guard but you have to understand it's for your own safety. The chances of Behar trying anything on are remote but he's there just in case.'

He went on: 'I've been thinking about this and I think it would be a good idea if you moved in with me, at least until this is all over. That way I'll be around all the time.

We can travel to work together. And it means you have to spend less time with the minder. We could even spend some time on my boat to really get away from it all. What do you think?'

His proposal – for that's the way Karen's mind interpreted the suggestion – momentarily shocked her. On the face of it, it seemed a sensible suggestion. They would be physically together, which would make them both stronger, better able to face whatever was coming their way. They would have each other to lean upon, to rely upon. And yet deep down she knew that if she moved into his home in Fulbourn she would probably never move out again. Was that a commitment she could handle? More importantly, was it a commitment he could handle?

'Karen?' She heard his voice at a distance.

'Karen? You OK?'

'Sorry Ray, I was miles away for a second there. I think it's a good idea. We'll call by mine after work and I'll pick up a few things. Then I'll move the rest of my stuff into yours at weekend. But only until this is done and dusted. Then I'm moving back to Sawston.' She knew the last statement was a lie. 'Deal?'

'Deal,' Ray agreed, his mind rapidly planning and plotting how he could make her stay a permanent one.

One hundred and sixty miles north, in an interview room at Millgarth, Leeds' central police station, Ann Massey was undergoing her second day of questioning by SOCA agents Wetherby and Barker. For the second day in succession they asked her the same questions. And for the second day in succession she gave them the same answers.

She had never heard of Kamil Behar. The man with whom she had spent the weekend – and the man whose photograph the agents had shown her – was known to her as Amir Nazari, an Arab, born and raised in Dubai. As far as she knew he lived in The Hague, Holland, from where, he told her, he ran a network of companies selling jewellery on the Internet. She had never been to his home. They had met at a jewellery fair in Amsterdam which she had visited during a hen weekend in a vain attempt to give her liver a rest. He had been charming and generous and she had slept with him for the first time that weekend. His work sometimes brought him to the UK and when it did, he would call at her home in Thomas Place. He never wrote, not even e-mails, and very rarely phoned. He would just turn up on the doorstep. And no, she didn't think that was odd. When you love someone you don't think about things like that. There was no possibility of her being compromised because she only loved Amir and was faithful to him. In return he paid all her bills, including her mortgage. Every three months, on dates agreed in advance, he would, without fail, turn up at the Cavendish Hotel in York and they would spend the weekend drinking champagne and making love. He always paid the bill, in cash. She used a false name because he'd asked her to. He said it increased the excitement. And how many more bloody times did she have to tell them? Amir was a lovely and loving man who didn't have a violent bone in his body. Any suggestion that he was mixed up in crime of any sort was ludicrous. No, he'd never mentioned Turkey – how could he be a Turk, he was born in Dubai. No, he'd never spoken of illegal immigrants or of black market body parts. Where had they got all this rubbish?

'Interview suspended 1421,' Wetherby said for the benefit if the tape recorder in the corner.

A young police woman stepped into the room to keep an eye on Ann Massey and her solicitor while Wetherby and Barker went for coffee in the canteen.

'Well,' said Barker, the cappuccino foam forming a pale moustache on his top lip, 'she's either telling us the truth as she knows it or she deserves an Oscar. Those are exactly the same answers she gave us yesterday and I have to say I think I believe her.'

Wetherby grimaced. 'I know what you mean but I've still got a gut feeling about our Miss Massey. There's something not right about an attractive young girl who's happy with a tumble every three months in return for getting all her bills paid by a bloke she hardly knows. It's just odd.'

'Yeah, but fortunately being odd isn't a crime, otherwise half the bastards we know would be behind bars. What do you reckon we should do? We can't keep her much longer without charging her with something. Question is what?'

'I don't think we can nail anything on her with unless there's something in the Naivety Thy Name Is Woman Act we can use. I suggest we thank her for her help, let her go and keep the intercepts and surveillance on for a while longer. If I'm right she'll go running to Mr Behar or Nazari or whatever his name is this week.'

Wetherby entered the interview room alone, nodding to the policewoman to stay put.

'Well Miss Massey, I think you've told us everything we need to know for the moment so I don't propose to detain you any longer. You're free to go. Would you like us to ring a taxi?'

'That won't be necessary Mr Wetherby. My lawyer will give me a lift home, thank you.'

Even as Ann Massey gathered her belongings Wetherby and Barker sat on opposite sides a borrowed desk in the CID room reassessing everything they knew about her and Kamil Behar, looking for the one tiny thing that wasn't right.

Chapter Twenty-Four

It had been a good after-work session in Davy's Bar, the modern, waterfront bar that served as the office pub for the Daily Mirror journalists incarcerated in their soulless Canada Square office block that was part of London's Canary Wharf development. Now Dominic McVitie, unsteady on his feet after more than two hours continuous drinking, was ready for home. Sensibly he opted to leave his car behind and take the Docklands Light Railway and then the underground back to his flat in Camden.

As he wobbled towards the Canary Wharf DLR station Dominic giggled to himself at the thought that no matter how sophisticated he tried to be when travelling on the light railway, the realisation that there was no driver other than a computer chip always startled and worried him. The time he spent in the otherwise light, airy and not-too-unpleasant carriages was always tense and it was always with a feeling of immense relief that he made his way from the DLR to the Northern Line at Bank Station.

It was this nervous distraction, coupled with the fact that he was drunk, that had caused Dominic to lower his defences, to be less observant than he would normally have been. And it was why he had failed to spot the two young men waiting outside Davy's, who seemed to take a more than passing interest in him and who even now were keeping a close eye on him as they stood in the carriage entrance, balancing themselves against the swaying motion of the train, ignoring the fact that there were plenty of empty seats.

Dressed in the uniform of the young, trainers, baggy jeans and hooded tops, they could have been anybody, going anywhere. Except that these two had a very specific task to perform, one for which they had been well briefed and handsomely rewarded in advance.

They stayed close to Dominic as he made his way up the escalator from the DLR halt at Bank Station to the Northern Line where he boarded an underground train to Camden Town.

He was still unaware of their presence as he left the underground station and crossed Kentish Town Road, close to its junction with Camden Road, and headed off on the half mile walk to his home in Georgina Street. His thoughts were of what he would say to Maria, his Australian girlfriend, if she had gone to his flat after work as she'd promised and, more importantly, if she'd stayed.

He would never know whether she had or not and his carefully rehearsed excuses would never be needed. For somewhere en route, the two young men who had followed him from Canary Wharf, approached from behind and struck him a violent blow with a short length of pickaxe handle, knocking him out cold. Dominic heard their footsteps but before he could turn, his world filled with intense pain and spiralling darkness.

When Dominic hadn't appeared in the Daily Mirror newsroom fifteen minutes after he was due to start work, no one batted an eyelid. Journalism wasn't a job that happened nine to five and even in a climate governed by bean counters, there was still room for a little bit of leeway, unspoken recognition that journalists – especially the reporters and photographers out on the road – worked long hours, much longer than the hours for which they were paid. When he hadn't turned up after half an hour, Charlie White, the news editor, was anticipating every telephone call to be from Dominic, calling in sick after a night on the piss, using some spurious excuse such as 'a migraine' or 'a tummy bug.' But when that half hour turned to an hour without so much as a call, Charlie White's anxiety level began to rise.

'Has anybody heard from that twat McVitie?' he said out loud to no one in particular.

The only response was a disembodied: 'Not seen him since last night in the pub,' which came from behind a computer terminal and was not instantly identifiable.

White waited until Dominic was two hours overdue before he made a positive move, calling Jason Thornley, another reporter who he knew was a friend of Dominic's, into his office. Fearing a dressing down for some unremembered misdemeanour, Thornley closed the office door behind with a degree of trepidation.

'You know where McVitie lives, don't you?' began White.

'Er, yeah. In Camden. I've been to his flat a couple of times.'

'Well look – and this needs to be kept discrete – I may be going soft in my old age but I'm worried about him. He should have been here two hours ago. He's not turned up and we've not heard from him, which is unlike him. He's normally very reliable. I need you to do a bit of digging. Find out where he is.'

'He was OK when he left the pub last night. He was a bit pissed and said he was leaving his car and going home on the DLR. Do you think something's happened to him?'

'I don't know,' said White. 'Start off with the car park. If his car's not there he may have tried to drive home, in which case ring round all the hospitals, see if they've got any road accident victims that match Dominic. If it is there, get out to his flat. You know the score.'

'Right. I'll call you when I know something.'

Thornley collected his jacket from the back of his chair and vanished through the newsroom door in the direction of the lift. White returned to the newsdesk and tried to get on with the business of gathering in the day's news.

Thornley had a rough idea whereabouts in the vast, hideously expensive Canada Square underground car park Dominic would have left his prized Audi with its leather seats and metallic dark blue paintwork, but he was saved the search when he met Arthur, the car park attendant who, even in these days of automatic payment machines, credit cards and contracts, was still deemed a necessity to ensure the smooth running of the facility.

'Morning Arthur. Don't suppose you've seen Dom this morning have you?' asked Thornley.

'Sorry mate, I haven't. But he must have been pretty leathered last night – his car's not moved. It's still on Level 2 where he parked it yesterday morning. Must have more money than sense to do something like at these prices.'

Minutes later Thornley was in his own car, picking his way through the London traffic heading for Camden and Dominic's flat in Georgina Street. As he turned the corner into the street, his mobile rang and was automatically answered by the Bluetooth system in his car. The voice of a near-hysterical female replaced the pop music he'd been listening to as he drove.

'Jason? Is that you? It's Maria. Where's Dom? Have you any idea?'

'Maria, yes it's Jason. Just calm down a minute. I'm actually outside Dom's flat right now. The office has sent me to see if he's here.'

She butted in before he could continue. 'Jason, thank God. I'm in the flat now. Come up.'

By the time he'd parked the car, Maria was standing on the doorstep. He was struck by her plainness, her dark, unkempt hair and the freckles across the bridge of her nose, undisguised by any hint of make up. She hugged him like a long lost brother, even though they met no more than half a dozen times.

'Jason, I'm so worried. I think something awful has happened to him,' she started.

'OK, OK, let's go inside and have a cup of tea and we can talk.' His tabloid-acquired expertise at getting across doorsteps unwittingly kicking in.

Inside, they sat in facing armchairs, each holding a mug of strong tea, as they tried to piece together the previous evening.

Thornley told Maria how Dominic had left Davy's Bar at about 8.30pm, saying he was going home on the DLR because he'd drunk too much to drive. That was the last time he had seen his friend, although his Audi was still in the underground car park.

For Maria's part she explained that she had gone straight to Georgina Street after finishing work at 6.00pm. When

Dom wasn't home by 7.30pm she guessed he was having a drink with his colleagues but when he still hadn't arrived at 9.00pm she rang his mobile but got no reply, the phone tripping straight to the answer message.

'He could well have been on the Tube by then, so there wouldn't have been any reception,' put forward Thornley.

'Yes, I thought that. But I tried again every 15 minutes until about ten o'clock and there was still no reply so I decided he was probably roaring drunk and I went home to my place. I called back here about half an hour ago but he still hadn't been home. The bed's not been slept in and there are no dirty dishes. I'm really worried Jason.'

'So am I. You stay here for a bit and I'll go and knock on a few neighbours' doors, see if they've seen anything of him.'

His first call was at the ground floor flat immediately below Dominic's and the houses either side, both of which were also split into two flats. But deep down he knew it was pointless. London, especially those parts of it that consisted mainly of old houses turned into flats, was an anonymous place. People came and people went unnoticed. No one saw anything, or if they did, they kept it to themselves. And so it proved. After half an hour he discovered that only the man who lived in the flat directly below Dominic had ever spoken to him. He knew that his name was Dominic and that he worked for the Daily Mirror. Apart from that, Dominic was just another unknown in the city of the unacknowledged.

Thornley and Maria drove together to the police station in Kentish Town, where they added Dominic's name to the list of almost 30,000 souls who vanish in London every year. But even as they answered the questions posed by the officer who took them into a discreet interview room, they were both secretly aware that there would be no high profile search, no national media appeal, no television pictures of divers dragging lakes or policemen searching fields.

Among the wealth of information his friends were able to give to the police – his mobile number, his photograph, his medical condition, his parents' address, his brother's address, the places he liked to visit – three facts doomed Dominic McVitie to remain, in the peculiar vernacular of the police service, a 'MisPer.' He was 34 years old. He was single. And he'd been missing for less than a day. Despite the reassurances of the interviewing officer, Thornley knew that the undeclared thought at the back of the policeman's mind was: He's old enough to look after himself.

For once, Jonathan McVitie dropped any attempt at American slang, speaking instead in his native tongue, complete with Fenland accent.

'Ray. I need to talk to you. Dominic's disappeared.' Even over a mobile telephone connection that was not the sharpest, the distress in his voice could not be disguised.

'He's what? When?'

'Night before last. Apparently he went to the pub after work and got a bit pissed. He set off to catch the Tube home but he never arrived. His car's still where he left it. His girlfriend's reported him missing. What can I do?'

A scene too ghastly to contemplate flickered briefly through Ray Wilson's mind and was quickly buried.

'First thing is don't worry,' he tried to reassure his friend. 'I'm sure he'll be alright. He's probably with one of his mates somewhere. Or he picked up a girl on his way home. There could be any number of explanations.'

'Yea, but it's not like Dom. He's the sensible one. He's not the type to pick up girls on the Tube and if he was staying with a mate he'd have let someone know by now. He didn't turn up for work yesterday and it was the Mirror that raised the alarm.'

'Look, I'll do what I can,' said Ray. 'I'll put a call into the Met to see if they've found out anything and I'll ask them if they can make Dom a bit of a priority. I can't promise anything, but I'll do my best.'

'Thanks mate. I appreciate that. Call me when you know anything yeah?'

But Ray's first call was to Karen, even though he had only dropped her at the Fitzwilliam an hour earlier. He had to know that she was safe. Not wanting to frighten her unduly, he didn't mention Dom or the fact that he was missing. Instead he suggested eating at the Prince Regent on the way home that night.

Then he opened the Police and Constabulary Almanac,

found the number he was looking for and dialled the headquarters of Operation Compass, the specialist unit established by the Metropolitan Police to give strategic direction to the investigation of missing people in London.

Within minutes he found himself speaking to man of his own rank, a DI Mike Park. He told Park how Dominic had been reported missing the previous day; about how he had broken the story of the mummy factory that supplied body parts for transplant on a bizarre black market; about how Kamil Behar, the man thought to be behind the mummy factory, was known to be in the country; about the SOCA inquiry and about his own previous dealings with the Turk. He didn't tell Park that he had been the sole source of Dominic's story.

Park listened to his counterpart intently and without interruption. When he'd finished Park asked: 'So, do you think this Behar is linked to Mr McVitie's disappearance?'

'I don't know,' replied Ray. 'But it's a possibility. Behar is evil walking and he's capable of just about anything. You should know that my force has authorised me to carry a firearm at all times and has assigned a close protection officer to my girlfriend when I'm not with her.'

It was impossible to tell whether Park's silence was incredulity or simply disbelief.

'What I'm struggling with Ray is that if this Behar is as bad as you say, why hasn't he been picked up?'

'No one knew he was in the country until Sunday. There's an All Ports Alert out for him but he somehow managed to evade that. SOCA came close to him in York on Sunday but he escaped dressed as a woman.'

'Christ Ray. This just gets better and better,' said Park. 'Your man will already be registered as a MisPer on the Police National Computer so I'll send a message out from Operation Compass to every force in the country, asking for special attention to be given to finding him. Any information will come back to me and I'll keep you informed. In the meantime, if you come across anything that you think might be useful, please let me know at once.'

'Will do Mike. And thanks for your help. I just hope we get a positive result.'

As Labrador's go, Jake was a particularly inquisitive individual, no more so than when he was off the lead, running free in the open countryside. And today, his owner, Frank Palmer, had every reason to give him his freedom. At 52 he should have known better and he should certainly have known how long it took him to recover these days, but Friday night was still a night for excesses. Pint followed pint followed pint during his weekly get-together with his mates at the bar of The Chequers, his favourite pub in the West Sussex village of Steyning, where he lived. And when the pub eventually closed, there was always the Indian restaurant across the street for a prawn tikka masala with nan bread, washed down by even more beer.

Now he was out walking on the South Downs Way,

the ancient track that snakes its way across 90 miles of Sussex, breathing deeply and trying to walk briskly as he fought with the after affects of overindulgence. Jake scurried back and forth, this way and that, nose to the ground or sniffing the air, his muscular tail beating its own silent tattoo.

As the pair approached the Chanctonbury Ring, Jake became even more excited, running on ahead and then returning to his master, as if urging him to hurry. The Ring was an Iron Age fort but in 1760 a young local man named Charles Goring had planted the fort with a crown of beech trees. Down the decades the Ring had acquired a reputation for mysterious and ghostly happenings. Some people claimed it was haunted. Others claimed that the Devil himself could be raised there. Many believed it was a place of witchcraft and still others that it was a magnet for unidentified flying objects.

But on that Saturday, Frank Palmer had no thoughts of little green men, witches or ghosts. His plan was to simply walk around the ring and then head off back towards Steyning and maybe a livener in The Chequers.

Jake, tail still thrashing the air, ran ahead, weaving in and out of the beeches, up and down the remains of the earthworks. When Frank caught him up he could see his dog was nuzzling what looked like a bundle of rags, albeit a pretty big one. Instinct told him to call Jake back but curiosity lead him onwards towards the pile of clothes.

Closer, he realised with a start that far from being a

bundle of rags, what Jake had found was a man. A man, apparently asleep on his side, and dressed in what appeared to be an expensive overcoat. But silent. Unmoving.

Frank bent and shook the man's shoulder. 'You all right mate?'

He pulled on the shoulder, turning the man on to his back and found himself staring into unseeing eyes. Beneath the overcoat the man was naked. And where his vital organs should have been there was nothing but a gaping, crimson cavity.

Frank felt his own stomach give one enormous heave as the whole of Friday night splattered onto the ground.

And onto the mutilated corpse of Dominic McVitie.

Chapter Twenty-Five

Mike Park hated being the bearer of bad news. The fact that he was about to deliver it a fellow policeman should have made it easier somehow but it didn't. He had guessed from the tone of Ray Wilson's original conversation that he was closer to Dominic McVitie than him just being the brother of a mate and he wasn't sure how the detective would take the news. It had taken police in West Sussex until Sunday evening to match the body in Chanctonbury Ring to Dominic McVitie's description on the Police National Computer. Park had been given the news as soon as he walked into his office on Monday morning. And now he had to make a call that he didn't want to make.

The mobile number that Ray Wilson had given him rang and rang and he was just on the verge of hanging up when it was answered. Park deliberately kept the pleasantries to a minimum, anxious to get straight to the point of his call.

'Ray, I've got some bad news I'm afraid,' he began. 'A body's been found. And it fits the description of your friend Dominic.'

'What? Where? When? How?' Park could almost hearing Ray's mind whizzing through the thousand and one questions he wanted to ask, questions to which, as yet, there were few answers.

'Look, I'm sorry to have to be the one to tell you this. The body was found at a local beauty spot in West Sussex. Man out walking his dog apparently. What's not clear yet is how he got there. The doc reckons he wasn't killed where he was found. From what the local CID tell me the track's pretty wide and could be accessed by a four-wheel drive vehicle, which means he could have been killed pretty much anywhere. Have you any idea what he could have been doing in West Sussex? Did he have any friends or relatives there?'

'I, I really I . . . Sorry. I really don't know. I'm afraid I didn't know him all that well. I can ask his brother if you like.'

'Yes, thank you. That would be useful,' replied Park. 'The other thing is, somebody needs to make a formal identification.'

'Yes, of course. I'll ask his brother is he's up to it.'

'Ray before you do that, there's something else you need to know.' Park steeled himself to reveal the grisly details he had been given by West Sussex police. 'The thing is . . . the body had been eviscerated.'

'Oh fuck, Mike. What . . .?'

'I know, I know. It's not pleasant. Apparently all the major organs, including the heart, were missing. The doc reckons they had been surgically removed. From what you told me last time we spoke that puts your mysterious Turk right in the middle of the frame. And by the sounds of it, he had some expert help. Sussex police have already started a murder inquiry and they're planning a Press conference tomorrow morning. They need somebody to ID the body as soon as.'

'OK. In the circumstances I don't think it would be fair to ask Jonathan to do it. I'll do it myself. Have you got a contact at West Sussex CID?'

His first call after hanging up was to Karen. Right now she was the most precious thing in his life and he wanted to keep it that way. He told her that Dominic's body had been found but not the gruesome details of his death. He told her that he was going to Worthing to formally identify the remains, but not the reason why. He told her he would try to get back that night; that she shouldn't wait up for him, but that her close protection officer shouldn't leave her alone. And he told her he loved her.

In her office at the Fitzwilliam, Karen knew from his voice that he wasn't telling her everything but she would never have guessed in a thousand years exactly what it was he was keeping to himself. All she could do was reassure him that she would be alright; that the bodyguard would stay with her until he got home. And then she did something she had thought she would probably never do again. Clearly, and in the full hearing of her bodyguard and of Margaret Jones, who was fussing around in the outer office, she told him she loved him. Until then, they had been personal words that only passed between them in privacy. But now she was worried about him and he was worried about her. She wanted to bolster his spirits. She loved him – and she didn't care who heard her say it.

His next call, the one he'd dreaded having to make, was to Jonathan McVitie, who, not unexpectedly, crumpled on hearing the news that his brother was dead. As with Karen, Ray spared him the abominable aspects but felt forced to share with him the fact that Dominic had been murdered. He didn't want his friend to hear it from an anonymous news bulletin or a stark newspaper report.

In his shock, Jonathan started to fire off questions, the very same questions that Ray had started to ask of Mike Park.

Ray interrupted him. 'Jonathan, right now, there's not a lot I can tell you. I don't have the answers to all your questions. But can you think of any reason why Dom would be in West Sussex? Did he have any friends or relatives down there?'

'No. Not that I know of at least. I know we don't have any family in Sussex but I suppose he could have friends there that I don't know about. Is it important?'

Ray could see why the information might initially strike Jonathan as trivial, but knowing what the dead man was doing nearly 60 miles from his home could be vital to the murder inquiry that was about to burst into the media.

'Well, it could be Jonathan. Think about it. Dom disappears on his way home from work in London and turns up three days later in a spot where he has no known connections. Knowing where he was in those three days could be key to helping us find whoever did this so anything you tell us will be very useful.'

'Yeah, sorry Ray. I just can't get my mind to function right now. I'm still trying to take in what you've just told me. I can't believe Dom's dead. He's my brother. Why would anyone want to kill my brother?'

'I know it's very hard to accept, but the thing is, it's going to get worse before it gets better,' said Ray. 'Sussex police are holding a Press conference tomorrow to appeal for information. You know the kind of thing . . . did anybody see Dom after he left the pub? Did anybody see him in West Sussex? The other thing you need to know is that they need the body to be formally identified so I'm setting off for the hospital in Worthing in a minute to do just that.'

'I'm coming with you then. Wait for me.'

'Jonathan, I don't think that's a good idea. It can be a very trying experience and one that you don't need to put yourself through. I can identify him easily enough and I promise I'll let you know if I glean any more information. Best for you to remember Dom as he was.'

'What does that mean? What did the bastard do to him?'

Ray recognised his error in an instant. 'I don't have the details, like I said. But I believe Dom was very badly injured. He'd obviously been violently attacked.'

'Ray I want you to get this bastard. Promise you'll get him. I want the fucker to suffer.'

'I know how you're feeling. But you have to remember it's not my inquiry. It's not even on my patch. It's another force's area and they'll be running it. But I promise you I will do everything I can to help. And I'll keep you up to speed with what they tell me.'

It was lunchtime when Ray arrived at the hospital in Worthing, West Sussex, where Dominic McVitie's remains lay in the mortuary. A telephone call to a number that Mike Park had given him ensured he was expected and as he gave his name to the receptionist he found himself flanked by two men. He had no idea where they came from and had not seen anyone hanging around when he arrived. You're losing your touch, he thought.

'Detective Inspector Wilson?' enquired the older of the pair. 'I'm Stuart Hodgson, the coroner's liaison officer. And this is Detective Chief Inspector Hamish MacLean from our major incident team. He's the senior investigating officer.'

'Pleased to meet you,' said Ray, shaking hands with both men.

'You must have had a long journey Inspector. Would you like some lunch?' MacLean's voice carried a Highland lilt.

'Thanks but if it's all the same to you I rather just get this over with.'

'Aye. I understand,' answered MacLean. 'Lead on Stuart.'

Hodgson lead the way through a maze of corridors and down two flights of stairs into the bowels of the hospital. Another corridor brought them to a pair of swing doors which had the word 'Mortuary' starkly printed in black over the top.

Inside, the walls and floor were tiled in clinical white, the brilliance of which was accentuated by powerful neon strip lighting barely concealed behind diffusing plastic sheeting. Along the wall to the left was a series of large drawers which gave the room the appearance of an over-sized filing cabinet. The right wall was empty except for a door with frosted glass panels on which were etched the words: 'Examination Room.'

Hodgson nodded to a green-gowned assistant without bothering to introduce him. The man turned and walked to the wall of drawers and, pausing only to check it was the correct one, pulled on a handle one row up from the bottom. The huge drawer slid silently open, allowing a whisper of chilled air to escape, revealing the naked body of a man.

'Mr Wilson,' intoned Hodgson, obviously the veteran of a thousand such moments, 'can you please confirm that this body is that of Dominic McVitie?'

Ray's eyes took in the harrowing sight. Dominic's face was swollen and badly bruised. There was a cut over his left eye, his nose was clearly broken in several places and in his partially-open mouth, he could see teeth were missing. And then there was the cavity; the pit where the parts that once gave Dominic life had been, now nothing more than an angry, livid void.

It was as if the Devil's hand had clenched Ray's stomach. His first instinct was to vomit but, miraculously, he managed to hold on to his dignity and he heard a hoarse voice, a voice choked with emotion, a voice strangled by hatred for the unknown person who could do this to another human being. The voice said: 'It is.'

He didn't remember leaving the mortuary, or the long walk back along the maze of passages. He couldn't recall agreeing when Hamish MacLean suggested a cup of tea but now here he was, sitting in the hospital canteen, sharing a table with his fellow police officer and Stuart Hodgson. And it felt like everybody else in the place was staring at him, that they were aware of the ordeal he had just undergone, that they knew what he had just been shown.

'The post mortem is scheduled for three o'clock this afternoon,' Hodgson told him. 'But I'm not sure whether the results will contribute anything to the inquiry.'

Both men saw the wince of anguish that creased Ray's face.

'The thing is, we're having the Press conference tomorrow,' said MacLean. 'Anything you can tell me, anything at all that might shed a bit of light on how Mr McVitie came to be in Sussex would be appreciated.'

It was time to behave like a professional, Ray decided. The best thing he could do to help Dominic was to share with MacLean everything he knew. So yet again he recounted the story of the fake Persian mummy and how it became linked to Kamil Behar and of Behar's connections with the black market in body parts. He told MacLean how Dominic McVitie had broken the story in the Daily Mirror and how that had lead to SOCA's involvement. He told how Behar had managed to evade SOCA and that he believed the Turk was still in the country. But yet again, he didn't disclose that he had been Dominic's source.

MacLean studied Ray carefully. This was a story that was as bizarre as they come and the fact that it was being related by another senior police officer only increased its outlandishness.

At last he spoke.

'Ray, you are aware that I'm going to have to give all this to the Press tomorrow? It strikes me that everything you've told me is material to the murder.'

'Yes, I know that. It's not a problem because it's all been used before – it's probably the reason poor Dominic was killed.'

'So you think this Behar character is responsible?'

'Even if he didn't actually murder Dominic himself I'd put money on the fact that he paid someone else to do it for him. Remember, it was Dominic who first brought

Behar's name to public attention and in a business as ruthless as the one he's in, that's probably a good enough reason to get rid of somebody.'

'Do you want to stay for the Press conference? It might be helpful if you were there,' asked MacLean.

'No thanks. I didn't come prepared for an overnight and anyway, I think I'd be better closer to Dominic's brother when this lot breaks. Are you going to describe the extent of his injuries?'

'Not in detail. I was going to say that the body had been badly mutilated.'

'What about the fact that his organs had been surgically removed?'

'Well, that was only the doctor's interpretation of the injuries. We'll have to see if the autopsy confirms them. But if it does then, no, I won't be revealing the fact. You know the old saying: there always has to be something only him and me know.'

Ray left Worthing with DCI MacLean's promise to keep him updated with any developments but it did little to assuage the guilt he was beginning to feel. If he hadn't been selfish enough to want justice for the poor mummified creature they'd found in the coffin, Dominic would be alive right now. If only he'd obeyed his ACC Crime, Dominic would be alive right now. If only he'd followed his first instinct and not gone to that bloody Rugby match, Dominic would be alive right now.

The thought ate deeper and deeper into him as he drove the Saab back North towards Cambridge. As the dismal winter day gave way to a shadow-filled twilight his tired eyes began to play tricks. Reflections of other vehicles' headlights, rain on the windscreen, the looming blackness of unlit stretches of road, all of them became the same nightmare vision. He saw Dominic, cold, beaten, broken and empty, lying in his impersonal, temperature-regulated drawer in an anonymous cellar in an anonymous hospital in a part of the country where he knew no one, where he was alone. Where he was anonymous. Just as he'd been in Camden.

A blast from a truck air horn focussed his attention back on the road and he forced himself to concentrate. Not far to go now. Another 30 minutes would see him in Cambridge. He called Karen.

'Ray! Hi. How did it go? I've been worried about you.'

'Hi babe.' It sounded vaguely childish, loosely teenager-in-love, and he didn't know why he'd said it. This woman was beginning to change everything about him, the way he felt, the way he acted, the way he spoke. It was, he realised, a consequence of being in love. 'I've had better days. Actually, it's been bloody awful. How about you?'

'It's been good. Rather exciting really. I've opened negotiations with the National Museum in Cairo to borrow some of their Egyptology collection, stuff that's never been seen in this country before. Not exactly Tutankhamen but it will be quite a coup if I can pull it off. But tell me how you've got on. Was it Dominic they found?'

'Yes it was unfortunately. Listen, I'm less than half an hour away. I'll pick you up and we can talk about it on the way home.

'OK. See you then.'

Later, outside the Fitzwilliam, he waited, illegally, on double-yellow lines. She opened the passenger door and he heard her say 'Yes, I'll be fine. Goodnight' to someone before climbing in. Looking back in the mirror as the Saab pulled out into the traffic he recognised the body-guard standing on the pavement.

She gave him a peck on the cheek and started the conversation he really didn't want to have. 'Go on then. Tell me all about it . . .'

'I don't know what to say, I really don't. It was horrible.'

She tried to make it easier, knowing deep down that she couldn't. 'Has anybody any idea what Dominic was doing in West Sussex?'

'No. That's the thing. According to Jonathan they don't have family in that part of the country. It's possible he had friends in the area but, if he had, he'd never mentioned them to Jonathan. The other thing is, the doc's fairly certain he wasn't killed where he was found, at this Chanctonbury Ring or whatever it's called. Apparently it's right on the South Downs Way. Local CID says a four-wheel-drive could get up there so whoever killed Dom could have driven his body there from anywhere.'

He hesitated. He didn't want to, but he had to tell her everything. He couldn't protect her from it. In 24 hours it would be all over the news. She had to hear it from him.

'And it gets worse,' he began. 'In fact, it gets pretty bloody revolting. Some of it's going to be on the news but I want you to know it all. It might help you deal with me in the next few days. But it really is unpleasant.'

'Go on. I was half expecting something like this so, go on. I'm ready.'

'The thing is . . . he . . . well . . . see . . .' Ray was struggling to communicate the vision of Dominic that was still raging around his mind. 'The thing is, all his major organs had been removed. Everything. And the doc reckons it had been done surgically. The post mortem was this afternoon and it was expected to confirm the preliminary findings.'

'What? You mean everything? Like Rhodugune?'

'Exactly like Rhodugune. Except Dom wasn't being prepared for mummification. He was just butchered.'

'And is Behar behind it?'

'I think he is. And I bet the bastard took a great deal of satisfaction out of selling Dom's organs. It just doesn't bear thinking about but the next problem I've got is telling Jonathan. I just know he'll blame me.'

'He might not . . .'

'Oh, he will. I'm the one that got his little brother into all this in the first place, don't forget. But I have to tell him tonight. I can't let him hear it on the news. I owe him that much at least. Will you come with me?'

One phone call and an hour later, Ray and Karen were sitting with Jonathan in the kitchen of his bungalow home, the mounting fury within him manifesting itself in the deepening red spreading upwards from his neck and across his face. Ray had held nothing back. He had told Jonathan exactly what he'd told Karen, including that he believed Behar was the man behind the murder.

'I'll fucking kill him. I'll tear his fucking throat out,' Jonathan exploded.

Then he rounded on Ray.

'This is all your fucking fault. If you hadn't given him that fucking story, he would still be alive. But he's been torn to pieces and for what? For some poxy fucking notion about black market body parts. Well, I hope you're fucking satisfied, you twat. Now get out of my fucking house before I start with you.'

A sonorous sob that could have been the death cry of a wounded beast burst from deep in his chest and he collapsed, head on arms, onto the kitchen table.

'Don't you think I know that Jonathan?' It wasn't meant to sound like an excuse. 'Don't you think I'm very aware of my role in all this? It's breaking me up inside too you know.'

Then, without another word, almost guiltily, Ray and Karen climbed back into the car and drove away. The silence between them lasted until they reached Ray's cottage where, in the dim glow of the street light, Karen noticed that tears had been coursing down his cheeks.

Frozen pizza provided them both with their first sustenance of the day, after which Karen went upstairs to run a bath.

'I've run you a nice hot bath and lit some scented candles,' she said when she returned. 'Off you go and have a good soak. It will do you a world of good.'

Tired, distraught and depressed, Ray was beyond arguing and simply did as he was told. He hung his suit back in the wardrobe and threw his dirty clothes in the washing basket. Then he picked up a towelling robe and the Glock G17 in its shoulder holster, both of which he hung on the hook behind the bathroom door. He sank slowly into the comforting embrace of the deep, hot water and closed his eyes.

He was stirred by the sound of the door opening again. His eyes flickered open and took in the vision of Karen standing in the doorway, her naked body silhouetted against the light from the stairs, the auburn hair she normally wore tight to her head in a scholarly bun, loose and flowing across her shoulders. In her left hand was a bottle of port, in her right, two glasses.

She crossed to the bath and lowering herself slowly into the tub murmured to him: 'I know what'll cheer you up' and began by pouring them each a glass of port.

Chapter Twenty-Six

The Press conference had been scheduled to begin at 10.00am. The clock was ticking towards 11.30am when Ray Wilson answered his office 'phone and found himself speaking to DCI Hamish MacLean.

'I thought I'd better let you know what happened,' said MacLean. 'We got a good turn out from the local media – radio, TV, evening newspaper, local freelance – but then we always do. The Daily Mirror sent a chap down from London and I think that alerted the locals to the fact that we were going to give them something big.

'In the end I told them everything. Everything except the full extent of McVitie's injuries. I confined myself that to the fact that the body had been mutilated and refused to elaborate. But I told them how McVitie had broken the story of Behar's links to your Persian princess and said that I was very anxious to speak to him regarding

Mr McVitie's death because right now I considered him to be the prime suspect.

'The other thing you ought to be aware of is that the Daily Mirror reporter told me privately that the Mirror is going to offer a £50,000 reward for information leading to the arrest and conviction of McVitie's killer. So I expect it will be a big story in the paper tomorrow and I believe it will also be on national television news tonight, so you may want to alert anybody up there you think should know.'

Ray was taken aback by news of the Mirror's reward but otherwise he hadn't heard anything he hadn't expected.

'Hamish I really appreciate the call. Will you keep me up to speed with any developments?'

'Of course. Bye for now Ray.'

The first call Ray made was to ACC Rafferty's office where he left a message with Veronica Barnes, updating Rafferty with the news from Sussex. Then he called Karen to share with her what Hamish MacLean had told him.

And then he called Jonathan McVitie.

Three times his call was rejected, tripping straight to Jonathan's voicemail box. When it happened a fourth time he left a message saying that Dominic's murder was likely to feature heavily on the night's television news and that it would also probably be given a lot of space in tomorrow's newspapers. He also advised Jonathan that he could evade the hordes of journalists who would undoubtedly be beating a path to his door by moving out of his house for a few days. And he added: 'You're welcome to stay at my place if you want.'

His next call was to Gaston Terray at Interpol in Lyon. He had a lot to tell him.

Once again the polite Frenchman listened patiently as Ray recounted how Behar had somehow sneaked into Britain; had evaded SOCA by dressing as a woman and was now implicated in the murder of Dominic McVitie and in the removal of his major organs. He explained that Behar's name was, for the second time, going to be all over the UK media, especially the Daily Mirror, which was to offer its handsome reward the following morning.

'Thank you for sharing that with me, Inspector,' said Terray when he'd finished. 'What you say about Behar being in York is very interesting. In a way it solves a little mystery for us and I think, for you also.'

'That being . . .?'

'How Behar managed to evade a pan-European All Ports Alert. You see, in the early part of last week, border control CCTV filmed a man crossing from Turkey into Bulgaria in a Lamborghini sports car. A couple of days later the same car and driver were pictured entering Austria, but this time the number plate was different. It showed up again some 30 hours later crossing from Germany into France on yet another set of number plates. But this time, the Automatic Number Plate Recognition System flagged up the plate as one that had been used in the past by Kamil Behar.

'Unfortunately the border guards knew nothing of the All Ports Alert out for Behar and allowed the vehicle to pass unmolested. It was next seen by a camera on the Paris Peripherique and then disappeared.

'A few hours later, the pilot of a twin-engined light aircraft in Dunkerque logged a flight plan to Norwich in your country. It never arrived. The pilot radioed Norwich to say he was diverting to another airfield for unspecified but non-emergency reasons. A little later, the aircraft landed at a place called Pocklington, which I believe is near York. The pilot told ground control that he was in-bound from Norwich and would be on the ground for only a few minutes to drop a passenger before making the return flight. Sometime later he returned to Dunkerque without landing at Norwich.

'From what you've just told me Inspector Wilson, I suspect that the man in the Lamborghini and the man in the aeroplane were one and the same. And that man was Behar.'

Ray replied: 'I think you're probably right Gaston but I'm amazed that one of the most wanted men in the world could evade a police network the size of Interpol so easily.'

'I agree,' said Terray. 'But then, your SOCA came within touching distance of Behar and they lost him. There is a very great deal of luck involved in these things. And when it comes to Mr Behar it seems luck isn't on our side.'

That evening, the BBC chose to lead its 6.00pm news with the story of a Government crisis. But the second item was the hunt for Kamil Behar following the murder of the national newspaper journalist who had exposed him as a dealer in death. ITV and Sky News both decided that the killing and mutilation of a journalist just doing his job was the most important story of the day.

Ray and Karen watched every news bulletin in fascinated horror. The story remained unchanged throughout the night but nonetheless they both felt compelled to watch, as if doing so would suddenly make things alright again; as if telling the world about Dominic's gruesome butchering would somehow bring him back.

The BBC 10 o'clock news had just gone off air when Ray's mobile rang. He looked at the screen and hesitated. The caller ID showed 'Jonathan McV.' After half a dozen rings he answered with a quiet, almost whispered: 'Hi.'

'Hi Ray, it's me.' Although introductions were unnecessary. 'Listen, I picked up your message earlier and I just want to say thanks. I really appreciate your offer but actually, the Daily Mirror sent a couple of blokes to look after me. I'm in a hotel with them now. They're going to keep other journalists away from me and I've agreed to talk to them about Dom.'

'OK Jonathan. If that's what you want. As long as you're safe . . .'

'I'm fine. And listen. I want to apologise to you and Karen for the way I reacted last night. It was uncalled for but you know full well I can be a twat without trying. Anyway, I just want to say sorry.'

'Listen mate, I was half expecting your reaction. I just wanted you to know that you weren't the only one feeling angry. Apology accepted. Let's forget it and I'll see you when the dust settles.'

'Yeah. Let's do that. Goodnight Ray.'

The following morning's papers all carried stories of Dominic's murder on their front pages and, as expected, the Daily Mirror gave it the biggest show of all. The announcement of the £50,000 reward for information leading to the conviction of Dominic's killer occupied a single column but almost the whole of page one was given over to a banner headline that read:

FEARLESS
MIRRORMAN
SLAIN

The story that accompanied it carried the by-line of Jason Thornley and recounted how Dominic had first told the world of the links between a mummified body in Cambridge and a world-wide trade in human organs and how, police believed, that story had marked him down for death. Pictures of Dominic and Kamil Behar dominated pages two and three. The story carried over to pages four and five where there was an aerial picture of Chanctonbury Ring accompanied by a story explaining how police were working on the theory that more than one person must have been involved in transporting the body. There was an interview with Frank Palmer, the man who found the body and a picture of him and his dog. And there was a first-person piece, again by-lined Jason Thornley, headlined: 'My Mate Dom.'

On the leader pager an editorial declared that Dominic McVitie had been a fearless reporter; that his dogged pursuit of the truth had lead to his killing; that he had died upholding the finest traditions of British journalism and, in particular, those of the Daily Mirror; that he was a hero among journalists and would never be forgotten.

It didn't say that when Dominic had regained consciousness after being knocked out in the street and discovered he was bound hand and foot in a chair with four hooded men surrounding him, he had soiled himself. It didn't say that he had begged for mercy when the four men took it in turns to beat him with pick axe handles.

And it didn't say that he'd cried out for his mother when one of the men stuck a six inch blade into his stomach and pulled it upwards, leaving him to bleed slowly and agonisingly to death.

Secure in the cottage in Fulbourn, Karen was growing to enjoy her new-found domesticity, even though it had been virtually forced upon her by a set of bizarre circumstances. The Friday night port and poker sessions with the girls were long gone. She kept in touch, of course – just in case things went sour – but she really didn't miss those Saturday mornings that felt like her head was immersed in a bowl of cold porridge. And she was a different person at work. She knew this because Margaret Jones, the forthright, tell-it-like-it-is Margaret Jones, had told her so. She was happier, smiled more, didn't shout as much and was altogether a more pleasant person, Margaret had said. The next step was probably a weekend on his boat and she shivered at the thought. Maybe when it gets a bit warmer . . .

But right now the man she loved, the man who had made her feel like she'd never felt before in her life, was in anguish. She knew Ray had been deeply affected by Dominic's death and tried her best to comfort him and makes things as easy as possible. And she also knew it would, as her mother had always told her, get worse before it got better.

An inquest into Dominic's death opened in Worthing a week after the body had been found and, after hearing the evidence of identification provided by Ray Wilson to Stuart Hodgson, the coroner's liaison officer and DCI MacLean, was adjourned to an unspecified date, pending the result of the murder inquiry. Although it was not revealed to the inquest, the Home Office pathologist who had conducted the post mortem examination of Dominic's remains had written to the coroner explaining that the condition of the body was such that the precise cause of death would probably never be known. He suggested that the corpse could yield nothing more that would be of benefit to the murder investigation. Armed with this information, the coroner issued a certificate allowing the burial, but not the cremation, of Dominic's brutalised body.

Although the Daily Mirror hierarchy tried to persuade Dominic's devastated parents to go for a full-blown funeral at the journalists' church, St Bride's, Fleet Street, so that his colleagues from every national newspaper could pay their proper respects, Peter and Doreen McVitie decided on a more private affair at the parish church in St Neots, where their son had been born and raised. They knew that, given the nature of their son's death, they could not avoid the funeral becoming a media magnet but their hope was that by holding it in their home town, at least they would be among people they knew and trusted and the service would be something they wanted and agreed upon, not something imposed upon them by a giant corporation, no matter how well meaning.

Two days before the funeral was due to take place, Jonathan McVitie rang his old friend Ray Wilson and asked him to be one of the six pall bearers. Ray was dumbfounded.

'Jonathan, I don't know what to say . . . I can't . . . I mean, I hardly knew him. There must be somebody else more appropriate.'

'No. I've talked it over with Mum and Dad and they would both like you to carry the coffin. And so would I. It would mean a lot to me and to them too.'

Ray was silent. He still blamed himself for Dominic's death and he knew that deep down so did Jonathan. But he was being offered an opportunity to do something more than simply pay his respects, more than share the family's grief. In his mind, carrying Dominic's desecrated body would be cathartic, almost an act of atonement.

'OK Jonathan, if you're absolutely sure it's what you want, I'll do it.'

'Thanks Ray, I really appreciate it,' said Jonathan. 'We'll reserve seats for you and Karen at the front of the church so you can be together during the service. You'll need to be at the church at least 20 minutes before the service starts and probably a lot earlier of you want somewhere to park.'

'Yeah, good point. See you Thursday then.'

Chapter Twenty-Seven

Thursday dawned the kind of day about which ex-patriots reminisce and poets are inspired to write – still, crystal clear, bright sunshine contrasting with the biting cold and hints of frost playing around the edges of leaves in the sheltered places. A good day for a funeral.

Ray and Karen arrived in St Neots 45 minutes before the service was scheduled to begin at 2.00pm. They managed to find a parking space close to the church and decided to wait in the car, Karen absorbing the magnificent architecture of the late medieval church with its 128-foot tower, while Ray watched those gathering around it, some to say their last farewells, others to report those last farewells to the wider world. Finally, it was time to go.

On the pavement outside the church's main entrance, he gave Karen a peck on the cheek and waited for the cortege while she went inside to occupy their reserved seats. He watched her walk slowly and calmly towards the oak doors and couldn't help but think that even dressed in mourning she was beautiful. Once again he told himself how lucky he was to have found her.

And then the cortege was upon him; the hearse carrying the simple oak coffin, surrounded by wreaths; two official cars carrying the grieving family and a countless number of other private cars carrying friends and distant relatives who simply wanted to be part of the cavalcade of sorrow.

The senior undertaker called the pallbearers together. Jonathan was the only one Ray knew. Slowly, the coffin was withdrawn from the hearse and instructions given, quietly but firmly, on how it should be safely raised and carried. The vicar lead the way up the long path to the large doors that only a few minutes earlier he had watched swallow Karen. As the procession passed through the doors, the vicar began his intonation:

'I am the resurrection and the life saith the Lord. He that believeth in me, though he were dead, yet shall he live: and whosoever liveth and believeth in me shall never die.'

The coffin was safely placed on the two stands where it would remain for the rest of the service, as the weakening afternoon sun shone through the myriad of stained glass windows that encircled the church of St Mary the Virgin, dappling the mourners in a kaleidoscope of colour. Ray was only vaguely aware of proceedings. He wasn't paying full attention when Jonathan spoke of his younger brother; of their shared interest in Rugby; how Dominic had hated the boats he loved so much; how they had been so much more than brothers; how they been mates and good mates at that. Nor was he paying attention when the Daily Mirror's editor Jim Garside spoke of what a courageous reporter Dominic had been and tried his best to lift some of the gloom with a few light hearted tales of Dominic's time on his newspaper. Ray could only think of how he had drawn Dominic in and used him for his own ends. Ends that even though they began as right and noble, now seemed trivial and worthless.

And then it was time to make the long walk to the graveside.

The six pall bearers once again picked up their burden and followed the vicar outside into the churchyard, where a yawning hole had been dug, the edges thoughtfully covered in planking. On one side lay the three sturdy lengths of fabric which would be used to lower Dominic to his final resting place. On the other, a pile of freshly dug soil, shielded from view by several square yards of imitation grass as if, somehow, the very earth in which Dominic would lie was offensive to the eye.

'Man that is born of woman hath but a short time to live and is full of misery,' recited the vicar. 'In the midst of life we are in death . . .'

A barely perceptible signal from the vicar caused the pallbearers to each pick up one of one of the lengths of fabric that now ran beneath the coffin.

'Oh holy and most merciful Saviour, deliver us not into the bitter pains of eternal death.'

The coffin was now resting on the bottom of the grave. Tears flowed freely down Ray's cheeks.

Then, Dominic's parents were at his side, each clutching a pathetic handful of soil.

'. . . Earth to earth, ashes to ashes, dust to dust; in sure and certain hope of the resurrection to eternal life . . .'

And it was over.

Karen slid her arm through his and kissed him gently. Jonathan held out his hand: 'Thanks mate. You have no idea how much it meant to me for you to do that. We're all going back to Mum and Dad's place for a drink. Will you join us?'

As the trio walked slowly back towards the church gate, Ray switched his mobile back on. At once it beeped the strange tone that indicated he had a text message. He pressed the 'show' button and read the words: 'Your lady looks good in black.'

His initial reaction was that it was somebody playing a joke. A pretty bloody sick one, but a joke all the same.

He looked again. It was a number he didn't recognise. He stared around the mourners, many of whom were just standing around in that slightly embarrassed aftermath that accompanies all funerals. He stared at the men individually, hoping for a wink, a smile, a nod that would reveal the joker. But there was none.

As he and Karen reached the Saab, the text message

tone went off again. It was from the same number, but this time the message was much more sinister.

'And she'd make a beautiful mummy.'

This time he knew who had sent the message and he knew the sender wasn't extolling Karen's virtues as a potential parent. Behar. It had to be Behar who had sent the texts. And he had to be there, in St Neots, probably watching them at that very moment. Ray's first move was to open the glove box and slide the Glock back into its discrete shoulder holster. Then he jumped back out of the car and began to stare hard at every corner, every car, every tree, every shadow, but he saw nothing.

Karen also knew there was something seriously wrong. She had never seen him as agitated as he was at that moment. This was caused by something more than the simple act of carrying a body to its burial place but what?

'Ray, what's happened? What's the matter?'

'We need to get away from here. Right now. Get back in the car.'

'Where are we going?'

'I don't know, just away . . . home first . . . then I'll decide.'

Clouds of dust kicked up from the Saab's wheels as he accelerated hard across the loose-surface car park, at the same time as he hit the abbreviated dialling button that would connect him to Jonathan McVitie.

The conversation was brief. 'Jonathan, I've got a problem and I've got to go. Apologise to your Mum and Dad for me and I'll ring you later. I might need your help.'

'What's the problem. Is there . . .'

'I can't talk about it now.' And he hit the 'off' button.

Beside him, Karen was trying desperately to stay calm. His behaviour was beginning to frighten her.

'Ray you have to tell me what's going on,' she pleaded. 'Was it that text message? Who was it from? What did it say?'

Every few seconds his eyes flicked to the rear view mirror as he constantly checked whether he was being followed. He said nothing.

'Ray, please. I'm frightened.'

'I know. So am I,' he confided. 'From now on you and I go everywhere together. We'll take time off work if we have to. And I'm getting your close protection officer back 24 hours a day.'

'What's happened? It's Behar isn't it? Tell me. I have to know.'

'Listen, it might just be somebody's idea of a very sick joke but I don't know for sure, so until we do, I'm leaving nothing to chance.'

'For fuck's sake tell me,' her voice almost at screaming pitch.

Driving with one hand, he retrieved the mobile from his inside jacket pocket and opened the text message inbox. He scrolled to the first message and passed it to her.

'Read that. That's the message I got as we were leaving the churchyard.'

From the corner of his eye he could see the beginnings of a smile play around the corners of her mouth. She had read the message as a compliment. She was flattered.

'Now scroll down one.'

The smile swiftly dissolved into a grimace of abject terror.

'He's going to kill me. He's going to turn me into one of his fucking mummies. Ray, you have to do something. He's going to kill me.'

'No he's not. He's not going to get anywhere near you. But there are things we need to do. You have to trust me and do whatever I tell you without argument. Understand? It's the only way I can keep you safe.'

The remainder of the 30 minute journey back to Parkside police station passed in silence, Karen staring fixedly ahead, nervously kneading her fingers, Ray's eyes constantly darting to the rear view mirror, fully expecting that any second . . . actually he had no idea what he was expecting. He just wanted the security of knowing what was behind them.

Safely inside his office, Ray rang ACC Bill Rafferty to tell him of the text messages and their latent threat, while Karen embraced the calming cup of tea made for her by the unit secretary as if it was the last thing she would ever consume in this life.

Ten minutes after the end of his conversation with Rafferty, Ray's office telephone rang.

'Ah, DI Wilson,' said an unknown voice. 'Superintendent Tony Whittle, Serious Organised Crime Agency. Your ACC Rafferty has just called me. I believe our friend Mr Behar has surfaced again.'

'Thanks for calling sir. There's no proof it's Behar but the text messages are very unnerving, especially for my partner. She's terrified, as you can imagine.'

On the other side of the office Karen's ears pricked up. Partner. That was a new one. Did she like being called a partner? It smacked of permanence. But wasn't that what she wanted? Her mind raced as she heard Ray reading the content of the two text messages to whoever he was speaking to. Then she heard him read over the number from which the texts had been sent.

'Pretty careless of him to leave the number visible,' said Whittle. 'I'll get it checked out but it's a reasonable assumption that it's a pay-as-you-go phone so there won't be a subscriber name attached to the number. And I'll get a tracker put on it so if it's switched on we can identify his whereabouts and lift him. We can always think of a charge once we've got him off the streets. I'll keep you posted.'

'Thank you, sir. I appreciate that.'

On the way back to Fulbourn, Karen's mind kept returning to the telephone conversation she had overheard in Ray's office. She decided it was only a word; that it meant nothing. Then she decided it had implications. He'd called her his partner. And that suggested commitment. Finally, she voiced her disquiet.

'Ray,' she began, extending the vowel in the manner of a child about to ask for something she knows is forbidden. 'When you were on the phone to whoever it was, you called me your partner.'

'Yeah. So?'

'Well, is that how you think of me? As your partner? Not just your girlfriend?'

'Why, is it a problem?'

He's getting all defensive on me, she thought.

'No. Not at all. I was just wondering.'

'The way I see it we're both too far out of our teens for all that boyfriend, girlfriend stuff. We've been virtually living together for months and now you've moved in. To my mind that makes us partners.'

Before she could make a response, she found his left arm pinning her into the seat as the car came swiftly to a stop.

'Get down, quickly,' he ordered.

They were only a few hundred yards from the cottage in Fulbourn but parked outside it was a car with a solitary male occupant. Ray drove on, past his home, to see whether the car would follow him. It didn't. Nor did it move when he drove back in the opposite direction. On the third pass he reversed up to the parked car's rear, a manoeuvre that would gain him valuable seconds if he was forced to make a run for it.

'Stay here and keep down,' he told Karen. 'I'm going to see who chummy is.'

He left the car with the engine running, slipping his hand inside his jacket and unfastening the short leather strap that secured the Glock in its holster as he did so. His hand was curled around the warm plastic grip as he approached the parked car, hoping he was in the wing mirror's blind spot.

The man in the car had been enjoying a quiet cigarette, the driver's window wound fully down, and would later swear he felt his heart stop when he suddenly found himself staring at the business end of the world's deadliest handgun.

'Right. Who the fuck are you and what do you want?' barked Ray.

'Shit. They didn't tell me I was going to be in a gangster movie. I'm PC Ed Kelly, Cambridgeshire Police firearms unit. I could ask you the same question.'

'Let me see some ID.' Ray was establishing his authority.

Slowly, Kelly produced a slim, black leather folder from his pocket which he flicked open with practised ease to show his warrant card.

Ray immediately put the Glock back in its holster. 'Sorry mate. DI Ray Wilson. Sorry, but I just couldn't take any chances.'

'It's OK. No hard feelings boss,' said Kelly, attempting

to make light of one of the biggest scares he had ever experienced.

'I assume you're Karen's new close protection officer.'

'If that's Karen Bowen, aged 36 and, from what I'm told, very pretty, then yes. I'm her CPO.'

'Careful Kelly. That's my partner you're talking about.' There. He'd said it again.

'Sorry boss. Didn't realise. Is the lady around?'

'Yes, she's in my car. I'll get her.'

Inside the cottage, introductions complete, the three of them managed to share the joke of how Karen's lover had nearly shot her bodyguard. But despite the jocularity, Kelly was under no illusions. His charge was attached to a senior officer. A senior officer who also happened to be carrying a firearm. He would have to ensure there were no cock-ups on this one.

'Right boss,' he said eventually. 'How do you want to play this?'

'Well, when she's in here with me, I can take care of her and that's the way it's been up until now,' said Ray. 'But now the threat level has increased so she needs round the clock cover. As long as we're together, I only need you to look after the outside – the front and back of the house. You know the kind of thing. But when I'm at work – if I go in, that is – you will need to be with her constantly. What's going to happen tonight? I assume you'll be going off for some kip?'

'Yes. I'll be relieved by an armed response vehicle that

will stay outside the house until I return in the morning. If I'm going to be outside while you're inside, better give me your mobile number in case I need to reach you.'

The men exchanged numbers and Kelly retreated to his car.

As darkness fell Kelly's anonymous saloon was replaced by a Range Rover sporting a vivid lime green, blue and white paint job, complete with Cambridgeshire Constabulary badges on the doors and a blue light array across its roof. It was manned by two officers, each wearing dark blue combat clothing and bullet proof vests and carrying Glock G17 pistols – identical to Ray's – in open holsters at their waists. In addition, they had rapid access to two Heckler & Koch MP5 automatic weapons. At the very least, the Range Rover's presence would ensure the street stayed free of burglaries or vandalism that night.

Chapter Twenty-Eight

There were odds and ends that Ray needed to clear up before he could devote all his energies to the care and protection of Karen as she struggled to come to terms with the fact that her life was under threat. That's why the following morning found him in his office at Parkside while Ed Kelly was in his house in Fulbourn, safeguarding the security of the one person that now meant more to him than any other. And that's why he was able to answer the call from Tony Whittle at SOCA.

'Thought I'd better let you know that the tracker's picked up the mobile that was used to send you those text messages,' he began. 'It's just been activated – in Leeds. We've got men on their way to the spot now. And West Yorkshire's firearms unit is responding too. If he's there, we should have him pretty soon.'

'Thanks for letting me know sir. I don't know

whether it's a comfort or not. How accurate is this tracker?'

'Tracker's maybe the wrong description. It's a system that triangulates the source of a mobile phone signal from the masts it uses – you don't have to ring anyone, just having it switched on is enough. In cities and built up areas it's more accurate than in the country so I'd say we can probably locate him to within a few metres.'

'The wonders of technology eh? I assume you're aware that Behar has a girlfriend in Leeds and that your guys have had her under surveillance for weeks?'

'Yes Wilson, I'm aware of that. I can tell you that he's not been seen anywhere near her since he gave us the slip in York and she's not done anything out of the ordinary. To be honest, we're on the verge of calling off that particular exercise. It's very expensive and, so far, not very fruitful.'

'The problem is,' said Ray, 'that Behar is a slippery character who seems to be able to come and go at will. You can bet eggs are eggs that if you pull out, he'll be round there like a shot.'

'Thanks for that advice Inspector.' The tone was just short of condescending. 'I'll let you know what develops.'

SOCA agents Dennis Wetherby and Don Barker had organised an 11.45am rendezvous with units of the West Yorkshire Police firearms unit in Headingley, the area of Leeds in which the tracker had shown the mobile used to text Ray Wilson had been activated. It was little over a mile from Thomas Place, where other SOCA agents still had Ann Massey's home under round the clock surveillance.

Two dark blue, unmarked Ford Transit personnel carriers with blacked out windows pulled in behind the SOCA men's car and a man wearing the rank badges of an Inspector but dressed in full NATO kit – flame retardant overalls, flak jacket, combat boots, carbon-fibre helmet – jumped into the back seat.

'OK, what have we got?' he asked without the courtesy of introductions.

Dennis Wetherby kept it brief. 'Mobile phone known to be used by a particularly nasty individual, wanted for people smuggling and potentially murder, has been activated in this area, which is very close to where his girlfriend lives. I've got the location programmed into this.' He produced a handheld GPS receiver. 'We've been told it's accurate to within 10 metres or so. If our man – his name's Kamil Behar by the way – is there, we need to take him down swiftly. He's already got away from us once and I don't intend to let it happen again. Follow us to the location. Silent approach. Not even headlights. Any questions?'

'Is this chap armed?'

'We don't know for sure but we have to assume he is. Right, let's go.'

The convoy set off along Otley Road and after 300

metres made a right turn followed by a left and another right. Suddenly the GPS receiver began to beep, indicating they had arrived at the phone's location. Wetherby and Barker stared at each other slack-jawed.

They were outside a junior school.

'Christ, Dennis. It's a school. It must be a mistake,' said Barker.

'Well, this is the location the tracker has given,' replied Wetherby. 'We can't assume it's wrong just because it's a school. Anything could be going on in there. Anything. He might have taken hostages for all we know.'

'I think that's a bit over the top.'

'It might be but we'd look like a right bunch of dick-heads if he's in there and we didn't bother going in because it was a school and we thought it was a mistake. Listen Don, I don't like this any more than you do but the way I see it we don't have a choice.'

With that he got out of the car and went to speak to the firearms unit Inspector.

'As you can see, the given location is a school so we need to be very careful,' he said through the open window of the Transit. 'We have no idea what we'll find in there. We don't know whether Behar is in there or not but we've got to take a look. So, how are you going to do it?'

The Inspector glanced over his shoulder at the six men in the back of the vehicle.

'There's only one way. In situations like this, shock and

surprise are the elements that win the day. If he's in there we have to catch him off guard.'

'OK, you're the experts,' said Wetherby. 'How many men have you got?'

'There are seven armed men in each vehicle, plus Charlie here,' indicating the driver with his thumb. 'He's our WamRam man.'

'He's your what?'

'WamRam man. You know, the big weight with handles on that open doors people don't want us to open. Believe it or not, it's a specialist job. He's been on a course and everything.'

'Right. Well, hopefully, we won't need Charlie's talents. Don and I will stand back and let you boys go in first. Good luck.'

The Inspector spoke into the radio clipped to his flak jacket. 'OK guys we're going in. But softly, softly 'till we know exactly what's going. Bill, bring the infra-red camera so we can have a look in the classrooms before we make a move. OK. Let's do it.'

The rear doors of the two Transits burst open and the 14 police marksmen, each wearing the full NATO kit like their Inspector and carrying their trusted Heckler & Koch MP5s poured on to the pavement and melted into the playground, crouching, out of sight, under the classroom windows of the Victorian building.

The infra-red camera that could detect body heat was switched on and held against the exterior wall. No heat sources were detected. Moving onto the next classroom produced the same result. When the third room to be checked was also empty Don Barker felt the bile beginning to rise in his stomach.

Bill, the camera operator, reported to the Inspector: 'There's residual heat in all three rooms boss. But there's no kids.'

Shit, thought Barker. *The bastard's taken them hostage.*

'Right guys. We're going to have to go in and have a look. Let's go.'

Quietly, the column of armed men moved round to the main door of the red-brick school. Charlie stood by with his WamRam as the Inspector tried the door. It opened outwards, silently, releasing as it did so an unmistakable aroma that immediately sent the officers closest to it back to their childhoods. It was a mixture of furniture polish, boiled cabbage and sweaty bodies.

Without a sound, the men lined each side of the corridor. Snatches of instructions being issued could be heard and it took only a few seconds for the source to be identified as the school hall.

Still crouching, but now advancing at the run, the armed men burst through the double swing doors into the hall, each one yelling 'Armed police. Don't move' at the top of their voices.

Inside, 120 children aged from four to 10 were having lunch. Several of them screamed. At least three of them wet themselves and many more burst into tears.

A short man with an unfashionable moustache and even more unfashionable long hair, leapt to his feet.

'What the hell is going? What's the meaning of this?' he shouted over the cacophony of crying kids.

'Serious Organised Crime Agency,' said Wetherby, holding out his identification card for inspection. 'And you are?'

'Chris Liddle. Headmaster. What on earth do you think you're doing? You're terrifying the children.'

'Mr Liddle, we are on the trail of a notorious international criminal whose mind, even now, might be filled with murderous intent.' The sarcasm heavy and deliberate. 'So if we've made one or two of your precious charges cry, I apologise. Otherwise I would advise you not to get in the way.'

Liddle backed down from confrontation immediately. 'Er. Yes. Of course. Sorry. What can I do to help?'

'We've traced a mobile phone that has been used by the wanted man to your school. We thought he may still have it in his possession, which is why we have armed officers in attendance. When we found your classrooms empty, we assumed the worst I'm afraid. I need you to brief your children not to be worried, that no harm is going to come to them but that they need to do everything we ask them to do. Then we will leave you in peace.'

Liddle did as he was told, after which Wetherby spoke to the still frightened children.

'I'm going to dial a mobile phone number,' he told them, waving his own mobile in the air. 'And I want you all to be very quiet and listen so we can find out whether the phone I am calling is in the school.'

He dialled the number that had been used to send the text messages to Ray Wilson and was promptly rewarded with the metallic chimes of a ring tone. A dozen little heads swivelled in the direction of a boy sitting in the centre of one of the trestle tables that had temporarily transformed the school hall into a dining room. The boy blushed and lowered his shaved head to avoid the gaze of friends and acquaintances alike.

'OK son. There's nothing to worry about. You're not in any trouble,' assured Wetherby. 'Just bring the phone out to me. I need to ask you a few questions.'

The boy, Wetherby, Barker and Liddle went off to the headmaster's office, while the armed police officers returned disappointedly, to their vans.

In the cramped office, Wetherby explained to the lad that he and his colleague were special policemen who needed his help to catch a very bad man and started by asking the boy his name.

'Kyle Davies,' he said.

'Right then Kyle,' Barker began. 'Can you tell us where you got that mobile from?'

'Some bloke,' said Kyle. 'He gave it to us.'

'And where was this?'

'On the park.'

'When?'

'At the weekend.'

'And did you know this man?'

'No. He was just walking across the park.'

'What did he do?'

'He came over to us and asked if I wanted a new mobile. He gave it to us. He said there was £20 credit still on it but that I hadn't to switch it on until this morning. He said it wouldn't work if I turned it on earlier.'

'Did you not show it anybody? Your parents for instance?' Wetherby intervened.

'Kyle lives with his Mum. He doesn't see much of his Dad,' Liddle explained for no obvious reason.

'Did you show it to your Mum then?'

'No. She would have taken it off us and flogged it.'

'So have you made any calls or sent text messages to anybody,' asked Wetherby.

'No. I just switched it on this morning.'

Barker jumped back in. 'What did this man look like? The one who gave you the phone.'

'Don't know really,' answered Kyle. 'He was just an Asian bloke.'

'Asian? What, Indian, Pakistani?'

'Just Asian.'

'Can you describe him?'

'No. I've told you. He was just Asian.'

Wetherby produced a sheet of folded paper from his inside pocket, opened it out and held it in front of Kyle.

'Do you recognise this chap?' he asked.

'That's him. That's the bloke who gave us the phone.'

He was looking at a photocopy of the Sunday Mirror picture of Kamil Behar.

Chapter Twenty-Nine

The news was no more and no less than Ray Wilson had anticipated. Behar was no longer in possession of the mobile he'd used to send the intimidating texts but at least they now knew he was still in the country – or, more correctly, he was over the weekend. It was this knowledge that made Ray very nervous indeed.

'I don't know what to do for the best now,' he confided to Tony Whittle of SOCA, who had called Ray to tell him of Kyle Davies and how he came to have Behar's telephone in his pocket. 'Part of me wants to take Karen and run but another part of me is saying 'stay.' We both have jobs to do but the constant threat from Behar is making it impossible to do them. Karen's a nervous wreck and I'm not sure how much longer she can stand it. But I know it's all my fault. She's only in this position because of me. If only I'd gone somewhere else with that bloody mummy . . .'

'Then somebody else would probably be in this position,' interrupted Whittle. 'You can't think like that Ray. You're not to blame for any of this. You followed your instincts and uncovered what looks like a major international crime so now you've got to take a step back and let us get on with things. We will do everything we possibly can to ensure your safety and Karen's so for now I suggest you just try to get on with your lives as best you can.'

It wasn't what Ray wanted to hear. He wanted someone to tell him to grab Karen and run. To get as far away from Behar as possible. America. Australia. It didn't matter. Just run. But in his heart of hearts he knew that wasn't the solution because no matter where they went, no matter what they did, as long as Kamil Behar was free to walk the streets, they would not be safe.

The clock on his office wall was showing 4.30pm. He picked up his mobile and rang Karen.

'Ray. Is everything OK?' He could hear the anxiety rising in her voice.

'Yeah, yeah. Everything's fine. Can you make an early cut?'

'A what?'

'Finish early. Like now.'

'What for?'

'I just fancy finishing work early, going to the pub and drinking lots of beer. Then we can go home and drink port 'till we break into smiles. Then we'll go to bed and do unspeakably dirty things to each other.'

'Oh Mr Wilson. You really know how to romance a girl.'

'I know. It's a gift. What do think?'

'Pick me up in ten minutes.'

And so it was that half an hour later Ray and Karen were snuggled into a corner of the bar at the Bakers Arms in Fulbourn, while the ever-present Ed Kelly sat on a bar stool sipping Coca-Cola. To Ray's mind, the Bakers had two things going for it. First of all, it sold his favourite Greene King IPA and, almost as importantly, it was only five minutes walk from the cottage he now shared – and looked like continuing to share – with Karen.

They had four or five drinks each and decided to make life easier by eating in the pub's dining room. Kelly moved to a position from which he could still keep them under observation but did not join them.

Both of them began with spicy Thai fish cakes and for his main course, Ray chose the 10oz rib-eye steak cooked, as he liked to describe it, 'just on the bloody side of medium.' Karen opted for the mushroom stroganoff. A bottle of house red ensured they were both in mellow mood by the time Kelly insisted on driving them home, where he waited in his car until the brightly liveried Range Rover and its heavily armed occupants arrived.

The next morning Ray dropped Karen off at the Fitzwilliam Museum and into the care, once more, of Ed Kelly. Then, virtually on auto-pilot he made his way to

Parkside police station where he parked his car in its reserved spot and went upstairs to his office. Booting his computer into life was almost a reflex action, after which he hung up his coat and wandered off towards the tiny kitchen in search of a reviving cup of coffee.

Back in his office, he opened his e-mail and watched as the in-box loaded with 12 messages that had been sent overnight. The majority of them were routine, internal messages from his own force. One was from the Home Office about yet another change to performance targets. But the one that caught his eye had a blank 'Subject' box.

Clutching his coffee cup to his chest, he double clicked the message and read its brief contents:

'Such a pretty face. It's a shame to swathe it in bandages.'

Fear was the only noun that came to his mind that even adequately began to describe the feeling that gripped him in that instant. Fear for Karen. Fear for himself. Fear of Behar.

Apart from the terror of the text, there was no indication that Behar was behind the message – it had been sent using a Hotmail account in the name of 'Zerohour' – but Ray was in no doubt. It was a crude form of psychological warfare and it was giving Behar the upper hand.

His trembling fingers dialled Tony Whittle at SOCA.

'I've had another message from Behar,' he told the Superintendent. 'This time it's an e-mail but it's just as threatening. He's close, I know it. I'm sorry sir but I can't put Karen through any more of this. I'm going to have to disappear for while. Until Behar's nicked at least.'

'Ray, listen to me. I've promised you we'll do everything we can to protect you and Karen but if you want to run for it, then it's up to you but I think you will be of more help to me if you stay put. At least if we know where you are we can guard you.'

'Yes but Behar's got me so bloody jumpy I'm beginning to doubt that anybody can protect us.'

'Look, here's my advice. Don't delete the message. Contact your IT department and ask them if they can trace the source. E-mails leave all sorts of information about where they came from and where they've been. It might give us a lead.'

'OK,' replied Ray. 'But I want you to know that I'm rapidly reaching the point where I can't go on while he's still out there.'

'I understand. Call me and let me know what the IT people say.'

Whoever Ray spoke to in the IT department at Headquarters told him he was in luck. There was a technician in Cambridge at that moment. They'd call him and get him to call in to Parkside.

Ray had never met anyone who 'worked in IT.' To him technology was a tool. He didn't want to understand it. He didn't want to know how it worked or why it worked. As long as it was available when he wanted it and it did what he wanted it to do, he was quite content. Computers, the internet, e-mails, mobile phones, even VHF radio, all fell within the 'don't know, don't want to know' category.

So he was taken slightly aback when the technician finally turned up. His arrival was announced by a call from the front desk: 'Inspector Wilson, there's a young man from the IT department at headquarters here to see you.'

Five minutes later, duly signed in, Julian Head, IT expert, was ushered into Ray's office by Marilyn Forbes, one of the team of civilian support staff – 'shiny arses' to serving police officers because they mainly occupied jobs that involved sitting down – who manned the front desk.

Head's hair was greasy and probably shoulder-length, but the ponytail in which it was held made estimating its true length difficult. Each ear sported two rings and a double ended stud pierced his left eyebrow.

The hand that he offered to Ray was warm, moist and limp. 'Hi man. Call me Jules,' Head said, doing nothing to endear himself to this senior officer who literally had a life or death situation on his hands. 'What's the problem?'

'I've received an e-mail which I believe is connected to an inquiry I'm involved with. I won't bore you with the details but I need to know what you can tell about who wrote the message and where it came from.'

'OK. Let's take a look at the box of magic tricks,' said Head, stepping, uninvited, around to Ray's side of the desk. 'Any chance of a coffee?'

Ray passed the request to the unit secretary then sat back to watch Julian Head at work and for no discernable reason took an increasing dislike to the young man.

He opened the e-mail from 'Zerohour' and keyed in several commands. He watched the screen – which was out of Ray's line of sight – for several seconds before muttering something under his breath and keying in even more commands. More clicks, more commands and more curses followed. The coffee arrived and went cold by his right hand.

Finally, he looked up from the keyboard. 'Well, I've got something. Look, I'll show you,' he said, turning the screen so that Ray could see it too. It was filled with lines of what appeared to be random numbers and letters.

'Because it came from a Hotmail account, the most important thing I was looking for is this, the X-Originating IP which . . .'

Ray interrupted him. 'Look, I'm sorry but you may as well be speaking in Swahili for all the sense you're making. I'm a detective, not a techie. Can you give it to me simply, in plain English?'

'Sorry man. Yeah, of course. The problem in trying to trace a message from a Hotmail account is this. Anyone, anywhere, can open a Hotmail account for free. You just have to give it a name and think of an address such as this one, 'Zerohour.' If no one else has got it, it's yours to use. All you have to do is log onto the Hotmail website from any computer.'

'OK. I understand that. What do all these numbers and letters mean?'

'Right. Keeping it simple, they tell me where the message was sent from, where it's been on its way to you and who sent it.'

'Great. So what's it telling you?'

Head could see the need to control Ray's expectations. 'Well, bearing in mind what I said about you being able to use any name to open a Hotmail account . . . This message was sent at 10.30 last night from an internet café in Tottenham Court Road, central London. The sender, as we know, calls himself 'Zerohour.' And the name of the account holder is Ronald Reagan.'

'Which tells us absolutely fuck all.' Ray's frustrations were coming close to the surface.

'Got it in one man. Any chance of another coffee? This one kinda went cold on me.'

Before Ray could order the second cup, his computer issued the familiar pinging sound that heralded the arrival of another e-mail.

'Can I just read that? It might be important.'

Julian Head watched as the colour drained from Ray Wilson's face in the 20 seconds or so it took him to open and read the message.

'You OK man?' he asked.

Ray looked at him uncomprehendingly and weakly waved his hand towards the screen. 'It's another. He's sent me another message.'

Once more the message had no subject. But the subject of the message was all too clear to Ray. It was Karen.

Julian quickly assimilated what was on screen. It too was from a Hotmail account only this time the sender called himself 'Zeroplusone.' The words of the message didn't make any sense but he could see the affect they'd had on Ray Wilson.

It read: 'And her pretty little heart will make me even richer.'

'Right. Let me see what I can find out about this one,' he said, virtually elbowing Ray out of his seat.

Again, there followed a series of keyed commands, of clicks and mouse movements before Julian was able to announce what he'd found.

'It's not good I'm afraid,' he began. 'It's just like the last one except this one was sent 20 minutes ago from an internet café in Charing Cross Road. And the account holder is different. This account belongs to John F. Kennedy.'

Ray stared blankly at Head, numb with shock. He might just as well have been told the Four Horsemen of the Apocalypse were waiting to see him. He'd heard what Head had said. He'd understood what Head had said. It just hadn't sunk in.

'You alright Mr Wilson?' The voice was far away, as if he was coming round from an anaesthetic. 'Mr Wilson? Is there something wrong?'

'Er, yes. Well, no. It's just . . . It's nothing you need be concerned about son. Like I said, it's related to an enquiry I'm working on. I just wasn't expecting that second message, that's all.'

'OK then, if you're sure,' said Head. 'If you get any more messages from a Hotmail account and you need my help, just call me.' He held out a business card. 'My mobile number's on there and you can call any time. I don't mind.'

'Right. Well thanks for your help,' said Ray. 'Do you mind showing yourself out? I've got a lot of things to get my head round right now.'

'No probs. See ya around man.' And he was gone, leaving behind a slightly musty aroma which could have been a very expensive aftershave, a notion which, on reflection, Ray dismissed.

On a whim, he put on his coat and walked out of the building. He crossed the road and entered Parkers Piece. He needed to make sense of what was happening, to gather his thoughts, collect himself, before he rang Tony Whittle for the second time that day. As he walked an idea entered his head, an idea so blatantly stupid it might just work but one which would require Karen's full co-operation and consent. He decided not to breathe a word of it to anybody for now. He would, however, ring Whittle immediately and bring him up to speed with developments.

'Yes sir. He's using Hotmail, which is virtually untraceable because according to our IT boffin, anybody can use the system using any name they like. It would appear the information you have to give to start an account is unchecked and, indeed, uncheckable.' Ray was desperately trying to remain calm, to act like a policeman, while he briefed Tony Whittle at SOCA on what Julian Head had told him.

'He's sent two messages, approximately 12 hours apart. One from an internet café in Tottenham Court Road and the second from another internet café in Charing Cross Road.

Both of them refer to Karen without naming her. And he's used two different address names – Zerohour and Zeroplusone. It's as if he's started a countdown. The question is countdown to what? And how long do we have before time runs out?'

Whittle's voice was calm and reassuring. 'OK Ray. I'll get the Met to collect whatever CCTV footage there might be from the locations of the two internet cafes and surrounding streets. At least if Behar shows up on them it will prove that your theory is right. I'll let you know what we find, if anything. In the meantime, try to leave the worrying to us. You've got round-the-clock armed protection. I don't think even Behar would be stupid enough to try anything while you're being looked after to that extent.'

'Yes sir. I appreciate that. But like I said this morning, it's Karen I'm really worried about. She's putting a brave face on it but I know that underneath she's terrified.'

'That's understandable too. Just keep reassuring her. I'll

call you when we know something.' And with that he was gone, leaving Ray to work out more details of his plan.

A rumble in his tummy reminded him that he'd not yet had lunch, even though the afternoon was well advanced. So he asked the unit secretary to pop down to the canteen and get a corned beef and Branston pickle sandwich while he tried to give his full attention to the minutiae of his daily routine in the arts and antiques squad, something which he had lately neglected.

As he ate, he reopened the Microsoft Outlook e-mail system on his computer which had been closed since Julian Head's departure. One, then two, then three unread messages dropped into view, none of which was flagged as urgent, so he chose to ignore them all until the following morning. Then, a fourth message appeared. And this one had an empty subject box.

Even as his finger hovered over the mouse button, he knew who had sent it. Equally, he knew that its contents would cause him great distress. Yet he was unable to stop himself. Click, click. In less time than it took to blink the message was open. His eyes read the words. His brain absorbed them. And his heart cried out. A pitiful sound, a half-strangled, injured animal wail. He read the words again:

'What shall I call your pretty princess? I'm bored with Rhodugune.'

Ray's cry caused a young constable in the unit's main office to run to the DI's door.

'You alright boss? Sounded like you were in pain.'

'I'm fine thanks Jon. Just choking on a canteen sarnie. Should've known better really.'

He rose from his desk and quietly closed his office door. The Hotmail message, this one sent from 'Zeroplustwo,' was still open on his desktop as he reached for his mobile and called Julian Head.

'Listen, I'm sorry to bother you, but I've had another message,' he began when the IT whiz-kid answered. 'It's another Hotmail message but this time the sender's calling himself Zeroplustwo.'

'OK. Look, I'm back at headquarters now so I can tap into your e-mail from the main server. I'll find out what I can and call you back in a couple of minutes.'

'Won't you need my password to do that?'

'No. I'm an authorised administrator. And anyway, we've got the entire force's passwords logged here.'

Ultimately, nothing is secret, Ray thought to himself, pressing the 'end call' button.

True to his word, Head called back very quickly indeed.

'Mr Wilson, I've looked at the coded info on your last message and you're quite right, it is from a Hotmail account. The account belongs to a Franklin D. Roosevelt and it was sent at three o'clock today from an internet café. In Cambridge.'

The last two words hit Ray with the force of a falling jet. In Cambridge. There was only one interpretation to put on those words. Behar was back in Cambridge and he could only have returned for one reason.

For Karen. His germ of a plan was suddenly catapulted to priority level.

Chapter Thirty

Secure in the sanctuary of the cottage, with the now well-established armed response vehicle parked outside, Karen knew there was something wrong. On the short drive back from Cambridge, Ray had tried to be his normal self, lively, chatty, interested in her day, fending off questions about his own. But she could tell it was an act. Even though they had been together for just a handful of months, she knew enough about him to recognise when he was keeping something from her – and that he was doing it right now.

Sipping the gin and tonic that was becoming a routine of arriving home after work, she asked him straight out: 'Ray, what's wrong?'

'Nothing darling. Why?'

'You just don't seem yourself. Is something bothering you?'

'No. Why should there be anything bothering me?'

'I don't know but just listen to yourself,' she said 'You're being very defensive. It's almost as if you'd done something you didn't want me to find out about.'

'Karen, I assure you, I haven't. Top up?'

They both began a second gin and the topic of conversation moved on. He told her about his desire to sail in a competition called The Scottish Series, which took place every May on Loch Fyne, one of the giant sea lochs that spreads its fingers inland from the Firth of Clyde. He knew some people who had competed on several occasions and they'd told him of the well-organised racing and the fantastic social scene.

'How are you going to get the boat up there? It's a long way to take a small yacht,' she asked, not unreasonably.

'No. My idea is to put my name down as available crew on the Scottish Series website and see what response I get. Then we could both go to Tarbet for the week. You can do some walking while I'm out sailing. I think we'd both enjoy it.'

'We'll have to see about that,' she replied. 'The west of Scotland in May? Have you seen the midges they have up there? They're the size of sparrows and have armour piercing teeth.'

At dinner – pan-fried cod fillets with stir-fried vegetables – he uncharacteristically refused a glass of wine. She knew in that instant she was right. Something was troubling him.

'Ray, you have to tell me. What's wrong?'

'I . . . I . . .' She'd already noticed his tendency to stammer slightly when he felt under pressure. 'It may be nothing. I'm not sure. But I think we need to get away.'

'What? To Loch Fyne? Now you are joking.'

'No. Anywhere. I just think we need to be away from here. For a while at least.'

The penny dropped and in a split second she knew what, or rather who, the problem was.

'It's Behar isn't it?' she asked. 'What's happened? What's he done?'

Ray recognised that there was now no going back; no point in holding anything from her; no point in trying to protect her from what had taken place that day. It was, after all, her life that was in danger.

'Yes, it's Behar,' he started. 'I've had three e-mails from him today.'

'Oh my God, Ray. What did they say? How did he get your e-mail address?'

'Getting hold of my e-mail address wouldn't be difficult for anybody with half a brain. All he'd need to do would be to go on the force website. It's littered with e-mail addresses and they're all configured the same way. It wouldn't take a master cryptographer to work out what my individual address would be. But that's not what's concerning me. It's what he said.'

'Which was what?'

'They were all veiled threats. Against you.'

'What kind of threats?'

'They weren't specific. Erm . . . one talked about wrapping you in bandages and the other asked what he should call you. Said he was bored with the name Rhodugune.'

'And the third? You said there were three.'

There was a moment's hesitation and he exhaled deeply as if forcing the breath from his body would make everything go away. It didn't.

'He said your pretty little heart would make him even richer.'

'He said what?' Her voice was bordering on the hysterical. 'Fucking hell Ray. I told you he was going to kill me. Now he wants to chop me up and sell what's left to a fucking museum. Oh fuck.'

'Karen, Karen. Nothing's going to happen to you. But now do you understand why we need to get away? All the e-mails he sent came from different Hotmail addresses. The first one was from 'Zerohour' and came from an internet café in central London about 10.30 last night. The second one came about 10.30 this morning from 'Zeroplusone' and came from a different internet café but still in London. The third one turned up this afternoon. The address line was 'Zeroplustwo.' It came from an internet café here in Cambridge.'

She had the look of a cornered beast.

'What the fuck does it all mean Ray?'

'I don't know. He's obviously begun some sort of

countdown in his twisted little mind. But we don't know when the countdown ends or what happens when it does. That's why we've got to get away.'

'But where will we go? Behar seems to be everywhere.'

'I've thought of that,' said Ray. 'We'll go to my boat on the Norfolk Broads. We can get out on the water and just motor around. We'll just look like any other tourists. I know it's a bit early but there will be other boats about, trust me. We'll just blend in.'

'What about Ed Kelly and those two outside the front door in their little tank? They'd stop us.'

'Not if we go in the early hours. They won't be fully functioning. They won't even know we've gone.'

'Like hell they wouldn't. They're parked right behind your car, in case you hadn't noticed.'

'Yes, but they don't know about your car. And you car's parked round the back, out of sight. All we have to do is get in it and drive away.'

Karen thought for a minute. If she fled, she'd be as good as admitting that Behar had scared her away. But at least there was a good chance she'd be alive. If she stayed, there was a strong possibility she would end up dead and butchered like poor Dominic.

'Alright. Let's do it. What time do we need to leave?'

'It takes about two hours to get to the boatyard. I'd like to get there just before daybreak so I reckon if we left about five o'clock that would be fine.'

'OK. I'll start packing,' she said, not altogether convinced that the plan would work but equally realising that staying put wasn't an option to Ray.

'Just take enough for a few days,' he said. 'We don't need a lot. There's sleeping bags and stuff already on the boat.'

He was awake soon after 4am but decided to leave Karen asleep for a while longer. He dressed quickly in the dark, conscious of the need not to show any lights, and opted to wear his leather, Gore-Tex lined sailing boots rather than let them take up valuable space in his already full kit bag. Downstairs, he made sure the kitchen door was securely closed behind him before switching on the under-unit florescent tubes which provided just enough light to enable him to make a pot of tea and a few slices of toast. He turned out the lights and allowed his eyes to readjust themselves to the darkness before taking the tea and toast back to the bedroom for Karen.

'When you get up, don't turn the light on,' he said, finding himself whispering conspiratorially in case the slightest noise alerted the guardians at the gate. 'We need to be leaving in 20 minutes or so.'

Ten minutes later she stumbled into the kitchen, still half asleep, clutching a small, sturdy, canvas bag into which she had managed to cram enough clothes for five days, which meant the bag contained mainly changes of underwear, a couple of pairs of socks, T-shirts and a spare sweater. Her natural instinct when she had begun to pack the previous evening was to include her hair drier, hair straighteners and full make-up bag. She was having second thoughts about the wisdom of taking the electrical kit when their fate was sealed by Ray.

'No point in taking those,' he'd said. 'There's nowhere to plug them in.'

Ray slipped his arm gently around her waist and kissed her lightly on the forehead.

'Don't worry. Everything's going to be alright. I promise.'

She didn't answer but her look said I hope you're right. It's my life on the line.

Then he was rummaging in a cupboard, finally emerging with a box from which he took two hand-held VHF radios and two spare batteries, all of which he slotted into pockets around his bag.

'Right. Let's go,' he said, holding out his hand for her car keys. 'I'll drive.'

He took her hand and guided her down the narrow garden path and out of the back gate to where her MG TF sports car, her pride and joy, had stood, unused, for more than two weeks.

'I hope the bloody thing starts,' he said, thumbing the key fob button which activated the central locking system. The action also switched off the car's alarm with a beep that in the silence of the pre-dawn darkness sounded loud enough to arouse the entire village. For a second neither of them moved, straining their ears for the echo of footsteps running to investigate. They realised the pointlessness together and giggled at each other.

Within minutes, the MG was heading towards the A14, the first of the five trunk roads that would take them to Wroxham, away from the care and protection of their armed guards but also, Ray hoped, from the all-seeing eyes of Kamil Behar. The road was busy with heavy goods vehicles heading for the ports of Felixstowe and Harwich but the little sports car was small enough and fast enough for them not to pose a problem. The trucks also meant that if anybody had seen them leave and decided to follow, keeping them in sight would have proved extremely difficult.

One hour and fifty two minutes after leaving Fulbourn, the MG was bumping down a roughly surfaced, narrow lane as the first fingers of daylight pushed red and yellow streaks into the lightening sky. Ray stopped under a sign that read: 'Charley's Marina. Private Moorings. Berth Holders Only.'

'This is it,' he announced. 'The boat's just over there. We'll leave the car here for now. I'll shift it later.'

Karen cautiously glanced around, just to confirm to herself that they really were alone, that nobody had followed them. Then she grabbed her bag and slipped her hand into his as they headed towards a locked gate where Ray punched an entry code into a keypad allowing the heavy metal gate to swing silently open.

Two, long, low wooden buildings, one of which

appeared to serve as an office, gave way to a relatively small riverside bay, sheltered on two sides by trees, in which floating pontoons provided moorings for about 100 boats, mainly motor cruisers in the classic Norfolk Broads style. Ray led her along the shore to the third pontoon then out past four moored boats until they came to a wooden cruiser named 'Lady Mary' which, even in the weak early morning light, she could see was finished in gleaming varnish from stem to stern with highly polished, heavy brass deck fittings.

'Lady Mary?' she asked, almost mockingly.

'It was my mother's name. My mother was called Mary.' A brief flush of embarrassment coloured her cheeks.

'I never had you down for a sentimentalist.'

'Oh, I didn't name her. She was my father's boat. He bought her new in 1962, before I was even born. He used to bring us out here every weekend and for most holidays. When he died I was the only one of the family with even a vague interest in sailing so Mum decided I should look after her. But come on, let's get aboard. I could do with a couple of hours kip.'

From the cockpit, a short companionway led down to the forecabin with its double berth, ensuite shower, toilet, wardrobe, small dressing table and storage space.

'Quite the little home from home,' said Karen, who had not known what to expect but, in her mind's eye had fashioned a picture of something sleeker, more modern than this.

Ray produced two sleeping bags from the storage cupboard. 'Here. Get some shut-eye. Then when we waken up I'll show you where the galley is and you can make me a fat boy's full English breakfast.'

A feeling akin to blind panic descended on Ed Kelly when he realised the cottage in Fulbourn was deserted. He had rolled up as usual at 8.00am and had a brief chat with the ARV crew, ascertaining that the night had, yet again, been a quiet one. They hadn't even seen a chink of light from the cottage. It was that statement that triggered the trepidation in Kelly. Occupied homes usually showed at least slight signs that somebody was in, even if it was only a sliver of light in the darkness. He asked the ARV crew to stand by.

Using the heavy brass knocker fashioned in the shape of a ring of twisted rope he knocked loudly on the front door. He hammered twice more but with no response. The downstairs curtains were closed, denying him a view inside, so he tried around the back of the cottage but found that there, too, the curtains were closed and the door securely locked. He called the house 'phone from his mobile and was rewarded with the sound of ringing from somewhere inside, a ringing that went unanswered.

Back at the front, he confirmed Ray's car was still parked in the street. He could feel the adrenalin starting to pump through his body. He spoke again to the ARV driver. 'You guys got a WamRam in there?'

The driver gave him an odd look. 'Yes. But neither of us has done the course. Why?'

'It looks like the place is empty. It's all locked up but that's DI Wilson's car. I need to get inside to take a look.'

'But neither of us can use the WamRam.'

'Fuck that for a game of soldiers. Give it me. I'll use it. I've never understood why you need to go on course to learn how to batter a fucking door down. I just need you two to go in with me. You know, just in case.'

The solid, hardwood door splintered under the impact of the WhamRam and the firearms men rushed in, the under-barrel torches on their sub machine guns illuminating the gloom. The initial, cursory search revealed the house was empty but there were no obvious signs of a struggle or a break-in. Upstairs, Kelly noticed that some drawers had been left partially open, as if someone had left in a rush.

He sat on the edge of the unmade bed, his mind churning with possibilities and probabilities. He called Ray's mobile then Karen's. Both were switched off and tripped straight to voicemail. On a whim, he used his mobile to dial the Fitzwilliam Museum and got put through to Margaret Jones who confirmed Karen wasn't yet in the office.

'Does she have a car?' he asked.

'Of course,' she answered in a manner that implied owning a car was as natural as owning clothes.

'Do you know what kind of car?'

'It's a little dark green MG sports car.'

'And where will that car be right now?'

'Well, Ray's been bringing her into work, as you know. So it should be at Ray's place somewhere. If not, it will be at her place in Sawston.'

'Thank you Margaret, you've been very helpful.'

There was no MG sports car, dark green or any other colour, anywhere near the Fulbourn cottage, he was certain of that.

Fifteen minutes later, accompanied by the armed response vehicle, he pulled up outside Karen's cottage in Sawston. The car was not there, nor was it parked in any of the surrounding streets.

His next call was to ACC Bill Rafferty, an act which he later likened to sitting on a powder keg farting flames.

ACC Bill Rafferty was still puce with fury when he called Detective Superintendent Tony Whittle at SOCA. The bollocking he had just handed down to PC Ed Kelly had been delivered with hurricane strength rage. Kelly would be lucky if he ever so much as handed out a single parking ticket again. Of all the incompetent arseholes he'd known . . .

But however intense his anger had been, it was more than matched by the tempestuousness of Whittle's response. It seemed obvious to all that Ray and Karen had run away together. After all, hadn't Ray suggested that was what it might take to calm Karen down? So how had they managed to run away from under the noses of personal bodyguards? And what sort of amateur organisation was Rafferty running when he couldn't even keep tabs on one of his own men? Anyway, where would Wilson and the girl be likely to run to – assuming, of course, that they actually had done a runner and hadn't already fallen into the hands of Behar and his cronies?

Bill Rafferty, no stranger to handing out verbal monsterings, put down the receiver with quaking hands, not from fear but from his own anger. Nobody had ever spoken to him in that tone before. Certainly nobody had ever accused him of incompetence. He'd show these flash SOCA bastards. He'd find Wilson. And God help him when he was found.

Within an hour, Rafferty had established that Wilson owned a boat on the Norfolk Broads and that the man most likely to be able to give him more detailed information was Jonathan McVitie, the brother of the murdered Daily Mirror journalist who had been in all the papers recently. He reached McVitie with one call and minutes later was speaking to Charley Parker at his small marina in Wroxham. Ninety minutes after being on the receiving end of Tony Whittle's bollocking, he was able to tell the SOCA boss that Wilson had a small cruiser called Lady Mary and that he and somebody he'd described as 'my new partner' had taken the boat out three hours earlier, saying they would be back in about a week.

Chapter Thirty-One

The sun had climbed a long way into the morning sky and a weak, hazy light was dappling the lustrous wooden interior of the boat when Ray and Karen awoke, for the second time that day. Apart from the singing of the birds, there was not a sound to be heard; nothing to disturb their peace. Ray peeked cautiously through the cabin port-hole before climbing out of his sleeping bag.

'Right, come on,' he said, playfully slapping Karen on the bottom. 'There's work to do. I'll show you where the galley is, then I'll go and move the car and get something for breakfast.'

To reach the galley and saloon, they had to cross back across the cockpit where she noticed a small steering wheel and instrument panel on the left hand side of the boat and a bench seat on the right. By the end of the day she would be referring to port and starboard like a seasoned sailor. It was the kind of thing that Ray only said once.

For a few seconds he disappeared through a pair of small stern doors.

'OK, I've turned the gas on,' he said when he returned. 'There should be plenty water in the tank so you put the kettle on while I just nip to the shop. I'll leave this for you just in case . . .' He carefully placed the Glock on the galley table but pointedly did not tell her how to use it. 'I'll be back in 10 minutes.'

His first stop was the marina office. A man in his 60s with a weather beaten face, crowned by a grimy Breton fisherman's cap looked up from a desk as Ray walked in.

'Ray Wilson as I live and breathe. To what do we owe this honour? It's a bit early in the year for you.' Charley Parker owned the small marina and boatyard. The attitude with which he ran his business – treating all his berth holders like friends – meant that the same people had been in his marina for years and he liked it that way.

'Morning Charley. Thought I'd just pop down to make sure you hadn't sold my boat.' Ray liked to banter with the old man. 'Actually, I need a few days peace and quiet and I couldn't think of anywhere better than the Broads. I'm planning on taking the boat out later today, probably for about a week.'

'Well, as you can see we're blessed by the weather and there are a fair number of boats out there, given the time of year. You'll have a good time. I take it you're not alone?'

'Er, very perceptive of you Charley. I've brought my

new partner down. She's never been on the Broads before so it's an ideal opportunity to give her the introductory tour while it's reasonably quiet. As a matter of fact, that's her car outside the gate. Is there anywhere we can put it while we're away? It's a soft-top and I don't want to take the risk of some passing yob putting a knife through it.'

This last statement was a blatant lie. The MG was probably safer parked outside Charley's yard than it would be anywhere else in England. The truth was that Ray wanted it hidden from prying eyes.

'Yeah. You can stick it in the old boatshed next door if you want. It's empty and I don't need the space for another couple of weeks.'

'Thanks Charley. If I don't see you before we leave, see you in five days or so.'

On his way back to the Lady Mary, he called in the small shop which served the needs of the marina's guests and bought milk, bread, eggs, sausages and bacon as well as that day's Daily Telegraph.

He dropped his purchases on the galley work-top, saying only: 'I'm starving,' before lounging on the saloon's 'L' shaped seating and opening the paper.

Without a word Karen busied herself making breakfast. It had taken only a couple of minutes to familiarise herself with the tiny galley which occupied about six feet on both sides of the boat so that as the sausages and bacon sizzled away, she knew exactly where to look for plates, cutlery and place mats.

By early afternoon the Lady Mary was underway, heading east down the River Bure as it meandered gently in the general direction of Great Yarmouth. Even at this time of year there were a significant number of other boats around, enough at least to make Ray keep a weather eye open as he taught Karen the rudiments of handling the 35-foot craft. She sat in the helmsman's position – not unlike a barstool with a low back – while Ray stood close behind her, arms stretched around her as she grew accustomed to the feel of the boat through the wooden steering wheel. She could not remember the last time she had felt this contented. But then the sudden realisation of why they were there in the first place broke her reverie. They were, after all, hiding. In a very public place but, nonetheless, hiding.

'I've never been on the Broads before,' she said. 'It's beautiful.'

'Yes,' he agreed. 'This is one of the most beautiful stretches but in summer it gets very, very busy. You can get up to a thousand boats a day on here. It's a bit like the M1 at rush hour.'

'Pity we have to be here in these circumstances. It's difficult to relax.'

'Karen, I've told you. There's no need to worry. Behar would never find us down here in a month of Sundays. And when this is all over I promise I'll bring you back so you can enjoy it to the full.'

On they cruised, past the entrance to Salhouse Broad,

past Black Horse Broad until the river took a sharp turn to the right and brought them to the village of Horning, which stretched for over a mile along the river banks.

'I think we should tie up here for the night,' suggested Ray, even though the clock was not yet showing five o'clock. 'You can't get near here in summer but we can take advantage of the relative quiet. There are a couple of good pubs where we can get something to eat and take on copious amounts of attitude adjustment juice. Then we can have an early night.'

'Are you sure we'll be safe here?'

'Safe as anywhere. Trust me.'

He quickly explained to her how he would bring the boat alongside the staithe so she could jump off and secure the bow line to a mooring ring. He would then show her how to make the boat fast. In less than 15 minutes the Lady Mary was secured, the hatches locked and the pair of them had set off, arm-in-arm, for the Swan Inn. The New Inn followed. Then it was back to the Swan for something to eat. By 9.30pm they were back on board, snuggled down in their sleeping bags, which Ray had zipped together to make own, big, double bag. Karen was tightly tucked in between Ray and the hull; warm, cosy, comfortable – and aware that underneath the pillow on Ray's side of the berth was the loaded Glock.

After breakfast, they headed into the village to stock up on supplies. Enough for another four days, Ray had said. It was on the way back to the boat, heavily loaded with plastic bags that cut into her fingers, that it occurred to Karen just what an asset a car was when it came to shopping.

They spent the remainder of the morning simply lounging around the boat and then, after lunch in the New Inn, set out again. Within 20 minutes, Ray made a turn to starboard, into a narrow dyke which, after a few hundred yards, opened out into the expanse of Malthouse Broad. At the opposite end of the navigable stretch of the broad lay the village of Ranworth, where Ray expertly moored Lady Mary stern-to on the public staithe, within sight of the Broads Authority Information Centre.

'I think we should stay here,' announced Ray. 'At least for a couple of days. It's away from the mainstream of the river and it's going to be fairly quiet at this time of year. It will just give us chance to take stock of the situation and make a decision about where we go from here.'

'Did you have anywhere in particular in mind?'

'What? Course not. You know what I meant. There are going to be people back home who will be concerned that they haven't seen us or heard from us for a while. When we do we tell them we're OK? What do we do about work? At some point we're going to have to make contact.'

'I know. It's just that I'm having difficulty coming to terms with why we're here in the first place. I feel like a criminal. We're on the run and we haven't done anything wrong.'

'It will all be over soon, I'm certain of it. SOCA will catch Behar and then we can go back to our normal lives. In the meantime, we just need to stay under the radar. Alert, but out of sight.'

'You're right,' she agreed. 'What do you fancy doing for the rest of the day?'

'I thought you'd know better than to ask me a question like that,' he said, hooking his arm around her shoulders and pulling her into him.

Although Anne Massey and her home in Leeds were no longer under 24 hour surveillance, her telephones were still tapped and her mail and e-mail traffic were still being intercepted. Now, the patience of the watchers and listeners was about to be rewarded. Just after three o'clock in the afternoon and only a couple of hours after Lady Mary had pulled away from Charley Parker's marina, GCHQ in Cheltenham picked up an e-mail that was sent to her personal address. It came from a Hotmail account held in the name of George Bush and was sent from an Internet café in the West End of London. There were no greetings, no intimacies, no signatures but nevertheless the message triggered an alarm. It read: 'Need to be in Great Yarmouth this weekend. Take a week off. Meet me there then we'll catch a ferry to Denmark for a few days.'

Tony Whittle's first thought on being told of the message was: 'They all make one mistake sooner or later.' But now he was really worried. Great Yarmouth was where the Norfolk Broads met the North Sea. Behar was obviously several steps ahead of SOCA in locating his prey and the only reason for him to be in Yarmouth was to lay a trap for Ray and Karen. With Behar's contacts he could have the pair of them out of the country in the twinkling of an eye and a fate that did not bear any kind of thought.

Whittle's next call was to the Chief Constable of Norfolk Constabulary, asking that his entire force be alerted to look for the Lady Mary and also for a firearms unit to be placed on stand-by in Great Yarmouth and at SOCA's disposal for the next few days. The Chief Constable did not ask the reason why and was not given one. The only question he asked was: 'What do we do if we find this boat?'

'There should be a man and a woman on board,' answered Whittle. 'Take them into protective custody and hold them until I can get someone there.'

The Maltsters, just beyond the staithe where Lady Mary was moored, had provided a convivial evening, with good food, good beer and an enjoyable hour spent playing darts with the locals, but now Ray and Karen were heading back to the boat, content in each other's company. As they approached, Ray froze and tightened his grip on Karen's arm, holding her back. The doors which led from the aft deck into the saloon were slightly ajar. But he knew he had left them locked. Someone had been on board.

'Wait here and don't move,' he told her, drawing the Glock from its shoulder holster as he did so.

Carefully and quietly he stepped on to the boat and went in through the stern doors, his eyes taking in the familiar lines of the saloon with its leather upholstered banquettes, drop-leafed table and the small galley beyond. He could see that nothing had been disturbed. Clutching the pistol in both hands, arms locked straight, he cautiously mounted the three-step companionway up to the cockpit, then went down the other side into the forepeak berth. Both were empty and undisturbed, just like the saloon.

He relaxed, lowered the gun and was on his way back outside to collect Karen when he felt the Lady Mary roll slightly as somebody stepped on to the aft deck.

'I thought I told you to . . .' But the rebuke strangled in his chest as in the half shadows thrown by the street lights on the other side of the staithe, he came face-to-face with the burly figure of Kamil Behar. His left arm was crooked around Karen's neck and his right hand held a Glock – identical to the one now hanging loosely at Ray's side – to her temple.

'So, my friend. We meet again,' said Behar. 'And if you place any value whatsoever on the life of this lovely lady you will do exactly as I say. Do you understand?'

'Yes I understand. What is it you want from us?'

'Well Mr Wilson, once again you and your interfering ways have caused me a great deal of trouble. You have made it very difficult for me to go about my daily business. I have to admit that telling your journalist friend all about me and my mummy factory was a stroke of genius. It made it virtually impossible for me to travel anywhere and I was forced to resort to some, shall we say unorthodox, methods of transport.

'But your meddling has meant many, many problems for me; problems for which somebody must pay. That is why I am here. To collect payment.' He pushed the gun hard against Karen's temple.

'If you hurt her . . .' Ray began.

'You'll do what Mr Wilson?' Behar broke in. 'I don't believe you are in a position to do anything other than exactly what I tell you. I control the game. You have to play to my rules. Otherwise, I promise you, life will become extremely painful for both of you.'

'You bastard.' Ray felt his grip tighten around the stock of the pistol. He had no plan; no idea what to do next. But any thoughts that were forming in his head were cut short by Karen crying out.

'For God's sake Ray. Just do as he wants.'

'Ah, the lady has good sense as well as being very pretty,' said Behar. 'She understands the rules. You should take notice of her Mr Wilson. And you can start by putting down your gun.'

'OK, OK. Just don't hurt her,' said Ray, throwing the Glock onto the nearest banquette. 'Tell me what you want me to do.'

'I want you to sail this boat to Great Yarmouth where something bigger and considerably faster is waiting for us.'

'To take us where?'

'Come, come Mr Wilson. You cannot expect me to tell you that. Let me just say though that the mummy factory is not in England.'

A shrill, half-choked squeal emanated from somewhere deep inside Karen and she went limp in Behar's grasp.

'Let her go you bastard. Can't you see she's fainted?' demanded Ray.

Behar levelled the Glock at Ray's head as he let Karen's unconscious form slip gently to the cabin floor.

'Leave her,' he ordered as Ray made a move towards her. 'She will be alright in a moment or two. In the meantime, get this thing under way.'

'We can't. She has no navigation lights. I'm not allowed to move her by night.'

'In that case, sit down and make yourself comfortable. It's going to be a long night.' Behar tucked Ray's discarded Glock into his trouser band and settled himself between the policeman and the still-open stern doors.

Karen came to quickly and snuggled into the comfort of Ray's embrace where, unexpectedly, she fell asleep. Ray and Behar passed the night in silence, each man staring at the other.

The first arrows of daylight pierced the darkness with shots of pink, blue and gold just after 6.00am and in the gathering dawn, Ray made ready to move off. He went to the bow where, with a great of effort, he retrieved the 32-kilo mud weight which prevented the bows from yawing in the wind. Then, he fired up the 35 horsepower BMC marine diesel and brought in the fenders, three from each side, as the engine worked its way up to operating temperature. Finally, he cast off the stern mooring lines, retrieved the two aft fenders and made his way along the port deck to the cockpit.

Still holding the pistol, Behar had positioned himself at the top of the forward companionway while a terrified Karen sat on the bench seat on the starboard side of the cockpit. Ray eased the throttle lever forward and slowly the Lady Mary began to move.

PCs Des Wright and Barney Choudery were coming to the end of an uneventful night shift and, if the truth were known, were just killing time by driving through the village of Ranworth as dawn was finally giving way to recognisable daylight.

In the passenger seat, Wright's attention was caught by the movement of a boat away from the staithe. *Somebody's keen to get away*, he thought to himself. Then he spotted the name across the transom in nine inch high gold lettering. Lady Mary.

'Bloody hell Barney,' he yelled. 'That's it. That's the boat we've been told to watch out for.'

'Eh? What boat?'

'At the briefing yesterday. We were asked to watch out for a boat called Lady Mary. It's a SOCA request.'

'You sure that's it?'

'It bloody says so in the back. Look.'

Choudery could not quite make out the name but was prepared to take his mate's word for it. 'Better call it in then.' He came to a stop outside The Maltsters.

Wright picked up the VHF radio handset and pressed the transmit button. 'Norwich OCR, Norwich OCR, this is Tango Papa 25 over.'

The response was immediate. 'Go ahead Tango Papa 25.'

'Yeah, Norwich, we've just identified the boat Lady Mary that is the subject of a force-wide search. She's just left the public staithe at Ranworth on Malthouse Broad. Over.'

'Received Tango Papa 25. Stand by.' Almost two minutes passed before the radio operator in the Norwich Operational Control Room was back on air.

'Tango Papa 25, we believe the Lady Mary is heading for Yarmouth. Can you monitor her progress to make sure she doesn't turn off at either the River Ant or the Thurne?'

'OK Norwich. We'll see what we can do. Tango Papa 25 out.'

Turning to Choudery he said: 'Head for Acle Bridge and we'll see if she passes. If she doesn't, they'll have to get the air support unit to take over.'

*

From Malthouse Broad, a short dyke led back to the River Bure, where Ray made a turn to starboard and joined the main channel that would eventually take them all the way to Yarmouth. The tension in the tiny cockpit was palpable, the silence unrelieved until, after about half an hour, Behar spoke: 'How long will it be before we are in Yarmouth?'

'Five, maybe six hours,' answered Ray. 'The river is tidal beyond Stokesby. If the tide is running with us we can make decent time. We should be there about lunchtime. And there's something I need to know. How did you know where to find us?'

'I'm sure it will come as no surprise to you Mr Wilson, to learn that I know a great deal about you,' answered Behar. 'Maybe even as much as you know about me. So I was aware of the existence of this boat and of its location. But where to find you? Let me just say that for a capitalist society, you treat some people with a disagreeable amount of disdain. You place a very low value on their labours. Such people make ripe pickings for people like me.'

The marina. Some bastard at the marina had betrayed them. If Behar knew what time they left and the direction they'd taken, it wouldn't be difficult to work out where would offer the safest moorings. There wouldn't be many places to look.

Suddenly emboldened, Karen fired a question of her own, one which made Ray subconsciously grip the wheel even tighter as he anticipated Behar's response. 'So. Tell me,' she began, 'who was the girl you called Rhodugune?'

Behar's mouth played out into a grin that could, at best, be described as lascivious. 'That, my little princess, depends upon which Rhodugune you are referring to.'

'I'm talking about the poor soul in the coffin we examined in Cambridge.'

'Ah yes, that one. Of course. She was one of the first and probably the most beautiful. Until you that is.'

Karen's stomach wretched and it was only the fact that it was empty that prevented her from vomiting.

Behar ignored her. 'She took a long time to die, that one. I remember she did a great deal of damage to my Mercedes. The force of the impact should have killed her but it didn't. In the end we were forced to – how shall I say this? – help her on her way. It's surprising how effective a single stroke from a surgical instrument in trained hands can be.'

A feeling of revulsion crept through Ray as he struggled to concentrate on keeping his small craft in the safe waters away from the river bank. 'You mean that a doctor, a surgeon, killed that poor girl for you?'

'Well, yes,' answered Behar. 'I had booked him. Paid for his time, you see. But she wasn't dead. There was nothing else to do. The surgeon told me later that when he removed her heart and kidneys they were still warm.'

The knowledge was too much for Karen, even with an empty stomach. She bent at the waist and acrid, yellow bile spilled onto the cockpit sole.

'You bastard,' she spat.

'No, princess. You have to understand that I am a businessman. I buy and sell whatever commodity is in most demand. And right now the commodities that can earn me most money are human body parts. The demand in certain parts of the world is such that it cannot be met, even by people like me. I find it a very lucrative business but one which, unfortunately, has its less pleasant side.'

'You mean you have to kill people to make a profit,' said Ray.

'Regretfully, sometimes it is necessary to meet a particular requirement but in such cases I usually chose someone who will not be missed. There are many such people in the developing world. In other instances, people are willing to accept money for a kidney. I have been known to pay up to $300. To many of them that's more than they could earn in a year. And they get by perfectly well on one kidney.'

'And the mummies,' asked Karen. 'What are they for?'

'Ah yes, the mummies,' he answered. 'They were the idea of one of my associates. A stroke of genius. What do you do with a cadaver that's been stripped of its internal organs? His answer was 'Use it to make even more money.'

'It's highly profitable. Several museums around the world that were not as meticulous as you, princess, believe they own priceless Persian mummies. One very wealthy private collector in America paid $25 million for one, even though he knows he can never talk about it or show it to anyone. It wasn't even a particularly good one as I remember.'

The abominable horror of the sum of Behar's words stunned Ray and Karen into silence although both retreated into private thought. Retribution was the main thought in Ray's head. Retribution for those he had killed; for those he had maimed and for those he had simply used. What kind of society had spawned such a brutally cruel and pitiless human being? We need to do the world a favour and take this bastard out.

Karen's horror-struck mind raced with thoughts of what fate held in store for her. Despite all Ray's promises it was obvious that Behar was going to kill her. He was going to kill her then sell her organs and turn her into a mummy. But would he torture her? Would he rape her? Would he let his friends rape her? Where would he take her? Where would he kill? And when? She imagined his hot, fetid breath on her face. She imagined his hands running over her body, touching her, stroking her, fondling her. She imagined his friends submitting her to the same humiliation, in twos and threes and fours. How much degradation would she suffer before he finally put her out of her misery? The fear in her made her body tremble. *Ray you have to fucking do something. I'm too young to die.*

Just on the Yarmouth side of Acle Bridge, the Bridge Inn provided Wright and Choudery with the perfect place from which to observe the passage of the Lady Mary. They parked the police patrol car at the back of the car park, out of view of the river, swapped their uniform jackets and paraphernalia for civilian outerwear and wandered into the pub, where they bought two coffees and took a seat in the semi-circular, glass walled lounge that offered panoramic views of the River Bure and the countryside beyond.

They were contemplating a third cup and trying not to attract too much attention from the landlord – who obviously believed that not only were they skiving, they were also cluttering up his pub and not spending – when Lady Mary came into view. She appeared under the single concrete span of the bridge that carried the A1064 over the Bure, her wooden hull a burnished chocolate brown in the weak winter sun. She was well within the speed limit set for that part of the river and as close to the right hand bank as providence and good boat handling would allow. From their vantage point, they could see there were three people in the cockpit. They watched her disappear out of sight before wishing the landlord a cheery good morning and returning to the patrol car.

'Norwich OCR, Norwich OCR. Tango Papa 25 over.'

This time it took several seconds before the control room responded. Wright looked at his watch. No particular reason why they should be busy at this time of day, but who knew?

'Norwich, we've tracked the cruiser Lady Mary as requested. She's just passed under Acle Bridge and would appear to be heading for Yarmouth. Over.'

'Tango Papa 25, stand by.' Again, the interminable wait while the operator took instructions.

'Tango Papa 25, thank you for the information. Instructions are that SOCA will handle things from here. You're free to return to patrol. Over.'

'Norwich, we should have finished duty two hours ago, so if it's all the same to you, we'll return to station and book off. Over.'

'Tango Papa 25, message understood. And thanks again for your help. Norwich OCR out.'

Tony Whittle was growing more anxious with every hour that passed. It was now more than 18 hours since he asked Norfolk police to find the Lady Mary and still he'd heard nothing. *Surely it couldn't be that bloody difficult to find one boat on a few miles of river at this time of year?* The thought revealed his lack of knowledge of both the Broads and boats.

His anxiety manifested itself in the speed with which he picked up the ringing telephone. 'Whittle.' It wasn't quite a shout but it was loud enough to cause the duty inspector in the Norwich control room to move the phone away from his ear.

'Good morning sir. Inspector Jenkins, Norwich OCR here,' said the caller. 'We've found the boat you were looking for. The Lady Mary? She's currently on the River Bure and would appear to be heading for Yarmouth. Do you need us to do anything more?'

'That's great news Inspector. I don't think we need

trouble you further. Did your chaps happen to see anyone on board?'

'My information is that three people were seen in the cockpit but, of course, there could have been more people below.'

'Three people? That's worrying. Inspector, can you confirm that there is a firearms unit at our disposal in Yarmouth?'

'Er, I'll need to check. Stand by one sir.' And with that the line went dead as Whittle was put on hold.

Several minutes passed before the Inspector was back on the line. 'Sorry to have kept you sir. Yes, we have a firearms unit currently at Yarmouth Yacht Station and I'm told they have already linked up with four of your men.'

'Thank you Inspector.' The conversation ended with the same speed it began.

To describe the facilities he was looking at as a 'yacht station' struck SOCA agent Dennis Wetherby as something of an over-glamourisation. In his mind, a yacht station would be full of, well, yachts. And those yachts would be full of beautiful people, all dressed to the nines, sipping champagne and braying at each other. Instead, he saw a quay to which, he guessed, a considerable number of small cruising boats could be moored, and a shower block that contained public toilets. There was also an office for the full-time staff and volunteers that manned the station. His fellow agent Don Barker was right behind him as he pushed open the office door.

'Good morning. Agents Wetherby and Barker. Serious Organised Crime Agency,' he said to the weather-beaten man seated behind an old fashioned wooden desk. 'We need your assistance.' It was said in such a way that the man had little doubt it was an instruction, not a request.

'Yes gentlemen,' he answered. 'My name is Roy Woodhead and I'm the yacht station manager. How can I be of help?'

As usual, it was Wetherby who took the lead. 'There's a small boat heading down the river, we believe it's coming here to Yarmouth. One of the men on board is extremely dangerous and may very well be armed. We want to make sure it stops here.'

For a fraction of a second a puzzled expression crossed Woodhead's face. 'If you know this boat is definitely coming to Yarmouth then it can only come into the Yacht Station. There are no other moorings for pleasure craft except Marine Key but that's quite a long way back up the river.'

'So it can't get past here?' asked Wetherby.

'Well, yes. If it's going across Breydon Water and into the southern Broads. But if you're certain it's stopping here then you're in the right place.'

'We can't let it go past. It has to stop here. Is there any way we can ensure that it does?'

'You'll need to talk to the Harbour Master's office. He

could illuminate the three red lights on the road bridge which means that the river is not navigable beyond it. They usually only put them on when there's a freighter manoeuvring but if you explained, I'm sure they would help.'

Barker produced his mobile. 'I'll get onto it straight away. What's the number?'

While Barker spoke to the Harbour Master's office, Wetherby continued his conversation with Roy Woodhead. 'You need to know that when this boat arrives, it will be met by armed police so we need to have the area cleared. Can you organise that for me? We just need everybody to be out of harm's way, just in case.'

Woodhead looked suddenly worried. 'Er, yes. There are only a handful of boats moored up. But what shall I tell them?'

'Anything you like as long as you don't mention armed police. We need this to go off as quickly and as quietly as possible.'

'OK. Leave it with me.'

Wetherby gave Woodhead his card. 'My mobile number's on there. Ring me when the place is clear.'

Outside on the quay he called the Inspector in charge of the firearms unit and asked him to come to the Yacht Station office.

Ten minutes later the pair were standing on the quayside, weighing up the size of the task ahead of them.

'The immediately obvious problem is the size of the

quay,' said Inspector Harry Matthews. 'They could come in anywhere along the best part of a quarter of a mile.'

'As long as we can see them, I don't think that's an issue,' said Wetherby. 'Remember, we're only interested in Behar and we don't have to lift him the second he steps ashore. We can watch him and take him in our own time.

'Agreed. But what if comes ashore with a hostage?'

'That's a risk we're going to have to take. I suggest you put your men where they can see either end of the quay and you and I will be inside the office with a couple more.'

The relative snail's pace which the Lady Mary was making along the river towards Yarmouth was beginning to agitate Kamil Behar. His eyes constantly scanned the river banks looking for signs that they may have been spotted. The fingers of his left hand tapped constantly on the cockpit bulkhead while his right still kept a firm grip on the Glock. Not a word had passed between any of them for more than an hour.

'How much longer is this going to take?' he finally demanded of Ray.

'Not much. We're probably about 20 minutes away from Yarmouth Yacht Station.' He was desperately thinking of what to do; of a plan that would free them from the clutches of this madman, but every thought that crossed his mind was dismissed as unworkable or just too dangerous. 'What's going to happen when we arrive?'

'Mr Wilson, I would not want to spoil the surprise. But

just let me say that my plans do not involve all three of us.'

You bastard, thought Ray. *You're really good at this mind-bending stuff.*

Karen burst into tears, the terror and revulsion at the thoughts of what awaited her painting vivid, bloody and loathsome pictures in her brain.

Chapter Thirty-Two

Luke Burton was the model of disaffected youth. Seventeen years old, no job and no qualifications to get one, no ambition and no money. The world had, he believed, shit on him from a great height and all he could do was kick back. He couldn't remember the first time a policeman had knocked on the door of the council house where he lived with his mother, older brother and three younger sisters. But over the years it had become a common occurrence. He had stolen so many cars that he had earned himself a driving ban long before he was old enough to even apply for a driving licence. And now he was slouching along Yarmouth's Marine Drive looking for a way, any way, to punish the society that owed him a living.

The BMW 330 coupe didn't so much attract his attention as shout at him. Parked on the wrong side of the road; bright red; cream leather upholstery, low profile tyres on shiny alloy rims. Keys in the ignition. It was manna from Heaven and he didn't even have to break a window to enjoy the feast. In seconds he was roaring along Marine Drive, weaving in and out of the traffic, confirming at least three motorists' conceptions of all BMW drivers.

At Yarmouth Yacht Station, the firearms unit had been deployed. Two men waited inside the office with Wetherby and their boss, Inspector Matthews. Two more took advantage of vehicles on the car park to provide cover. At the northern end of the quay, where a narrow strip of grass separated it from a main road, a marksman equipped with a tripod-mounted LA96 sniper rifle was concealed under an old Land Rover that had been parked on the grass specifically for the purpose. Another marksman, similarly equipped, waited under the cover of a bush at the southern end of the quay. All they could do was wait.

On board Lady Mary, Karen was still crying, fearful of her fate and terrified of what might happen to the man who had called her his partner; the man to whom she had become inextricably bound. The 35-foot craft rounded a gentle right hand sweep in the river and ahead Ray saw the three red lights on the bridge. Behar saw them in the same instant.

'What do they mean?' he demanded. 'Is it a trick?'

'No it's not a trick. It means that we cannot go beyond the bridge until they go out. There's probably a freighter or something on the other side. But it doesn't matter. We're here.' Ray nodded to the quay on the opposite side of the river and its low red brick building.

Inside the office, Harry Matthews spoke into the tiny microphone that curled around his face from the single, high-amplification ear piece in his left ear. 'All Alpha units stand by. Target vessel is in sight.'

Ray took a quick glance all around to double check he had the river to himself. Then he put the boat's wheel down, crossed the river and brought Lady Mary up alongside the quay, bow into the running tide.

'I need Karen to go ashore and make the bow mooring line secure,' he said to Behar, rapidly thinking of what he could do to overpower the Turk once Karen was off the boat.

'OK. But no one tries any stupid tricks,' said Behar without argument. 'I will be right behind you my friend and if there is any funny business I will blow your brains through the windscreen. Understood?'

Karen nodded, jumped ashore, made the bow line fast, then secured the stern line and – to the astonishment of the policemen watching from their hiding places – got back on board.

Luke Burton, by now accompanied by two of his equally disenfranchised friends, was causing so much mayhem behind the wheel of the BMW that a Norfolk Police traffic car had picked them up and was giving chase. The trio thrived on the thrill. Luke drove on, faster and faster, ignoring the flashing blue lights and wailing siren behind him.

Kamil Behar was calm, composed and dispassionate as he explained to Ray and Karen what was about to happen. He, Behar, and his princess would go ashore where she would call a taxi to take them to Lowestoft, a handful of miles down the coast, where one of his associates was waiting with a large, fast, off-shore cruiser – 'I believe you refer to them as "gin palaces" ' – which would whip them out of the country. Once abroad, his princess would provide him with hours of fun. Mr Wilson, on the other hand, had no further part to play in this little adventure but he had decided against killing him. There was more pleasure to be had from thinking of his torment as he tried – and failed – to track down the hiding place where his little princess would be providing so much entertainment for so many.

In Karen's mind the statement confirmed her worst fears. Not only was she to die, she was to provide a sexual spectacle before she did so. She dropped to her knees and vomited bile once more, secretly wishing for a rapid, less degrading end.

'Turn round and put your hands behind your back,' Behar ordered Ray.

He heard the familiar ripping sound of a roll of gaffer

tape being unwound. Then Behar wrapped each wrist several times before binding them both together. Just like wrapping a mummy. The next second Ray's world filled with flashing stars as Behar used the Glock to club him unconscious.

As he lay motionless, the Turk taped his legs together in the same way he had his arms then, using longer lengths of tape, secured both bindings together, ensuring Ray would be unable to move. Finally, he used even more tape as a gag.

He stood, levelling the pistol at Karen. 'Now princess. It is time.' She felt a warm stream of urine run down her leg. Behar ignored the puddle that formed at her feet and the accompanying odour. 'You will leave the boat in front of me. On shore you will walk very closely on my left remembering all the time that I have this gun just inches away from your spine. To kill you before I have taken my amusement would be a pity but, if I have to, I will not hesitate. Do you understand?'

'Yes.'

'Good. Let's go.'

The watching policemen saw Karen step ashore from the little cruiser's cockpit, followed very closely by Behar. They had to act now. Their resources were stretched so thinly the area could not be properly contained. If Behar and his hostage disappeared into the warren of streets that led into Yarmouth centre, they would be lost. It had to be now.

Wetherby gave Matthews the nod and he stepped out of the office door with his two armed colleagues behind.

'Kamil Behar. You are surrounded by armed police. Put down your weapon and let the girl go.'

Behar stopped dead. He glanced around but could see only the three men in front of him. To the right, the road seemed an impossible distance. But to his left, only a narrow strip of grass stood between him and the road, on the opposite side of which he could see streets that offered sanctuary.

There was an old four-wheel drive vehicle parked on the grass but there was no point in attempting to steal it – it would be more of a hindrance than a help.

He grabbed Karen around the neck and began to slowly back away towards the grass strip.

'Behar. If you do not stop we will open fire,' Matthews shouted.

Still Behar edged further away, unaware of what was behind him. Beneath the Land Rover, the marksman held Behar in his sights.

'This is Alpha Four. I have the shot. I repeat. I have the shot.'

Every man in the unit heard the call and the response. 'Stand by Alpha Four.'

Matthews tried to reason with Behar one more time. 'Do as I say and no one will get hurt. Put down your weapon and release the girl.'

Behar glanced behind him, estimating how far he had

to go to reach the safety of the streets opposite. He began to pull Karen faster.

'This is Alpha Four. I still have the shot.'

Through the telescopic sight of the LA96, a weapon designed to kill with pinpoint accuracy over long distances, the marksman had fixed on a point slightly behind and about an inch lower than the bottom of Behar's right ear.

This time Matthews had no hesitation.

'OK Alpha Four. Take the shot.'

Unlike the victims of his own barbarity, it took Kamil Behar less than one second to die. The 7.62 mm bullet left the rifle's barrel travelling at more than half a mile a second. It punched into Behar's neck, disintegrating his carotid artery and splintering his spine, severing the spinal chord as it did so. The impact with the bone of the spine deflected the bullet upwards so that it exited Behar's head just above his left ear, leaving behind a bloody, jagged-edge hole the size of a tennis ball.

The distant wail of a siren was almost drowned out by the intensity of Karen's screams as Behar fell dead at her feet. Shocked, stunned and stupefied by the events that surrounded her Karen had only one thought. To run. And she didn't care in which direction she fled.

Luke Burton was driving much faster than his capabilities in a bid to keep the police car behind him. The BMW hurtled around a long left hand bend on the wrong side of the road and on the very limit of its adhesion. Luke did not have the remotest possibility of avoiding the slightly built woman that ran, unseeing, into his path.

He hit the brakes but there was a sickening crunch and the windscreen exploded as one and a half tonnes of premium German engineering smashed into nine and a half stones of soft tissue, fat and bone at close on 70 miles per hour.

The crew of the pursuing police car radioed for an ambulance even before their vehicle came to a standstill.

The initial impact of the BMW splintered the bones in both Karen's legs and flipped her slender frame into the air. She landed face down on the bonnet, disintegrating her facial bones and fracturing her skull. Her ribs snapped like twigs, puncturing both lungs. The momentum of the car lifted her body so that it fell backwards against the windscreen, causing it to shatter. Smashing into the edge of the roof broke Karen's back, severing her spinal cord. Her stomach wall and spleen both ruptured causing massive internal bleeding. Her body continued to slide across the roof and over the boot, landing heavily on the ground, breaking her pelvis.

No one who witnessed the smash was surprised that the victim lay motionless.

At that moment, four armed policemen boarded Lady Mary to find Ray Wilson on the cockpit sole, conscious but unable to either move or speak because of his bindings. They removed the tape that was gagging him and as they set about cutting through the bonds that tied his hands and feet his only question was: 'Is Karen OK? I heard a shot. Is she alright? Take me to her. What was that crash?'

The officers had witnessed what had happened and although they were sure there could only have been one outcome they did not know for certain.

'You need to stay here for a few moments, sir,' said the leader. 'We need to be certain that everything is clear before we can take you outside. You just need to be patient. I'm sure everything will be alright.'

'But Karen . . . Is she alright? If that bastard's hurt her . . .'

'Just take it easy sir. We'll be able to move you out soon.'

Inside the BMW, Luke Burton and his front seat passenger were battered and bruised by the combination of seatbelts and air bags. But between them lay the bloodied body of their friend. Unrestrained by a seat belt, the impact had thrown him forward between the front seats where he hit the inside of the windscreen three thousandths of second before Karen's body hit the outside. The boy's face disappeared in a bloody pulp and his neck snapped.

The two policemen from the traffic patrol car radioed for another ambulance and a fire crew to help them extricate the three youths from the wreckage.

Chapter Thirty-Three

Harry Matthews and Dennis Wetherby decided that Ray should be taken to hospital for a check-up before they broke the tragic news. Even as a trained police officer used to dealing with death, he was likely to go into deep shock when he learned what had happened to Karen. A third ambulance was summoned but this one was directed to the quayside, alongside Lady Mary's berth, where Ray could be put on board without sight of what was going on less than 200 yards away.

'I don't need to go to hospital. I'm perfectly OK,' Ray was arguing with the ambulance crew.

'Mr Wilson, you've been through a terrible ordeal and I think it's wise that we let the doctors give you a quick once-over to make sure everything's OK before we proceed,' Wetherby reasoned in his calmest tone of voice. 'Don't you agree?'

Reluctantly Ray climbed abroad the ambulance and 10 minutes later was being assessed in the unusually quiet accident and emergency unit at Yarmouth's James Paget Hospital. A doctor checked his blood pressure and heart rate before declaring him unharmed.

But instead of allowing him to return to the public waiting area, a nurse took him by the elbow and gently guided him towards a room marked 'Relatives Room.' Inside it was comfortably furnished with two sofas and two armchairs in soothing pastel blues and greens. A small coffee table dominated the centre of the floor which itself was covered in a dark blue carpet. Dennis Wetherby slipped in behind him and closed the door.

By that simple act Ray knew something was very, very wrong.

'It's Karen isn't it? What's happened? Is she alright?'

Wetherby didn't speak a word. His eyes told Ray everything he needed to know.

'No, no. Not my Karen.' The cry was choked by a weeping that came from deep inside. 'That fucking bastard. I'll kill him with my bare hands. Oh, Karen, Karen.' He had fallen into the embrace of an armchair and was rocking to and fro, head held in his hands as his fingers clawed at his hair. 'Please tell me it's not true. Please tell me she's alright.'

'I'm so sorry sir,' said Wetherby. 'The lady stepped into the path of a stolen car and was killed instantly. There was nothing anybody could do.'

'And what about that bastard Behar? What happened to him?'

'He's dead too sir. Shot by a police marksman. Single shot to the head. Fine piece of shooting in the circumstances.' As soon as he'd said it he realised how unfeeling and unnecessary the last remark had been.

Ray was still rocking gently, muttering to himself. 'A joy rider. A fucking joy rider. After everything she went through. A fucking joy rider.'

He was still rocking when a nurse opened the door and brought him a cup of hot, sweet tea.

'The doctor wants a word with you Mr Wilson. He won't be a minute,' she said, placing the cup on the low table.

Five minutes later a young houseman, probably not much older than 25 walked in and introduced himself, although neither Ray nor Wetherby would later remember his name. Like every other worker in A&E he was dressed in a baggy, shapeless dark blue uniform that consisted of a smock top and trousers – the stethoscope casually draped around his neck was the only thing that differentiated him – but had the kind of reassuring demeanour that's sometimes called a 'good bedside manner.'

'Mr Wilson, I need to ask you about Kamil Behar, who was declared dead by me about an hour ago.'

'Behar? I don't want to talk about him. My Karen's dead because of him.'

The doctor carried on as if he hadn't heard: 'Do you

know if he had relatives and, if he had, where we could contact them?'

'My Karen's dead. What do you want to know about that bastard for?'

'Well, you're probably aware of the grave shortage of organ transplant donors that we have in the UK. Because he was shot cleanly in the head, Mr Behar's organs are undamaged and I wondered who we needed to talk to for permission to make use of them to offer others a chance of life.'

Even in his grief the irony of the request was not lost on Ray. Through his tears he realised it would be a fitting end for a man who had sown so much misery, harvested so much death. It wouldn't bring Karen back, or all the victims of his evilness; nor would it restore the health of those he cheated and abused. But, in a way, it would be a kind of atonement and Rhodugune would have her justice at last. For her and for Karen, he managed a calm, almost clinical response.

'No doctor, he doesn't have any family. But if you will accept me as someone who has responsibility for his remains, then feel free to take what you want.'

Before the doctor had even reached the door, Ray's sorrow overwhelmed him again and he collapsed, a gibbering wreck of tears, his life rendered meaningless.

Right then, he didn't want to carry on. He wanted to end it. He wanted to be with Karen.

A feeling of complete helplessness crushed Wetherby

as he witnessed Ray's suffering. In the darkness his mind focused on a memorial stone he had once seen. He had vague recollections of being on a hilltop up North somewhere. A memorial to people who had died in an air crash, he thought.

But the words carved on it were vivid in his memory and offered a crumb of comfort amid the horror he had just seen.

They said: 'Somewhere, around the corner, all is well.'

Chapter Thirty-Four

Dr Akar Kaplan carefully draped the jacket of his linen suit on a coat hanger and hooked it over the cupboard door immediately behind his desk. As head of the Western Australia Museum Centre for Egyptian Studies, just outside Perth, he was responsible for bringing together research, exhibitions and artefacts that would allow those Australians who wished to do so to study life in ancient Egypt.

He had just taken his first sip of koyu cay – the strong, black tea drunk from a glass cup that was a favourite refreshment in his native Turkey – when the telephone jangled.

'Akar Kaplan.'

'Ah, Dr Kaplan, my name is Osman Tabak and I represent a group of people who have made a discovery in which I think you may be interested.'

'Really. What is it?' Kaplan received many such calls.

Usually the find was of no interest except to the discoverer. He was finding it hard to disguise his annoyance.

'It's a mummy. And we have reason to believe that it is of Persian origin. I'm sure I don't have to spell out for you the significance of such a discovery.'

Akar Kaplan sat up and began to take notice.

If you enjoyed *Dead Harvest*, you might also enjoy *Dead Money*, also published by Endeavour Press.

Dead Money

Prologue

The dark came as a shock. It was obviously expected but there was no way of preparing for it, no way of practising for it.

Nor was there any going back. This might be the only opportunity and there was desperately little time.

The stairs were fairly easy, a regular height that could be taken with a steady step, touching the wall with the left hand to guide round corners. It was the level part at each floor and halfway up each flight that was tricky, the sudden lurch forward when the expected step up was missing.

Then came another shuffle round the corner until a toe end caught the next flight.

It was too risky to try counting the stairs. The important thing was to count the floors, to be sure of getting the right one. Two flat turns to each storey.

There was just enough light from the far end to find the door, to avoid clanging the bar against the wall as it was swapped to the left hand and the key to the right, to find the keyhole with a shaking hand and to turn the key.

The door clinked slightly as it was opened but the chain was not on. The curtains were open yet it still took a few precious seconds to make out the way through the lounge and into the short passage.

The door at the far left of the passage was open. The bedroom was dark and only the vaguest shape could be made out.

Down came the bar with a grunt. A pause for breath, then another blow. Then another, the series building up into a frenzy, striking all over the bed to be sure.

Not a sound came from the shape. The bar fell noiselessly onto the thick carpet.

An elbow caught with a start against something at the side. Eyes that were slowly adjusting to what little light crept through the curtains made out a bedside lamp.

One click of the switch revealed the full horror of what had happened.

Chapter One

"It's coming to something," grumbled Nick Foster as he brushed up the leaves. "Coming to something."

It's coming to something when you have to put a security barrier up, Foster thought. This is Lincolnshire in the 1990s, for heavens sake. Dull, quiet Lincolnshire. Killiney Court was just a small block of flats in a small town – well, a fairly large block in a fairly large town by Lincolnshire standards, Foster muttered away to himself, but hardly Chicago in the 1930s.

Killiney Court used to be council property but years of neglect, uncaring tenants of an uncaring council, had led to a decision to bulldoze the place. Sleathorpe Properties stepped in at the last minute, picked the place up for a nominal sum and spent millions on refurbishment.

Here was the result: 24 luxury flats, four to each floor,

in a solid brick and concrete building. It was a lifestyle that was beyond the hope of most of the surrounding populace but even paradise has its price. Killiney Court had been beset by petty thieving. It had caused tension among the residents as well as complaints that it was easy for envious outsiders to get in.

Hence the new sentry box that was being erected across the entrance. There a guard could sit all day and night, the tedium broken only by occasionally swinging the barrier up and down to let cars in and out of the short narrow drive.

Grumble and rustle, rustle and grumble, Foster edged his way round the bottom of the block. He was in no rush. He was 70 and would die leaning on his broom, though he did not intend that to happen for a long time yet. He had looked 70 since he was 50 and would still look 70 when he was 90.

His hair, though grey, was mainly intact. His face was chubby but lined. His body and clothes were indeterminate, as he hid them under an ill-fitting overall tied loosely at the waist.

The ground level at Killiney Court was open except for the lift in the centre at the back.

"Wind blows right through," he chuntered. "Brings all the dirt and leaves. Now we've got the building mess as well."

Foster had a point. One workman was drilling into tarmac and concrete while another stood supervising. They were making rather more mess than was necessary. No one, however, paid much attention to Foster's grumbles, which were in any case directed mainly to himself.

Even the security guard, sitting at his temporary desk under the shelter of the block where he had taken up his duties at the beginning of the week, had learned to turn a deaf ear by the fifth day.

"Just keep an eye on things, Nick, while I nip to the toilet," he said, easing off the chair and ambling round behind the lifts.

"Toilets aren't that way," Foster grumbled to himself. He knew the guard was going for a cigarette. Smoking on duty was a serious sin, a sackable offence. Some of the hoity toity residents didn't like to return to their palatial mansions to be confronted by a security guard with a cigarette protruding from his mouth, forcing them to run the gauntlet of a ring of smoke.

That was the fifth time the guard had "gone to the toilet" and it was still only midday.

"Friday the thirteenth," grumbled Foster. Rustle and grumble. "Unlucky for somebody."

It was 4.30 pm when the first car drove in and the new barrier was raised in earnest for its debut performance. Ray Jones, local businessman, entrepreneur with a finger in a dozen small-time enterprises dotted around the area, steered his BMW towards the barrier. He could afford a Mercedes, he told himself frequently, and others occasionally, but he did not like to display his wealth.

Jones, late fifties, stocky, heavily greying and slightly round-shouldered, waved peremptorily at the lone sentinel, now half way through his allotted shift and seated proudly, if a little uncomfortably, in his bright new sentry box. He pressed a button and the barrier swung up, just a little too late to avoid forcing Jones to slow almost to a halt.

Jones gave him a sharp look that meant "get the timing right", then he swung away into his parking slot down the left hand side of the block and under the high surrounding wall. As he got out and clicked the remote control key to lock the car, he heard a loud peep from another vehicle following him in.

The second car was a Mercedes. Scott Warren's signal had alerted the guard, who this time swung up the barrier far too soon. This incident annoyed Jones twice over: he hated people to misuse their horns and that guard, who would have to be paid out of the community fees, had got the timing on the barrier wrong again. Jones liked things in their proper place at their proper times just as God had intended them.

"Evening, Ray," Warren called cheerily from his open window as he drove past to his own bay two further on. Jones stood and watched the younger man with a mixture of contempt and annoyance.

He waited until Warren was getting out of the car and was caught in that awkward position with the door open, one leg out on the ground and one still in the well in front of the seat – the momentary pause before the driver summons the extra ounce of energy to rise to his feet.

"Christian names are for Christians," Jones remarked bluntly, "and horns are for warning other road users, not for greeting all and sundry."

Warren gave just a hint of being put out by this rebuke, then he sprang to his feet with a forced laugh. He was 30 years younger, tall, fit, well built and still tanned from a late summer holiday.

"What an old fusspot you are, Ray," he returned, deliberately using the familiar tone of address that he knew irked Jones. "What do they teach you at church on a Sunday night? Hate thy neighbour? Don't be so stuffy. It's all first names now."

Yet for all his bluster, Warren was clearly the lesser of the two men and both knew it.

There is a thin line between smugness and charisma and Jones was on the right side of it. He had a presence that Warren would never have, especially now Warren was struggling to fabricate the natural air that had come so readily when he and Jones had first met.

Warren ran one of those newfangled high tech operations that Jones fervently believed would never really catch on: his own small video recording company. Despite his reservations, Jones had backed it personally, hoping for a quick profit before the fad inevitably died a natural death.

Warren had shown a bit more respect then, when he needed the money. All that equipment was expensive and Jones had slowly turned the screw until Warren was finally reduced to grovelling for it.

Still, the operation had started to make its mark. Warren had contacts in London, from where most of the work emanated – work that could be done anywhere in the country, whizzed down high speed telephone wires or delivered in bubble wrapped packages by express couriers. The investment was beginning to come good and Jones had finally got a small dividend. It was a start, but not enough and not quickly enough.

The two men walked together nearly to the lift, side by side but a good yard apart. The awkwardness was broken when Jones spotted a third vehicle approaching down Killiney Road. As the car turned into the drive, the barrier swung up, nicely timed so that the Ford Mondeo eased through without having to change speed. The guard was getting the hang of it.

Joanna Stevens was a tall, handsome woman in her early 30s, as was readily apparent when she stepped from her car, which she parked on the opposite side from the two men. Warren hesitated and watched as Jones strode across to her.

Warren disliked the woman intensely but viewed her with trepidation. She was a jumped up little brat who interfered too much, who thought she knew it all but who hadn't the guts to drive a sports car. She dressed old for her age, too. Yet he almost feared her, for her command of figures was quite awesome and he was obliged to put his books at her mercy because Jones insisted on it as a condition of his investment.

Jones, on the other hand, held Stevens in great respect. She had saved him from one or two dubious investments and brought into line those company owners who thought they could take his money and do what they liked with it. Jones admired her choice of car, too: like him, she drove a less expensive vehicle than she could afford, avoiding attention by not flaunting her status.

Warren strained to hear what was being said but Jones spoke in low tones until the heathen videoman, as Jones called him behind his back, gave up and took the lift that had stood open and waiting for him for several seconds. The conversation between Jones and Stevens was, though, as Warren feared.

"Next week I want you to crawl through Warren's books," Jones said quietly but deliberately. "I think he is concealing something serious."

"You think he is hiding profits from you?" Stevens replied, more as a statement than a question.

"That, or he is in big trouble and manufactured this year's profit to appease me. I suspect the latter."

Steven nodded her agreement as they walked towards the lift that Warren had taken up. It had returned already. Warren must have considerately pressed the ground floor button as he vacated it, probably hoping that the lift's reappearance would cut short the conversation. Stevens and Jones moved towards it in silence. Foster leaned on his brush and watched. The security guard was heading back towards the sweeper.

It was the last time that anyone was prepared to admit to having seen the victim alive.

ENDEAVOUR
PRESS